David Merron was born and educated in London but left medical studies and went out to join a kibbutz on the Gaza border, where he lived for nearly twenty years, serving terms as general secretary and farm manager, as well as a spell in the army. He remarried, returned to England and worked as a construction projects' manager. He is the author of four novels and an anecdotal narrative of kibbutz life, as well as magazine articles and a collection of short stories. He is married with three children and lives in North London.

Previous Books

Collectively Yours. Tales from the Borderline
Delta. A Greek Triangle

Borderline

A Novel

By

David Merron

Cover Design, Text and Illustrations copyright David Merron

This first edition published in Great Britain in 2007 by
four o' clock press - a discovered authors imprint

ISBN13 978-1-906146-57-3

The right of David Merron to be identified as the Author of the
Work has been asserted by him in accordance with the Copyright,
Designs and Patent Act 1988

All rights reserved.
No part of this publication may be reproduced, stored in a retrieval system, or
transmitted, in any form or by any means without the prior written permission
of the Author

Further copies available from Discovered Authors Online –
All major online retailers and available to order through all UK bookshops

Or contact:

Books
Discovered Authors
50 Albemarle Street, London
W1S 4BD

+ (44) 207 529 37 49
books@discoveredauthors.co.uk
www.discoveredauthors.co.uk

Printed in the UK by BookForceUK. (BFUK)
BFUK policy is to use papers that are natural, renewable and recyclable products and made from wood grown in sustainable forests where ever possible

BookForce UK Ltd.
50 Albemarle Street
London W1S 4BD
www.bookforce.co.uk

'Sometimes there is no right or wrong – just right and right . . .'

anon

Similar events to those portrayed in the novel actually took place but the characters are entirely fictitious.

1

A star shell burst in the night sky, brilliant and dazzling. Darkness turned to day. Bushes and trees that an instant before had been just vague shadows took shape and quivered. Swinging from its parachute, the flare drifted down trailing a spiral of white smoke. Then, as suddenly as it had appeared, spluttered and went out, leaving the night darker than before.

The guard in the kibbutz saw it. So did those crouching in the dry riverbed of the *Wadi Shelaleh*. The sentry on the ridge along the border saw it too. But those who slept, slumbered on, drawing strength for the coming day.

The night paled, the stars faded and dawn broke over the mountains of Hebron. A grey light flowed down the foothills and across the dusty plain, lapping against a small hill that rose from mists still clinging to the hollows. Around the base, a necklace of fence lights still glimmered. In the stillness a generator purred and a cow lowed. Lights came on in the red roofed houses on the hilltop. A kibbutz woke up to the new day.

Uri, the night guard had made the last wake-up call. Sitting on the edge of his veranda, he eased the cold black magazine from a Sten gun and yawned as he unlaced his boots. Those shots and the Very Lights? Nothing special about those. But the star shell? That was different. Perhaps he ought to wake Itzik? At least go across and leave him a note.

Uri took off one boot and sock and rubbed between his toes, enjoying the tickling sensation. Itzik had been on late shift in the cowshed. He'd be dead beat, not at all pleased at being woken for nothing.

Pulling off the other boot and sock, Uri took up the magazine and flicked the nine-millimetre snub-nosed bullets into his woollen hat. It was growing lighter and in the daylight everything seemed more positive. No. No point in panicking. He'd leave it 'till they met at lunchtime.

As he stood up and stretched, Gavriel hurried past on his way to early milking.

'*Boker Tov,*' Uri called, smiling.

'*Boker Tov,*' muttered Gavriel. He scowled. 'Your watch is fast!' And carried on towards the dining hall.

Pursing his lips, Uri stood up. For a moment he felt uncomfortable. Then yawning, he shrugged, took up his hat, boots and gun and went into his room to undress for bed.

Gavriel paused by the dining hall as he crossed the courtyard. He looked over to the west. On the ridge of sand-hills that marked the border, all seemed quiet. That gunfire though? Could it have been in his dreams? Wouldn't be the first time.

Gavriel was tall, with a wide face with a prominent nose, his broad shoulders slightly stooped. He ran his fingers through his black, curly hair, glanced towards the ridge again then hurried away down the track towards the cowsheds.

A few minutes later, the sun rose fiery red over the distant mountains. The first sunbeams burnished the treetops copper then flowed down the hill, following a slight, hunched-up figure into the tall eucalyptus trees by the road.

Ella paused in the shadows. Tucking a wisp of hair under her red headscarf, she hesitated, wrinkling her nose at the sweet smell of silage carried on the cool, damp air. Dewdrops, condensing from the mist, hung from the tips of the foliage and dripped noisily onto the dry leaves beneath. One fell on her cheek and she started as it trickled through the freckles to her chin. Wiping it away with her sleeve, she walked on, bare soles slithering on her leather sandals.

At the fringe of the trees, Ella stopped again and listened. On the far side of the tyre-tracked yard, the whitewashed walls of the single storey milking-parlour glowed in the dawn light. Two brightly-lit windows cast incandescent squares on the sand. Beyond, the sharp angles of cowshed roofs were silhouetted jet black against the lightening sky.

Ella shivered and pulled her green cardigan tighter. Her light brown eyes, usually wide and bright were half closed. 'Please,' her brain cried out, 'please let someone else be there before me. Just this morning.'

On most days, she was only too keen to work the early shift, relishing the calm and the coolness before the mid-morning heat. Today though, she barely managed to pull herself out of bed. And now the morning chill seemed to seek out every weakness, penetrating right through to her bones. Even the fence lights, hanging like luminous puffballs in the mist seemed ominous. Sudden, unnerving fears gripped her: an infiltrator watching from the darkness beyond or a rabid jackal scavenging amongst the bales of straw in the shadows of the Dutch barn.

She was about to step out from the trees when the roar of a motor shattered the silence. Ella caught her breath then slowly relaxed. A warm sensation spread up from her stomach. Gavriel! Good old reliable Gavriel. She could hug him.

Running down the slope, she ducked under the cold steel rails into the collecting yard. Gingerly she eased herself through a steaming mass of black and white hulks as the cows humped and jostled, hooves clattering and slipping on the slimy concrete. The stragglers were pushing in from the walkway, metal ear-tags clinking against the fence.

At the far end of the yard, three small doors opened in a scuffed concrete wall. One on either side led to the raised milking stalls. Ella headed for the centre one, to the metal steps down into the pit.

Just before she reached the doorway, Gavriel clomped out in his heavy, rubber boots.

'*Boker Tov,* Gavriel,' she gasped and in the abrupt release of tension, her voice sounded high-pitched and sharp. 'Sorry I'm late.' Gavriel stopped short, his body awkwardly slanted and his head thrust forward.

'Hi. Er. Good morning to you too.' Regaining his balance, he snatched off a blue cloth hat and wiped his face. 'Actually, you're not late,' he continued. 'It's me that's early. That idiot night guard, Uri. Woke me quarter of an hour before time. Said his list was mixed up.' He jammed the hat on again. 'I didn't have the energy to argue with him just now. He shook his finger. 'Just wait 'till I see him at lunchtime!'

Ella smiled. Gavriel and his hours of sleep. It was a standing joke in the kibbutz.

'Why don't you use an alarm clock?' She smiled. 'More reliable.' And for her, definitely less disturbing than the night guard knocking at her thin plywood door in the dark.

'I would too,' he muttered, 'but it disturbs Rivka.' Then reaching out, he slapped the last straggler on the rump and swung home a small steel gate. 'Not that I blame her,' he muttered, turning back towards the doorway. No, he would never begrudge Rivka her sleep. Ever...

Ella followed him down the steps, the morning gloom falling from her shoulders with his genial company in the familiar surroundings. For a moment she even managed to forget the traumatic previous evening, Harold's bad fall, then Itzik turning up, she couldn't have had more than a few hours sleep.

'Anyway,' Gavriel called over the din of the compressor motors, 'with the early start, we should finish with time to spare.'

Ella smiled to herself. Good old Gavriel, always the optimist. Like her father, when they were seated behind a pier at the rear of the theatre in Melbourne. 'Never mind,' he said, 'we'll get out before the rush.'

Hurrying through to the office, she flopped down onto a metal chair and pulled a pair of blue rubber boots towards her. She glanced at the filing cabinet then at the desk. Five buff cards lay ready for the vet who would be coming later that morning.

When she'd first arrived, the herd record cards were kept in an old hand-grenade box. Every clumsy move sent the whole lot scattering across the muddy floor. 'You need a proper filing system,' she'd nagged. The boys resisted - as though something old and ex-army was an essential part of some pioneering ethos they wished to preserve. Even when she'd eventually worn them down, they'd bought this battered old cabinet at the flea market in Jaffa.

Despite their ideals and protestations about sex-equality, they were a macho crowd – except Gavriel with his old fashioned *noblesse oblige* – and of course Harold. The *Sabras*, the native born Israelis were most at fault. And Itzik, the worst of all. Oh, God. Itzik. She didn't need him in her head. Not now. Not this morning.

Ella pulled on one fluffy, grey, sock and wiggled her toes into the first boot. It took more effort than usual and she sat back before attempting the second one. At times like this, she questioned her decision to work with the dairy herd, the routine was so relentless and demanding. Yet she chose it herself and had fought hard to gain her place. And she knew why.

Cows were awkward and at first glance stupid, animals, yet each had her own character and temperament. And they weren't that stupid either when they wanted not to be. Then there were the horses. Ella had always loved horses, ever since Roger had taught her to ride up on the High Plains in New South Wales. So when she saw the cowmen out here taking the herd to pasture in the *wadi*, she was sure that this was the place she wanted to work.

It was just after she arrived, an early spring and the last rains still to come. From the top of the hill, the herd moved like a huge black and white quilt, flowing over the folds in the ground as it sought out the fresh grass that sprouted in the hollows. Two horsemen were riding round like a scene from a vintage Western, except that those weren't six-shooters they toted. And it wasn't the Comanches on the far side of that ridge.

The summer sun eventually burned off the last grazing and when deep fissures opened in the parched loess soil, the cattle were confined to the yards and the irrigated pasture. No more horse riding. But by then she had become hooked.

Ella pulled on the other sock and boot, then stood up and stamped on the tiled floor. A bright green Gecko lizard scurried across the fly screen over the high window and clamped a fluttering moth in its jaws. For a moment, she stared as they both struggled. Then jumped. What on earth was she doing, standing here idle and gawping?

Draping her cardigan over the back of the chair, she hurried through to the machine room. The vacuum motors throbbed and a giant paddle stirred the milk in the cooling tank. A defective fluorescent light reflected stroboscopically from the stainless steel sinks, making her eyes ache, she must get someone to change the tube later.

Straightening her headscarf, Ella clipped a bright steel container onto an overhead flange then, with a sharp twist of her wrist, flicked a lever. Immediately a soft hissing added to the general noise as the vacuum built up in the milking lines. Everything was now ready.

Outside in the yard, Gavriel was coaxing in the first cows.

'*Yalla. Yalla!*' Get a move on *nevelot*.'

Ella smiled to herself. *Nevelo*t: "rotten corpses". He loved the cows but was so fond of that curse. Plunging her hands into the sinks, she pulled out a tangle of umbilical black rubber tubing. It twisted and writhed as if with a life of its own as she carried them it into the milking parlour.

Gavriel's deep voice urged again from the yard outside and the first massive, angular heads poked through the doorways, eyes bulging, neck chains clinking as they sashayed onto the concrete ramps. Ella stepped down into the pit, slipped the tubes onto the steel nozzles of the six milking stalls then retied her headscarf. Above her, the frosted-glass windows lightened. Outside, the sky was growing brighter, soon it would be daylight. Another working day had begun. Already she felt better.

Less than a mile away to the north, a deep, dry riverbed still cloaked in shadow cut its winding way through the grey soil on its way to the sea. Hidden in a clump of bushes in a sharp bend of the *wadi*, four men anxiously watched the sky growing lighter.

Peering through the Tamarisk fronds at the edge of the thicket, Ahmed gripped a Carl Gustav sub-machine gun, his face taut, listening. With the sun rising, slowly the shadows were sinking down the far bank. Soon it would be broad daylight here too – and with it, their situation even more desperate.

2.

The early light flowed over the plain and across the border, out towards the still darkened sea. On the sand dunes by the shore, in the sprawling melange of tin huts and tattered tents of the Shaati refugee camp, Ibrahim rose for morning prayers.

Jamilla had risen too even though she had no need to. Like every morning, she wanted to start the day with him, she'd done this ever since they'd been dumped on these barren dunes. Despite her husband's optimism and wanting to be independent, Jamilla knew that each additional day of this miserable existence was gradually wearing Ibrahim down, eating away at his spirit.

Rolling up their bedding on the earthen floor they'd beaten down to cover the sand, Jamilla lit the small paraffin stove. She made them both a cup of coffee and insisted he munch a piece of *pitta* bread before going down to the town.

'Don't forget black olives,' she said, 'and the cardamom,' always seeking a way to make him feel he was doing something useful. The inactivity and boredom was destroying everyone's souls in the camp and with it, the expectation that they would return one day.

Jamilla glanced around the small hut of corrugated sheets and plywood that they had gradually cobbled together over years after they moved out of the tent. Across the rear was a half-open curtain where the children had once slept. Apart from a rickety chair that Ahmed found dumped and three small cupboards made from old orange boxes, the hut was bare. Just a faded poster of the sacred *Haram* in Al Quds on the wall and alongside, a framed photograph of the elder son and his family in Kuwait.

After a brief nod Ibrahim went out and wanting be busy doing something, Jamilla took up a small besom and brushed out the hut. Later she would go down to the strand to see if she could buy a few small fish to vary their monotonous diet of h*ummus* and *full*-beans, and whatever vegetables happened to be in season.

Settling a woollen cap on his sparse, white hair, Ibrahim set off from the camp and out along the road to Gaza, his tall, lean figure joining the day labourers on their way to the building sites and orange groves. Ahead of him to the east, the sandstone ridge stood silhouetted against the lightening sky, seeming even sharper and blacker than usual. Ahmed hadn't been home for over a week now and he was wondering why.

His son had never stayed away for so long, though as yet he was more puzzled than worried. If only the boy had gone to study in Egypt, like his brother. *Insh'allah,* he would soon be home, he'd tried to calm Jamilla last night.

Ibrahim entered the town just as the sun rose and headed for the Great Mosque. In the Alley of the Silversmiths, night still clung to the bolted doorways. Here and there, a shopkeeper was taking down his wooden shutters. From the tall minaret, the *muezzin's* loudspeaker called to the faithful and Ibrahim greeted fellow worshipers on their way to morning prayers. A laden donkey passed him on the way to the market. By the time he came out, the town would be bustling.

The sun climbed into a cloudless sky. Bright sunlight penetrated the alleyways of the ancient town then flowed across the dunes to Ibrahim's camp by the sea. It dazzled the Egyptian sentry raising President Nasser's new flag over the lookout post on the ridge and recognising no borders, began to burn off the night's dew from the corrugated roofs of the kibbutz cowsheds.

It sparkled through the frosted glass windows of the milking parlour where Ella was fitting the rubber hoses to the clusters of milking cups. Urged on by Gavriel, the next batch of six cows swung through the end doors, licking the steel yokes as they lumbered onto the concrete stalls, neck chains and identity tags clinking on the rails.

'*Yalla. Yalla!*' yelled Gavriel. 'Get a move on!' He hopped down the metal steps into the pit flush-faced, still annoyed at his untimely wakening. If that *schlemiel* Uri could keep his mind off Deborah for a few minutes he was thinking, he might manage to get the time right.

Gavriel was a creature of habit. Each morning after being wakened, he would lay back for a few precious moments, setting the coming day into some kind of frame. Then, before getting out of bed, he would turn and press his body against Rivka, holding her shoulder. Gently, she would take his hand and squeeze it, then reassured, drop off to sleep again. They had done that ever since... ever since.

Walking to the far end of the pit, Gavriel reached up and swung a long lever. The gates along his side closed with a sharp metallic clang, pinning three cows into their stalls. As Ella swung the lever on her side, their eyes met. Gavriel nodded and she smiled back.

Gavriel was a one-woman man, but he could easily see why Itzik had gone overboard. Even with this morning's puffy eyes and grey complexion, Ella still had that cheeky, attractive face. Yet he sometimes wondered about her and Harold. Platonic? Probably. People talked. Ella and Itzik. Ella and Harold. He couldn't stand gossip. If everyone had enough going in their own life, they wouldn't need to. Still, she seemed well able to handle it. Reminded him of the Bantam hen in the children's farmyard, small and pretty, but no nonsense.

When all six cows were ready, Ella turned a lever and a regular tsck, tsck, tsck, filled the room, the rhythm of vacuum pulsing through the pipes. Picking a small flannel from a wire basket hanging by the stalls she began to wipe down the first udder.

Ella liked working with Gavriel. Calm, confident movements, observing everything that went on down his long triangular nose. 'A real Rumanian nose this.' He would say, tapping the side with his finger, 'always tell a Rumanian by his nose!'

After fitting the cups to the first cow, Ella half turned towards him, hesitant.

'Don't think Harold will be down today,' she said, above the hiss of the pipelines. Gavriel was, squirting water from a hand jet and washing down his last cow.

'No. Don't suppose he will. Not after yesterday evening.' The cow kicked with its back foot. Gavriel swore. 'Still, Itzik will have arranged a replacement.' He wiped the udder dry, picked up a cluster of four milking cups and fitted them to the teats. 'By the way,' he called, 'watch that second one, Amira. She kicked off the cups yesterday.'

Ella glanced to her left. Like Itzik, Gavriel knew every one of their hundred odd milking cows by name. To Ella, a few months ago they all looked pretty much alike, black and white patches and snotty pink noses. But gradually, she'd learned to distinguish individual patterns, a single black spot here, a completely white leg there, a different shaped horn and so on. And with her growing confidence came the satisfaction of becoming accepted as one of the chosen few.

To work with the dairy herd, Harold joked, was as near to being part of an aristocracy as you could get in this egalitarian society. Harold. Would he ever feel like joking again after last night? She thought of his dry humour and restless intellect. Grey eyes twinkling through his steel framed glasses. Without his wry jokes and their endless discussions, even here the daily routine might easily have turned into a grinding monotony.

Ella began to wash down her second cow, rubbing and fondling the udder to draw down the milk. The swollen pink mass gave way to her hand, then returned to its shape. She found it pleasurable and soothing. 'Just Freudian,' Harold remarked one day, 'mother's breast and all that Melanie Klein stuff.'

'So what about you?' she'd countered. He'd just given that wry smile again and carried on working.

After washing down, came the testing: squirting from each teat onto a black plastic disc to look for telltale curds of mastitis. Then the milking itself, slipping on the rubber cups, taking the weight with her hand until the suction took over, sending the milk spurting and frothing into the glass container slung above her head. And then on to the next cow and the third before returning to the first to strip it down and remove the cups.

Gavriel worked with a steady rhythm, a method in every one of his deliberate movements. Ella bustled to and fro, desperately trying to keep up so that both sets of three cows would finish at the same time. Then together, they swung the levers overhead, the end gates opened and the six cows jostled and slithered down the concrete ramp that led back to their cowshed. After a quick hose down, the next batch was let in and the whole procedure started again.

As the routine took over, Ella began to feel more her usual self. Cocooned with Gavriel within their own world, she weaved back and forth along the concrete pit, dodging the air lines, watching the milk levels rising in the containers, then hand stripping the last drops before removing the cups.

Like most agricultural work, the cowshed routine was repetitive. But, unlike weeding or fruit picking, it was never boring.

Which was another reason why she had fought so hard to become a permanent worker in the dairy. The smiling girl holding a Jaffa orange looked enticing on the Israeli tourist board's posters, but humping bag after bag of fruit to the boxes day after day was soul destroying. And as for weeding, as far as she was concerned that was definitely for masochists.

Ella rested her back against the kerb of the concrete stall, waiting for the next batch of cows to take their places. For a moment, she closed her eyes, thinking of her first days in the cowshed. How quickly she had learned - and how overconfident she'd become, not appreciating just how much the others were helping her. Until that terrible day, during the second week.

She was on afternoon shift with Gavriel and all was going well until the third batch, when a young heifer kicked off the cups. Hurrying to refit them, she didn't notice that one hose was kinked, cutting off the vacuum. At that moment, another set of cups rattled to the concrete at the far end. Ella scurried back and slipped them on, again without checking. The udder was dry and they fell off straight away, just as the kinked set dropped into a dung pat.

Snatching at the hose to wash down, she tugged too hard. The gun came away from the water-hose and the pipe began to thrash and writhe as though alive, spurting water in all directions. Startled, the cows stamped and tossed their heads, eyes wild and bulging. Soaked to the skin, Ella jumped back fearing a kick from the sharp hooves, then completely loosing it, buried her head in her hands and froze.

Even now, Ella winced as she remembered standing, paralysed, tears streaming down her face. She had failed. They would throw her out and it would be back to weeding sugar beet or washing dishes. But she remembered too, how it had ended. Gavriel's warm hand on her shoulder, her turning round, unable to look him in the eye and burying her head on his chest.

Calmly, Gavriel had shut down the hosepipe and waited until she stopped crying. Then, without a word he turned away, replaced the fallen cups and washed out the second set, stripping and cleaning down along both sides, before sending all six cows away down the ramp.

Ella remembered too the sudden stillness, just the soft hiss of the vacuum lines and the sharp, damp smell from the stalls as he waited, silent, wiping his hands. In those few moments, she managed to compose herself and dry her eyes. And when she looked up, he was smiling.

'*Le'at. Le'at,*' he said with that fluid Russian 'L', 'Slowly. Slowly. Don't rush it.' Not patronising, just so caring. She grasped his hands, thanking him again and again. A surge of love, as for a brother - perhaps for the brother she had never had.

Ella wiped her hands on her trousers and straightened her headscarf. Poor Gavriel. He'd been so embarrassed, they were a puritan lot, the Rumanians, at times even prudish she thought. If only she hadn't taken Itzik's response a few weeks later to have been as brotherly.

It had been on the early morning shift, just she and Itzik, the head cowman. Suddenly everything went wrong just like that time with Gavriel - milking cups clattering to the concrete, cows stamping, vacuum lines tangled. The lot. Stifling the impulse to scream, she turned leaned against the rails, head in hands.

Itzik had rapidly sorted it out too, hands and arms moving like the pistons of a highly geared engine. Then those same hands resting on her shoulders, reassuring, slowly turning her around and holding her against his chest. And still in a state of panic she didn't resist. It was secure. Comforting. Strong arms and the smell of a man's body.

They could have only stood there like that for less than a minute before she realised that it was much more than just consoling, that he was pressing her tighter and tighter against him, her breasts squashed against his burning chest and his lips on her head.

Regaining her composure, slowly Ella disengaged and carried on with the milking, unable to look him in the eyes for the rest of the shift and praying for it to be over quickly without any more mishaps.

She should have made it clear there and then. But she didn't. Perhaps she was flattered, a leading member of the kibbutz, a *Sabra*, tall and good looking, head of the dairy, all sorts of reasons she could rationalise about now. But what a fool she'd been. Then there was that second occasion... But, no, she didn't want to think about that now. Today, she wanted just to get the work over with, to shower and get back to her room to sleep off the trauma and weariness of last night.

Ella glanced up at the windows, now bright with the sunlight, but it did little to ease the tiredness. She couldn't wait for this first batch to be over, to work through the second one then go up for breakfast. To get through the rest of the day, she so needed that break.

3.

The sun continued its climb into a cloudless sky, merging the clefts and folds in the ground into the violet and grey of the waking plain. Then that too blended in with the dull yellow of the parched expanse, broken only by a sporadic thorny-acacia tree.

The harsh morning sunlight struck the flank of a conical hill that rose from the bank of the wadi, *Tel Farah,* the ancient city of the Hyksos, its ruined mud-brick ramparts surveying the plain as they had done for over three thousand years.

With weapons of iron, these Shepherd Kings from the north had driven all before them and conquered the Nile valley. Driven out in turn by the Pharaohs they retreated across the wadi, and with them came the nomadic Habiru, who would later claim this land as their own.

Through the ages, the ancient Tel looked on, slowly crumbling as empire followed empire, the armies of Egypt and Babylon, Persia, Greece and Rome marching north and south across the plain, century after century, the sands drenched in a never-ending flow of blood.

Then came the sons of Mohammed and after them the Crusaders, their two centuries of wars laying waste the land, leaving it to the torpor and decay of the Ottoman empire. Across the silent plain wandered the nomad Bedouin with their flocks of black goats, overgrazing and spreading the wasteland ever westwards, up to the ridge of sand-hills that became a border between the desert and the sown - the fertile coastal strip with its mud-hut villages huddled around the sleepy town of Gaza.

Yet more destruction followed Napoleon's Grand Design and his retreat until finally, after Allenby's soldiers had driven out the Turks, for a while there was a kind of peace. Here and there, a Bedouin family dug a well, built a mud hut and settled. Jewish pioneers founded stockaded settlements and the sound of the tractor was heard in the land. A time of live and let live. But it was not to last.

In 1948, armies once again marched north from the Nile. A year later, they fled in retreat and a new state had been born. Generals and diplomats sat around a table on the island of Rhodes and drew a green line on the map. And again the border ran along the sand-hill ridge.

This too was called peace. Remnants of the Holocaust came to join the sons of the early pioneers. Kibbutzim, collective villages, sprang up along one side of the green line, new settlements bubbling with life and hope, bursting to make the desert bloom. New settlements also arose on the other side of that Green Line, but these were full of despair and desperation, Palestinian refugee camps of tents and tin huts.

And to all these, the old *Tel* bore silent witness, towering over the deep river bed of the Wadi Shelaleh that carried mighty winter floods from the mountains of Hebron to the sea, its swirling waters cutting ever deeper through the soft loëss soil around its base.

A mile downstream from the *Tel*, where the floodwaters had gouged a steep overhang in a bend of the wadi was a thicket of green reeds and tamarisk bushes. Having survived foraging camels and Bedouin women searching for tinder, its greenery provided welcome shade. Now, within its cover on the bed of dry tamarisk needles, a man lay groaning from the pain of a shattered leg. Close by the three others crouched, waiting and powerless, the last painkillers had gone.

Ahmed stared across the mud-crust and flood-smoothed pebbles of the dry riverbed. Stirred by the last breaths of the desert night breeze, tamarisk fronds brushed his cheek. Stockily built, with sharp, brown eyes and a bushy moustache, he glanced at his watch. Across the border, where the wadi continued its way past the town of Gaza towards the sea, his father would be in the mosque by now, praying. Much good praying had done. It would never get the *Yahud* off their land. No. It would be as Ismail always said: through the barrel of a gun.

Turning slowly, he beckoned to Ismail. The tall, lean figure, balding and long faced with a sharp nose crept forward. *El Aakil,* they called him - the cunning one. Together they looked and listened, their olive green denims merging with the bushes, boots caked with the white loëss soil through which they had walked all night.

Gripping his Carl Gustav, Ahmed glanced back up the wadi. The crest of the *Tel* shone in the sunlight, the Israelis were sure to have lookouts up there. He turned back. Their only escape was downstream. It was less than half a mile to the border. If only they could make it.

Ismail too was now staring down the wadi, cursing under his breath. Another hour of darkness and they would have done it. That brush with the patrol and having to carry the wounded Fais had delayed them until dawn. Now, any sudden move would give them away.

It would take a miracle for them to survive until nightfall and Ismail didn't believe in God or miracles. Their only hope lay with the Egyptian army up there on the ridge. Yet to rely on them, he would indeed have to begin to believe in miracles.

Brother Arabs, the Egyptians called them, but they behaved like an army of occupation, treated the refugees like outcasts and the *Fedayeen* fighters as a nuisance that served only to provoke Israeli reprisal raids. They had never helped before and probably wouldn't this time either. Yet perhaps, just this once, they might. *Insh'allah*. Though if He was up there, He hadn't ever helped much either...

From beyond the far bank, came the throb of an engine and whining gears. An Israeli half-tracked vehicle was edging towards the border to cut them off. Ismail nudged Ahmed's elbow and motioned him to get back into the bushes, his comrade had been on watch since they took shelter just before dawn. Ismail glanced up at the sky. It was getting lighter. They would all busy again soon enough.

The sun mounted higher, warming the parched soil and reflecting dazzling bright from the whitewashed walls of the dairy. Along the road, the eucalyptus leaves now hung dry and grey and listless.

Within the cool dampness of the milking parlour, as the machines pulsed and the routine continued, Ella mulled over her discussion with Gavriel and Rivka the week before. How anti-Semitism then disillusion with the Communist regime had driven them to leave Rumania and come out here. It made her think yet again of her own decision to join the kibbutz.

Nothing so dramatic had driven her, she hadn't fled persecution. True, she'd experienced some snide remarks in school and at university but her memories of Melbourne were overwhelmingly fond ones. And when she told them she was going to a kibbutz in Israel, her friends back home thought her absolutely crazy: 'If it's challenge and roughing it you're after,' they'd joked, 'there's plenty here in the Outback!'

But she had her own good reasons why she had chosen to settle in this place - perhaps some she wouldn't readily admit. And she supposed that despite the good times with Roger, precisely because they had been so good that those awkward incidents had awakened her consciousness.

It wasn't her first relationship, but it was the deepest. They met in the Socialist Society at Uni, he with his mop of fair hair and blue eyes and sunburned face. Came from a farming family up on the High Plains of New South Wales.

'Can't you find a nice Jewish boy in Melbourne', her mother moaned. Dad had been less critical. Seemed to trust her more.

Roger invited her for a weekend up to the farm. She loved horses and was thrilled at the idea.

'Does his family know?' asked Dad as if by the way, knowing they were Catholics.

'Doesn't matter to him,' she retorted. 'He's not their generation.'

'If he's the only son, it might, though,' Dad said but he patted her shoulder and wished her a good time. Mum refused to speak to her all that Thursday.

Ella remembered the thrill of riding at speed across the plains, wind in her hair and cheeks burning, then lying with Roger in the shade of a eucalypt. But afterwards there was the undisguised coldness of his mother and the strange way Roger had accepted – even excused it – making her, Ella feeling she was out of place.

When they got back to Uni, it wasn't as it had been. Something she couldn't pinpoint but it was there. And slowly they drifted apart, although at the time she hadn't fathomed why. And from, then on, more and more she wondered about the differences – and started thinking about her own identity.

Now, having arrived and settled in, Ella knew that she had been seeking a corner that was hers, a place where she would feel at peace and at home. Something with which she could identify, body and spirit. Like that stanza of a translation of a Hebrew poem she read: 'Do not question why they come or from where.

Those who in their hearts seek a purpose, whoever they are, let them come and join us . . .' Or something like that.

Even in the vibrant student life of Melbourne and all through her travels and backpacking, Ella had never felt so much at one with herself as she did here in this troubled corner of isolated desert...

A cluster of milking cups clattered to the concrete at the far end. In her daydreaming, she'd forgotten to keep an eye on the milk flow. Adjusting her headscarf again, Ella hurried to wash them out then she checked the other two cows. Yes, she mused as she washed them out, at one with herself - even with the aggravations of last night.

With the sun now shining directly through the high window, it was starting to grow warmer. Rolling up her sleeves Ella glanced up. The frosted glass had grown even brighter. Suddenly she noticed the empty stalls, the next batch hadn't come in. Having become accustomed to the new milking parlour the cows generally followed on in as each batch went out. Not now. The last stragglers must be hanging back.

Ella glanced at her watch. The time had flown, it always did at milking. She hopped up the steps into the collecting yard, squinting at the sudden glare. Half a dozen cows stood in the yard, motionless, heads hanging low in the heat. They were the heifers and new purchases, the lowest in the pecking order.

Each cow had its well-defined status in the herd, sorted out during the snortings and scufflings in the dung-strewn yards. Not a single beast would move out until the leading cow swung through the gateway and then, only in strict order of seniority. 'The perfect feudal society,' said Harold.

Down in the milking-parlour pit, Gavriel waited but no heads poked through the doorway. He breathed out, Ella would need help. Hopping up the steps too, he cautiously eased his way around to the far side of the yard. Any sudden movement and the cows would panic and slither all over the wet concrete.

'*Nu, nu, nu,*' he called softly as they both shepherded the first three towards the left-hand entry door, '*nu, nu, nu.*'

They managed to coax two inside but a third became wedged astride the opening.

'Haven't see this one before,' said Ella. It was almost completely white, just one small black eye-patch. Gavriel took hold of its neck chain and gently eased the head through the door.

'She's new,' he grunted, 'called Daliah. Itzik bought her in Dorot yesterday.'

At the mention of Itzik's name, Ella tensed. Gavriel appeared not to notice, as he manoeuvred the cow through the doorway and onto the stall. 'Say's she'll be a real champion.'

With the blockage resolved, Ella managed to bring in the last three by herself and quietly they recommenced the milking. But two minutes later, Gavriel cursed, above his head, the glass container was empty.

'*Neveilah srocha*,' he swore, 'she's holding back!'

Ella smiled to herself again at his favourite oath.

As if peeved at being rumbled, the cow kicked off the milking cups. Gavriel refitted them but a few seconds later, with a vicious kick they were off again.

'To hell with it,' he muttered, 'Itzik bought a load of trouble with this one, that's for sure.'

Slipping one arm in front of the cow's hind leg, he pressed his hand up against her belly. Then, holding the tail high with his other hand, he told Ella to refit the cups. The cow raised her leg to kick, but was immediately off balance and had to put it down again. It tried twice more, then resignedly stood still. Soon, milk began to flow into the container, higher and higher as though it would never stop. Gavriel winked at Ella.

'Bloody Itzik,' he muttered, 'got it right as usual!'

Ella leaned her head into the soft belly, her weariness returning with the gentle, rhythmic breathing. Itzik. God, hadn't she made it clear enough? Would she have to scream it out in single syllables for him to get the message?'

'Right.' Gavriel's voice cut in as he dropped the tail, 'she's almost finished.'

Ella pulled away from the steaming flank. The fluorescent light stung her eyes as she wrote the yield on the record card, but as Gavriel withdrew his arm the beast swished her tail and kicked out, the sharp hoof just missing his elbow.

'Neveilah!' he snapped, 'Did you see that?'

Ella grinned.

'Never mind. You won that round.'

Gavriel scratched his nose.

'Just about. But it will still take a few days for her to settle, that's for sure.'

The other cows had long finished and Ella raised her arm and swung the gate lever for them to exit. As the troublesome cow scuttled out and down the ramp with the others, Ella glanced at Gavriel.

'How much time did we lose?'

'About as much as we gained from the early start. Still,' he continued, 'that's the last of the awkward squad.' Ella washed her hands over the cleaning jets, smiling. Ever the optimist, Gavriel.

With the dairy empty, suddenly everything was so calm, just the soft pulsing of the vacuum lines and dripping hoses. Gavriel wiped his face with his blue, cloth hat, breathing deeply, then looked at Ella, his forehead furrowed.

'Well, if Harold won't be down, I wonder who Itzik has replaced him with?' He jammed the hat back on his head. 'Anyway, I'll go and bring along the next group along.' But as he turned and put his foot on the steps, a pale, thin face poked through the centre doorway, steel rimmed spectacles glinting in the fluorescent light.

Gavriel stiffened, then steadied himself, holding onto the rail beside him.

'Harold! Why.. ? Er. . . I . . .'

Ella looked up, mouth open, one hand gripping the concrete kerb to the stalls.

'*Boker Tov,*' drawled Harold in his Lancashire lilted Hebrew and his teeth set in a forced smile.

'Er. *Boker Tov,* Harold,' Gavriel managed to say as he stepped down again to regain his balance. Ella wanted to greet him too, but before she could speak, Harold had ducked out and was hurrying away, his rubber boots clomping across the empty yard.

Gavriel turned and shrugged, then Ella and he stood for a moment, neither saying a word, just the hiss of the vacuum filling the silence. Jumping up the steps, Gavriel looked out. Harold was walking swiftly down the straw-strewn walkway to the new cowshed, his woollen khaki hat bobbing between the rails. At the far end, the gates clanged.

Reassured he jumped back down into the pit.

'Right,' he said, shrugging in response to Ella's questioning eyes, 'That leaves us ready for the next lot.'

Picking up the hoses, they started to wash down the concrete stalls, staring at the muck and mud disappearing into the drains. Avoiding each other's eyes. And thoughts.

4.

Harold ducked away from the doorway as soon as he could, the astonished looks from Ella and Gavriel had been sufficient. He climbed through the rails of the yard and out onto the walkway. The last batch of cows sent out from the dairy stared at him with dark, bulging eyes, their hides damp and glistening

What did they sense, these dumb, placid creatures? His exhaustion? The sadness? The desperation? He smacked the last cow on her rump as it ambled off along the walkway then swung home the metal gate. The clang of metal on metal echoed across the sand and up through the trees.

On most days, this was the time he would go back to the dairy and brew coffee for the milkers and himself. They would take a brief rest, leaning back against the empty stalls in the cool isolation of the cool milking parlour, the hot sweet liquid seeping into their bodies as they chatted and joked. It was part of the camaraderie that made the early shift so special, no matter how many times. But not today. Ella's startled face, her white knuckles, Gavriel's mouth hanging open. No. Not now...

Harold gripped the cold steel tubing and wiped his free hand across his face. He didn't want to talk with anyone right now, nor think of last night. And as he followed the cows back to the sheds, he murmured: 'Please God - or anyone else - just let me get through the day.'

Harold had an uneven gait, his arms swinging from the elbows and seemingly out of synch with his footsteps. Heavy lensed spectacles were perched on his prominent nose, but his grey eyes missed nothing. Neither did the ever-whirring cogs of his mind.

'*Meshlumpar*', the Sabras called him, his sleeves always rolled up different lengths, shirttail flapping from his trousers. But they had a sneaking respect for him. For despite his slight frame, Harold could match any of them at work. And work was the criterion by which any *kibbutznik* was primarily judged.

They also admired him for the way he battled against his epilepsy for there was nothing they held in higher esteem than a fighter. And Harold had never fought harder than this morning to get up and come down to work.

At the end of the walkway, he shot home the long bolt. It had been welded on in addition to the gate-catch after a mischievous heifer had opened the gate, it had taken them the best part of a morning to round up the herd again. The cold metal was slimy where they licked the salt of sweaty hands. Wiping his hands on his navy-blue trousers, Harold swung open a wide gate to the yard of the second cowshed, calling and clapping his hands. Two black and white shapes heaved to their feet. The rest stayed on the ground, jaws incessantly chewing.

Harold waved his arms.

'*Yalla! Yalla!*' he shouted in his heavily accented Hebrew. '*Kumu. Kumu!*' get up! he called, urging them towards the gateway, envying the deep throaty roar of Itzik or Nahum and also their thick, leathery soles as they side-stepped the cowpats. Harold was not nearly so sure footed, he always wore gumboots.

The blood rose to his head. Every morning there was a similar farce to coax them to the milking parlour, despite it being the same routine day after day. Defies Pavlov, he would moan to Ella. This morning it seemed they were taunting him even more, testing to see if he would snap. He wouldn't. He'd show them.

Searching out the leading cow, he saw Carmella lying along the far side in the shade of the eaves. Harold felt murderous as he strode towards her. Observing him approach, the beast rose and snorted, stretched her neck and lowed, then swung leisurely through the open gate, pausing to lick the hinges then her leg before, in her own time, setting off up the walkway.

Slowly at first and then in an ever increasing rush, the rest of the group followed in order of seniority, stopping whenever she did, creating log jams of swishing tails and tossing heads between the steel fence rails.

As the last bunch squeezed through the gateway, one cow mounted another and hung there, its chin resting on the other's back. Harold looked for the tell tale markings on the one beneath. Could be Yardena. Then he saw the white star on her forehead and the downturned horns. It was Tzipora. On Heat! Itzik would be over the moon. She'd missed the vet last time and a whole month's milk had been lost.

Harold followed the last cows to the collecting yard, shut the gate, then walked round to the office and chalked Tzipora's name on the board alongside three others. Dusting the chalk from his fingers, he quickly hurried out, walking around the outside of the dairy to avoid meeting Gavriel or Ella, as if running away like some criminal. And he did feel guilty, the seizure last night was of his own stupid fault. He'd had fair warning - that dull headache between the eyes spreading out over his scalp. He knew the signs and should have gone straight to bed. Instead, he ignored it, his mind spinning and his whole body so worked-up after the argument with that soldier earlier in the evening.

It all started just after he finished supper with Ella and her friend Miriam. As the three came out onto the porch of the dining hall, two soldiers were hovering by the doors.

'Any chance of a cup of coffee,' called a tall, ginger-haired corporal, 'and there's three more of us below.'

'Sure.' Miriam nodded over her shoulder, 'ask inside.'

The corporal winked.

'What, by ourselves?'

'Why not?' Miriam countered in Sabra slang. 'You look old enough not to get lost.' And within a few seconds, they were bantering in rapid, colloquial Hebrew which neither Ella nor Harold completely understood. When Ella decided to go inside to sort out the coffee herself, gradually Harold began to get the gist of the conversation.

The patrol had caught an infiltrator in the nearby fields and had come up to telephone their base for transport.

'The older bastard got away,' the corporal was telling Miriam, 'but we managed to nab the boy.'

'Yes. And a bloody good beating will soon sort him out,' added the soldier.

Curious, Harold edged closer.

'The boy,' he asked, 'How old is he?'

'Who knows,' said the corporal. 'Ten, eleven. They start 'em young over there.' As he turned to Miriam to carry on flirting, Harold addressed the soldier. He was dark skinned with black, wavy hair.

'What was he doing?' Harold asked.

'Doing?' replied the soldier in the throaty accent of the oriental Jews, 'what does it matter? This one was collecting the binder twine off your hay bales. If we hadn't noticed them scattered all over the track, they'd have got away with the lot.'

At that moment Ella came out with an aluminium mug of steaming coffee and two cups.

'Here, grab it.' Miriam smiled, 'and just don't get used to the personal service.'

As the soldiers turned to go, Harold stepped forward.

'Where is the boy now?' he asked.

'Down by your silo, tied to a stanchion,' muttered the soldier.

'He won't get far.'

'Got a real chip on his shoulder, that one,' said Miriam after they'd gone 'Anyway, I'm on duty in the kindergarten. See you later Ella.'

As she walked off, Harold turned to Ella.

'That's just a kid they've got tied up down there. Who knows how long he's been like that?'

'Okay,' said Ella, reading his thoughts, 'let's go and see and take him some tucker.' In their personal conversations, Harold usually reverted back to English and she to her Aussie vernacular.

The boy was hunched up on the sand, his ankles tied together and his hands roped to the steel post. He was dressed in a torn green shirt and frayed trousers. A few yards away, the patrol sat in a circle, sipping coffee.

As they approached the boy, Ella holding a piece of bread smeared with soft cheese and Harold a mug of coffee, the soldier who had been up top, pointed to them.

'Hey look,' he scoffed, *'Kibbutzniks.* Sisters of mercy!'

Ella leaned down and placed the mug and the bread beside the boy. He curled up against the post, his eyes wide and white in the light of the grain store.

Harold turned to the corporal.

'That's no way to treat a kid. Trussing him up like a dog.'

The corporal shrugged. The soldier laughed,

'Huh. That 'kid', as you call him, would just as soon bury a *shabariyyeh* between your shoulder blades, as look as you.'

'Maybe,' said Harold, 'But if we treat him like a human being, he might grow up thinking differently. Accept that we Israelis are not monsters.'

'Okay, Moshe,' the Corporal called over. 'Untie his hands so he can eat. But keep his feet bound.' As the soldier untied one hand, leaving the other secured to the stanchion, the boy flinched and raised his free arm as if to protect himself. Slowly, he brought it down then grabbed the bread, biting off huge chunks as if to make sure he would finish it before someone took it away.

'Only a kid eh?' the soldier scoffed, hitching up his F.N. automatic. 'Feed him!' he spat on the sand then glanced at Ella. 'Know what they'd do to her if they caught her over their side? And to you?' He drew his hand across his throat. 'And they'd hand you back in a sack. In tiny pieces.'

The corporal walked across to stand by Ella and they watched the tableau, the soldier, short and squat, his face thrust towards Harold's slight frame and his glinting glasses. Two figures, silhouetted against the yellow lamplight.

'You and your principles, kibbutznik,' the soldier was saying. 'Those animals almost killed my mother in Algeria. That's why we left. And we didn't come here to be murdered in our beds like those poor kids in that village the other night!'

Harold took a step back.

'Look. I know what you're trying to say. But . . .' He stopped, trying to translate the idiom in his head, 'but two wrongs don't make a right. We are different. We live by certain principles don't we?'

'Sure. We are different,' snapped the soldier. 'Them, you can never trust, *habibi*.' He pointed at the boy. 'He'll be the same. Should have finished him off out there.'

Ella walked towards Harold. He turned to meet her, tense and frustrated. But the soldier blocked his way. Pulling up his sleeve, he turned his arm towards the light.

'See that?' A long, jagged scar ran from his wrist up to just below the elbow, 'Got that when I was only thirteen. Just a bit older than him down there. In Algiers, every day I tried a different way home from school. One day they caught me.' He coughed, 'the other bruises don't show now.' He spat on the ground again, 'Animals, the Arabs. That's what they are. And you and your principles won't ever change them, *habibi*. Never!'

Harold stared at the scar. What were his experiences of anti-Semitism compared to that? A few stones in Hightown? The snide comments at Grammar School, much as they hurt at the time? He suddenly felt humbled.

'When did you come to Israel,' he asked, taking off his glasses and wiping them.

'Nineteen Fifty-one. After the riots in the *Mellah* in Algiers,' the soldier answered. 'They looted my father's shop. We were lucky to escape with our lives. And you feed him?' Suddenly he turned away, hitched up his gun and walked off into the shadows.

The corporal strolled across to Harold.

'Look,' he said softly, 'don't think we all feel like Moshe. He's had a rough time and you won't change him.' Looking at Ella, he added, 'and with the new immigration from Morocco, Iraq and countries like that, there are many like him now.'

At that moment, two pencils of light swung through the main gate and a command car roared up to the silo, shattering the night's calm. Two soldiers grabbed the boy and dumped him in the rear, then they all climbed aboard. As the truck drew away, the soldier leaned out of the rear and waved.

'*Shalom,* kibbutzniks. Thanks for the coffee, anyway!'

Ella and Harold collected up the cups and plates and climbed the track to the dining hall. At the porch, Ella stood for a moment.

'I wonder what will happen to him? He was just a kid, Harold.' She paused and looked out to where the fence lights shone in the darkness, 'I was thinking of what you were saying the other day – about our two peoples having to live together in this land whether we like it or not. But are people like us are becoming a minority now?'

Harold didn't answer at once. He looked beyond the fence lights, out to the dark plain beyond.

'I don't know Ella. I just think that we have to keep our principles and influence others. Otherwise, what the hell am I doing here?'

By the dining hall doors, Ella took his plates and nodded towards the kitchen.

'Look. I'll take these in. I have to go and sort out the work rota for tomorrow anyway.' She looked into his face. 'You're dead beat, Harold. You ought to go and get some sleep.'

Yes, he mused, as he stood in the shade of the cowshed, that was exactly what he should have done. Then it wouldn't have happened.

Harold picked up a long handle broom and leaned on it. God knows how he'd managed to get up this morning. But he had to. Not to come down for work would be admitting defeat. No future. Nothing. And he had to get up even earlier to stop the night guard from waking someone in his place. Poor Uri, he looked as though he'd seen a ghost when he'd called to the guard from the veranda.

A ghost? Perhaps that was all he was? A tortured spirit in a hopeless frame.

Two sparrows flew in and chased one another in the dust. Harold jumped. What the heck was he standing dreaming. The vet would be here soon and everything had to be ready. Taking the broom, he began to sweep out the concrete troughs on either side of the central ramp with sharp, vigorous strokes, as if trying to brush away the trauma of the night - to let the routine take over and carry him through the day. And, for a while, it did.

5.

Uri had indeed been puzzled at Harold's sudden appearance on his veranda. Itzik told him to wake Yaacov in his place. And that wasn't the only thing that occupied his mind as he lay on his bed early that morning, waiting for that deep, untroubled sleep that came so easily and sweetly after a night of guard duty.

With the shutters closed to keep out the light as well as the heat that would grow during the morning, Uri could rise whenever he wanted and eat at leisure with all the time to himself until after supper. For Uri, as for all the field workers, a spell of night guard duty was almost a holiday. After weeks and weeks of long shifts getting in the harvest, it was a time to get the embedded grime from his hands and fingernails, the redness from his eyes and a chance to catch up on social life. And to try and see Deborah. Was she interested or wasn't she?

The question played through his mind again and again. He'd concluded some time ago that he didn't understand women. Did they or didn't they, yes or no? So he just tried one approach or another until it either worked - or didn't. Either way, some time during guard duty tonight, he would try again to see her.

As his eyes became accustomed to the dark room, the faint light seeping through the shutter-slats outlined the smooth curve of a Byzantine storage jar in the corner. Above it, small shelves held potsherds and scraps of bronze ornaments from his archaeological digs.

Uri was short and stocky, with bulging calf muscles that had hiked the length and breadth of the country. Like most Sabras, he had a passion for the geography and history of his country. There was hardly a hill or wadi through which he hadn't trudged or couldn't name and identify with some event in the Bible. Most of his next annual holiday was already booked for the Archaeological Society's meet in Eilat.

Now, as he lay back, the incident with Harold came to mind. Itzik had been so definite last night, to wake Yaacov for morning shift because Harold had had a relapse. Yet there he was, clear as a bell, standing on his veranda as though nothing had happened. What if he'd passed out again? He should have gone back to check. But he'd already been late on his rounds after watching that star shell and listening to the gunfire. Yes. The star shell. And again he agonised whether he should have woken Itzik. To hell with it. Lunchtime would do. And he turned on his side, his mind still going over the night

It had been quite a busy guard duty. After making his first rounds of the perimeter fence by ten thirty, he went to check with Dobush in the searchlight tower. The beam swept round beyond the barbed wire, picking out stunted trees and bushes in the scrub beyond. To the north, a pinpoint of light answered from another kibbutz. Along the distant main road, headlamps flickered between the trees. All was in darkness, apart from the soft glow of the half moonlight on the sand hills to the west.

Dobush teased him about his hots for Deborah. Nevertheless, Uri decided to call in on Miriam's party for a short while to see if she was there. She was, but there were too many people to get close and he soon left to make a round of the children's houses, before going up to eat.

Apart from the physical respite, the midnight meal was another reason for appreciating night duty. It was a chance to savour luxuries unavailable in the general run of the dining hall, as many chips as you could eat, a huge omelette of eggs too cracked to go to market as would fit in the large frying pan, salami offcuts left by the cooks. Wonderful.

With his stomach full, on his way out of the deserted dining hall, he took the early call list from the notice board before making a further round of the perimeter fence. The moon had set and all was dark and still, apart from the purr of the generator down by the cowsheds. When he finished, it was nearly two o'clock. Any infiltrators would be well on their way back over the border. Time for a cup of coffee.

Uri headed for the babies' house where the night-duty nurse was on duty, regretting that it wasn't Deborah's turn. As he allowed the fly mesh screen to clatter against the frame, Rivka put a finger to her lips.

'Shh. That racket wakes them up.' She nodded to the two doors that led off from the lobby where she sat. 'It's been an awful night as it is.'

'Sorry.' Uri winced as he sat onto a low, green-painted mothering chair and slipped the magazine from his Sten gun, 'won't do it again.'

For the children's nurse, night-duty was far from being a rest. Based in the babies' house, she made the rounds of the other children's houses from time to time, covering those whose blankets had slipped off, comforting any who had woken from a bad dream. Each event was recorded in the house notebook, to be read by the *Metapelet* when she came in the morning.

The night-duty nurse also had her hands full in the babies' house itself, changing those who woke and soothing them with a bottle of warm sugar water, or pressing a buzzer connected to the nursing mother's rooms, telling them it was time to feed, rocking the tiny bundles until they arrived.

Tonight had been even busier than usual and Rivka was beginning to feel the weariness that grew heavier and heavier during the last few hours before dawn. So, despite his clumsiness, she was glad of Uri's intrusion.

'Coffee?' she asked mechanically, plugging in the electric kettle, then adding more pointedly, 'who's down for morning milking with Gavriel and Ella?'

'Yaacov,' said Uri, glancing down at the list in his hand. 'Poor old Yankele. He will be pleased.' Uri grinned. 'He left Miriam's party real late, with . . ,' but didn't finish. You couldn't joke about things like that with Rivka. A bit of a puritan lot these Rumanians, despite their revolutionary ideas and phraseology, more like his mother's generation sometimes. And yet again he wished that it was Deborah on night duty with him.

As he sat back in the low chair, Uri fantasised snuggling close to her in the darkness of the babies' room. Things happened on night guard didn't they? 'At nights,' they joked, 'all cats are black.' In the stillness and the isolation, heightened by an ever-present sense of danger, new romances blossomed and discreet affairs flourished. And the following day, only the imperceptible wink or a tongue touching teeth as eyes met across the dining hall, betrayed the night's secrets. But not tonight. Not his luck.

Rivka made the coffee and pushed the mug across the marble worktop. She took up her knitting and stretched it over her fingers, only four rows the whole night and even they weren't regular. Tomorrow she'd have to unpick and start again.

Uri took a sip then looked more closely at the crumpled sheet of the early call list. He cursed, then glanced up at Rivka.

'Could you let me have a page of the notebook?' he asked softly, 'I'll have to rewrite the whole damn thing again. Just look at it!'

The list had started life as a whole sheet pinned to the notice board after supper. But throughout the evening it was reduced piecemeal by strips torn off for 'urgent' notes. On what remained, were scribbled names and times in a completely haphazard fashion until it looked more like some ancient papyrus.

The early call list was a vital part of kibbutz life, ensuring that key workers were woken each morning. Very few relied on alarm clocks that could be flicked off in a haze, allowing you to fall asleep again. But when the night guard thumped on the door then stood outside until a clear response came, you were well and truly awake.

Between sips of coffee, carefully Uri transcribed the names into a neat, chronological order, pursing his lips as he noticed one or two who were not in their own beds. Bachelors shared rooms and when one wanted privacy, the other moved out for the night. He smiled to himself, Len, in Nira's room. That was new!

Rivka reached out, took his cup and washed it under a running tap. She too was worried about Harold. He was a key worker, but if this happened too often, he wouldn't be able to continue in the cowshed. And Gavriel and Itzik wouldn't be able to carry it alone. True, there was Ella. But she was young and still quite new.

Uri finished writing, handed back the pencil and picked up his gun and the magazine. Thanking Rivka for the coffee, he went out, this time holding onto the screen until it closed quietly behind him.

'Oh,' Rivka called softly, 'Could you just pop in to the kindergarten on your way round, Uri?'

'Sure,' replied Uri, through the fly netting, *'Layla Tov.'*

Just then a wail split through the door to her right. Rivka rose and went in. The night still stretched away. Endless.

Clicking the loaded magazine into the Sten, Uri swung away down the path. The sky was now pitch black and very slowly, his eyes became adjusted to the faint starlight. Beyond the fence, bushes seemed to change shape. Was that a bush, or a figure? The more he looked, the more his eyes played tricks. He stopped staring and moved on. Only a couple of hours to dawn. Time to make a round of the cowsheds.

It had been an uneventful night. Not like two months ago when there had been a general alert. Shots had been fired through the fence by the garage so it was extra guards every night, with manned machine-gun emplacements behind the children's houses, everyone on a two hour stint after working a full day. By the end of the week, they were all wandering about like zombies, eyelids propped open with matchsticks. But since then, it had been quiet. Which made what happened next so strange.

On the way up from the cowsheds, a green Very light shot up to the north. As he looked, a red one arched into the sky followed by several bursts of automatic gunfire, one he couldn't recognise. Could have been a Carl Gustav, like the infiltrators used. Then came the star-shell. First, the faint plop of the mortar followed by the brilliant burst of the flare, high in the sky, silhouetting a nearby jacaranda tree like a black cardboard cutout.

Uri started to count staring at the white light. At five, came the sound of the explosion. That made it about two kilometres, he reckoned. Must be down by the wadi.

The flare spluttered, then fizzled out. In the pitch darkness that followed, he tried to explain to himself what was going on. It was now only an hour at the most, to dawn. No infiltrators would leave it that late to cross back. And if it were an ambush, there would have been many more shots. Probably more Very lights as well. Could have been a patrol of trigger-happy new recruits. But the flare?

Uri flicked up the leather flap of his watchstrap. Heck! He should have started on his waking up rota instead of gawping at that flare, the cooks would already be late. Running across the lawn to Ruth's room, he was stopped in his tracks. Harold was standing on his veranda? He was in his pyjamas and his room light was on.

'Hey. *Boker tov*, Uri,' he called softly. 'I was hoping to catch you.'

Uri skidded to a halt, swaying back and forth to catch his balance. ' Oh. Er. *Boker tov*. Harold. Itzik told me to wake Yaacov. It's .., I er...'

Harold half smiled as he raised his hand.

'No. No, it's okay. I'll do the early shift.' His voice was faint, but quite firm. Uri glanced down at his list again. There it was. In black and white, but .. ? When he looked up again, Harold was washing at the tap. Uri took out the stub of pencil from his pocket and crossed off Yaacov's name. What was Itzik on about?

After waking Ruth and Hedva, Uri turned to hurry to the far side of the kibbutz, then stopped. By the time he got back, he would be late in waking Gavriel. And there was no way you could wake a cowman late. But it was still fifteen minutes early. He hesitated, not knowing which way to move. In the distance, a jackal wailed. To hell with it. He walked back and knocked, Gavriel might not notice the time.

'Yes. Okay,' Gavriel answered, *'Boker Tov.'* By the time he turned over to look at the luminous dial of his watch, the night guard's footsteps were fading rapidly.

Lying on his bed, Uri felt his eyes closing, he turned on his side. Yes, it had been a good night - even with hell to pay from Gavriel later. Suddenly he thought again about the star-shell. But, no. Couldn't have been anything serious, it had remained so quiet afterwards. And poor Itzik, had enough on his plate: Ella. Shosh. The cows. No. Best let him sleep. He would catch him at lunchtime...

And while Uri fell into a deep, untroubled sleep, less than a mile away, in the bend of the wadi a man lay dying.

6

Stretched out on the dry tamarisk needles, the crumpled figure groaned. Ahmed looked down. Poor Fais. The first aid satchel had gone in their mad scramble down to the wadi in the dark. Somehow, half-dragging half-carrying him, they all managed to reach the cover of this thicket just before dawn. Now, the last desert breeze had whispered through the fronds. It was daylight.

Ahmed smoothed his moustache between thumb and forefinger. With his wide eyes and round face, babyface they'd called him at school - even into his teens. But he didn't care now. Two hard years slog in the blockmakers' yard had given him powerful shoulders and bulging muscles. That, and the moustache had settled the nickname forever. Except for his mother, to her, he would always be the baby.

She wanted him to study to be an accountant like his elder brother Naim. But to study for what? To look for a position in Kuwait, or Egypt? To be treated like a servant, or be on sufferance as a foreigner with no right of abode? No. The blockmakers' yard had been his college. To get anything from life, you had to work for it. Fight for it.

Ahmed still had vivid memories of their village but had been too young to understand why they had been expelled. He remembered being hoisted up onto the Israeli army lorries that morning and his mother hugging him with tears in her eyes all the hot dusty journey. Then jumping down onto the tarmac at the Red Cross post, being pushed across the border and trudging down to the sea, gripping his father's hand. Everyone was silent – apart from a few of the women still crying.

He would never forget that first day's exile. He'd gazed at the sea as they all sat on the dunes and – the first time he'd ever seen it. They'd had nothing to eat or drink the whole day since breakfast and all the time, he not understanding why he couldn't return to their village.

'There's been a terrible mistake,' the neighbouring Jewish *mukhtar* said to his father when the lorries came.

'Yes. A mistake,' echoed his father Ibrahim, even as they sat on the dunes. 'We shall soon go back.' But they never had...

The UNRWA brought tents and laid a water pipe, gave them food cards and regular rations. Soon more and more refugees joined them, from Majdal and Julis and Isdud and places he'd never heard of, the camp sprawling further and further north along the dunes, scorching in summer and cold and wet in the winters rain with strong winds from the sea.

Jamilla his mother tried to keep them all fed from the meagre rations. She sent him out to pick green *khubeza* buds from the bushes and made soup from them together with weeds, weeds they used to give to the chickens back in the village.

All this he remembered, as well as the arguments with his father and mother when he'd volunteered for the *Fedayeen*. He tried to push the thoughts from his mind, wanting to concentrate on what would happen now. It wasn't difficult. The sun rising higher, told him that the Israeli patrols out there wouldn't give them long.

Ahmed peered through the tracery of tamarisk fronds then looked up again to the ridge to the west, to the Egyptian positions along the border. He wondered whether they had been alerted, whether they might even be looking out for them. Like Ismail, he didn't hold out much hope from them. But even if they did react, their plight was desperate. Darkness had been their only real chance to get back safely.

As Fais moaned again, Ahmed winced. Had they left him behind, they might have made it over those last few miles. But there was no way they would. Fais, Ismail, him – they'd all been kids together in their village. They'd come this far and whatever happened, they would stay together. As he moistened Fais's lips with a few drops of water from his canteen - not much of that left either – Ahmed sat back on his haunches and closed his eyes, thinking of that first night when they crossed the border.

It hadn't been their first operation. But it was the first time they were to test Ismail's new strategy: to strike deep into enemy territory, stay hidden one day and return the following night. It was a risky plan, but if successful would sow panic far beyond the border areas where they had concentrated their attacks until now.

That first evening, they had crossed the Wadi Assi by the ruined village of Hurbiyeh, seven of them. After blowing up a water tower near Majdal, they knew that Israeli ambushes would be placed to the south, waiting for them to return. But this time, they carried on north.

All the next day, they lay up under piles of dead orange trees gathered for burning. At sunset, they moved off again heading east, until they reached a smallholders settlement. Unlike the kibbutzim near the border, the houses were strung out in one long line with small, individual fields on either side. There was little need for caution. Just one watchman who was probably dozing in the corner of a barn.

Slowly, they crept up to two end houses. They were larger than the others. The windows were open on the hot night and only the thin fly-mesh screens were closed. While Ahmed and Fais kept watch, Salim and Mahmud stole up to the walls and with all their might, hurled two grenades through the screens. As they ran back to join the others, flashes of flame and explosions ripped the night mingled with high-pitched screams and cries.

Quickly they moved off through the fields, with Fais muttering, '*Awlad. Awlad.* Kids. I could hear kids crying,' said Fais.

'So what,' snapped Ismail. 'Did anyone care when the kids cried in our village?'

Some five miles on and now well past midnight, they rested in a field of maize. The plants rose high above them and a short distance away, sprinklers ticked away in the darkness making the air cool and fresh.

'Kids,' Fais murmured again and amidst the smell of sweet-corn, Ahmed thought of his own childhood. Was it only seven years ago? He could still taste the cobs, fresh from his mother's pot on the fire, remember the prickly-pear cactus hedges where they knocked off the spiky yellow fruit, rolling it in the sand until all the barbed hairs had gone, before sucking out the juicy pulp. That too he could still taste.

Ismail gathered them around him in a tight circle and hitched his automatic on his shoulder.

'Listen,' he explained. 'The Israeli's will expect us to head for the nearest border. To Jordan.' He paused for a moment, his teeth glowing in the light of the quarter moon. 'But we shall lie low for yet another day. Then return across the Gaza border tomorrow night.'

'Huh. And they will think we have already escaped to Jordan,' said Mahmud his mind spinning as he thought of how the exploit would resound in the camps. How they would tell it in Gaza. And would Latifa's father be able to refuse him now? Ahmed was also listening intently, but as Ismail fleshed out his plan, a heavy lorry rumbled along the nearby road.

'*Ya, Ismail*,' he said, 'We could make a real night's work of it. That's the main road to Beer Sheba.'

Fais, ever cautious raised his hand.

'It might be too much. We ought to lie low.'

Ismail, flushed with their success so far, grinned and clenched his fist.

'No. It's a good idea. Still many hours of darkness until dawn.'

They walked on in single file along rough tracks between the fields, past the ruined village of Faluja and on south. Then, as the road curved to the right, a side track led off to the east. In the distance, glimmered the fence lights of a new kibbutz on the Jordanian border

'We are closer to Hebron than Gaza,' whispered Ahmed.

'Exactly,' said Ismail and they spread out into the shallow ditches on either side of the main road.

They waited. An hour went by. Then another. The moon set. Nothing passed along the road in either direction.

'*In an 'tiz,*' cursed Ahmed, 'it will soon be dawn.'

Just then, through the silence, came the distant throbbing of an engine. Pencils of light swept up and down and from side to side across the fields. Nearer and nearer they came, yet seeming to take a long, long time. The throbbing grew to a roar, the beams wider and brighter. Everyone crouched low, cocked their automatics and waited.

Avi leaned over the steering wheel, as though urging the truck onward, anxious to get home. The yellow headlamps danced over the featureless landscape, picking out the odd tree or prickly-pear cactus. Battling fatigue, he kept his eyes on the line of stones along the side of the road.

It was an old British military road, the tarmac edged with small, white limestone blocks. The shallow ditches beyond carried away the flash floods of winter that would otherwise have washed deep gullies across the road after the first rains. One moment of lost concentration and the truck would end up on its side before he could shout '*jimalayah*'.

Despite the weariness, Avi was pleased with himself. It couldn't have worked out better. The evening before, they loaded up twenty-six crates of broiler chickens for the market in Rechovot. Now he was on his way back. He glanced to his left. In the darkness, hidden by the scrub-covered hills, was his kibbutz. Soon, he should see the lights.

His own kibbutz was on the Gaza border, but during army service, he had met Orna. For months they had agonised over which kibbutz they would settle down on. He didn't remember what had decided it. Just that one morning he had woken with Orna tickling the hair on his chest - and he'd decided to go with her kibbutz.

Avi gripped the steering wheel, smiling to himself, remembering how they'd celebrated by staying in bed all day.

Cool, night air blew through the top of the side window. The new G.M.C truck was a beauty to drive. It hadn't really been his turn to do the night run, but Heskel, the regular driver had come in late with a load of phosphates from Haifa and Avi had been on standby.

At Rechovot, the broilers had gone for a really good price and quite quickly. That was when he'd decided to come back and be home before Orna woke. It would be such a surprise. With infiltrators coming over from time to time, she'd made him promise to stay in Rechovot until first light. But she would forgive him when he crawled in beside her, telling her that he had already fed the baby. He could already feel her warm, smooth skin against his body.

The baby had arrived five months ago, sooner than they had planned. But there were no regrets. His friends laughed at the way he talked non-stop about the kid. Still, most of them were still bachelors, they'd soon change. And getting back early would also give Orna a chance to lie in late, she was so worn out from months of trudging to the babies' house day and night to breast-feed. 'I'm like a damn milch-cow,' she would laugh. Now she had started working half a day and couldn't get rid of the constant tiredness.

Avi didn't find the morning feed a chore at all. There was something magical at that early hour when all the world seemed at peace, sitting with his warm wet bundle gulping her bottle, pinched face and screwed up eyes, her tiny hand gripping his finger.

After the feed, he would pace up and down, a napkin thrown over his shoulder to catch the burping, chatting quietly with the other fathers before they all went out to their work. Avi smiled again, his face reflected green in the windscreen from the glow of the dashboard.

A ruined house showed in the headlamps, another five kilometres to the turn off. He'd be home even earlier than he'd calculated. Yes, Orna would forgive him. She was still so anxious, despite the fact that they'd all lived with this tense situation ever since they were teenagers. But then most of the girls were, perhaps it was something to do with having babies.

At the market, he'd heard the news of a terrorist attack on a schoolhouse at Shamira. But any infiltrators would be well on their way across the border by now. He glanced to his left, imagining that he could see the first light of dawn over the jagged mountains.

Approaching the junction, his heart began to beat faster. Just ten kilometres along their dusty, potholed track and he'd be home. Already, he could see Orna's sleepy face smiling up at him, feel her warm kiss.

The headlamp beams swung and swirled in the sky then across the ground and along the road towards them. Ahmed was tense and ready, but also a little anxious. They had left it very, very late. He was sure he had seen the first glimmer of light to the east. The noise grew louder. It was a heavy truck. Perhaps an army lorry? *Ya'allah*, that would really make news in Gaza.

With a hiss of air brakes, the truck slowed down and the engine whined as the driver changed into low gear. Ahmed's pulse raced. This was the moment. This was it.

Avi braked hard. His hand dropped to the gear lever to change down again. A swift double-declutching and the first gear screamed in protest. At that moment, a dark shape moved in the nearside ditch. Before he could react, the windscreen shattered with a blinding light. A fierce pain shot through his head. And everything went black.

The truck careered across the road, the offside wheel spun into the ditch and threw the lorry on its side. As it lurched to a halt, the engine stalled. Ahmed leaped up and threw a grenade through the shattered windscreen. The explosion ripped open the roof of the cab with an orange flash and a shattering roar. Then all fell silent and dark - except for the tail-lamp, glowing firefly red. Ismail ran round and ripped at the cables, even that tiny light would show for a great distance in the darkness.

As the light went out, Mahmud, Fais and the others gathered around the truck. Heavy, steel crates were strewn everywhere, white chicken feathers, sticking to the bars and fluttering in the light breeze. And as the side ladders slowly creaked and collapsed, a sharp smell of chicken dung hung in the air.

'*Dejaj. Bas dejaj.*' Ismail spat in the dust, 'Chickens.' It was only a farmer's lorry instead of the army truck they'd been hoping for.

Ahmed stared at the white feathers, remembering the hens scuttling around his village roads on that day he would never forget. The day that had eventually spurred him to join the *Fedayeen* and had brought him here. He kicked at a crate and cursed, then went round to join the others.

7.

The sun rose higher. Down in the wadi, the first flies buzzed in the shade, settling on Fais's bloodstained trousers. Ahmed waved them away, then returned to think over the previous day.

Ismail had called a halt in a deep gully about a mile south of the ambush. The stars had vanished and the eastern sky was turning steely green.

'Very soon, if not already,' he said, 'the Israelis will be searching for us. We are too large a group. We must split up.' He nodded to Araf, 'You, Iqbal and Yusuf, will make for Hebron. You know who to contact there.' He looked up at the sky, *'Insh'allah,* we shall all meet again soon in Beit Hanun.

They clasped hands. Some hugged. Then the three made their way up a gully towards the no-man's land of rocks and scrub in the foothills around Tel Tziklag, the ruins of the ancient city where three thousand years before, the young David had taken refuge from the spite of king Saul. Now, as they passed silently by the fence lights of a new settlement, ahead of them dawn broke from the east.

By the main gate of the young kibbutz, Yossi the night guard looked out towards the main road, searching for a glimmer of the G.M.C.'s headlights. The night before, he'd helped to load the crates full of broilers, cursing as the droppings stuck to his trousers. He'd stunk of chicken shit the whole night.

Avi told him of his plan to get back early and surprise Orna, but if he were delayed at the market, Yossi was to wake her as usual to feed the baby. For the umpteenth time Yossi glanced at his watch then glanced down the road. No lights, there was no way now that Avi would get back in time.

Walking back through the gates, he headed towards Orna's room. As he reached her veranda, the sound of an engine came from the gate. He stopped and listened, but it was a light vehicle, not the roar of the G.M.C. Knocking on her door, he waited for the sleepy answer then hurried away.

A jeep whined down the track towards the dining hall, an army jeep. Yossi waved it down.

'Where's the local commander?' called a young lieutenant from the passenger seat as it braked beside him.

'Probably starting work in the garage,' replied Yossi. 'Why? What's up?'

'Truck ambushed at the turn off. Could be yours,' he muttered. 'I must get to a phone, quickly. Might still catch the bastards yet.'

The driver engaged gears, but Yossi held onto the windscreen top.

'What about the driver?' he pressed. The lieutenant winced, 'Not much left, I'm afraid. Didn't have a chance.' Seeing Yossi's horror stricken face, he added, 'sorry. Bloody murderers. We'll get them yet.'

The jeep sped down to the garage in a cloud of white dust. In the meantime, a small knot of people had gathered outside the dining hall. Out of the corner of his eyes, Yossi saw Orna in her blue dressing gown making her way to the babies' house. Please God, she would have those last moments of peace with the baby, before someone broke the news. And he prayed that he wouldn't have to be the one to do it.

On the far side of the main road, Ismail led his group towards the west. The light grew stronger and soon the sun was on the back of their necks. He reckoned that it was about thirty kilometres to the Gaza border but first they had to find a good place to lie up until nightfall. They were all fit and well trained and could easily make it comfortably under cover of darkness.

Buoyed up by their two successes, despite the risks Ismail decided to cover more ground in the stillness of the early morning. Everything had gone so well up till now, he was convinced that his luck would hold. Two hours later, he knew that he had made a terrible mistake.

Whilst crossing a dirt track through a banana plantation, a grey jeep shot out from behind a well house where an engineer had been taking water tests. As they dived into the elephant-grass windbreak, he wondered whether the driver had noticed.

'We haven't been spotted,' he tried to console Fais. But within half an hour, army trucks were rumbling along the nearby roads, dropping off foot patrols to pursue them.

Throughout the day, the Fedayeen played a deadly game of hide and seek, being forced further and further south, through the brown earth of Lakhish and into the badlands of the northern Negev, where gullies and cracks furrowed the parched grey loess soil.

The sun beat down mercilessly as they crawled in sweat-sodden denims through every shallow cleft and gully they could find, from time to time freezing into the nearest shade at the sound of a Piper Cub plane. And for the very first time, Ahmed felt a nagging doubt at the back of his mind.

Just after noon, when they sheltered in a clump of withered almond trees, Ahmed crawled to the crest of a small rise to see their way ahead. As he raised his head to look over, his heart missed a beat. A hedge of prickly-pear to his right ran down to a ruined mud hut. Beside it, a jasmine bush climbed up the wall of a large stone-built cistern. It was the well. The well they drew water from for their flocks. His old village!

Unable to contain himself, he slithered back and hissed to Ismail.

'*Shuf!* Look. *Shuf, ya Ismail.*' The commander went back up with him and together they looked out.

'The *hirbeh*,' murmured Ismail, 'old Abu Jamal's house.' Ahmed remembered the grey haired man sitting in his doorway, muttering to himself as they poured water into the troughs. *Al majnoon*, the crazy one, they used to called him. Ahmed wondered what had become of him. When they had to leave the village, he hid and stayed behind.

He felt a burning desire to go into the village. His village! This was where he grew up, where his family had lived for generations and where his father had been the highly respected headman, the *Mukhtar.* He hadn't seen it for seven years. At the same time he knew he mustn't. This same village would be a trap if a patrol located them in there.

His stomach aching and his head burning, Ahmed stared and stared, at the half-standing mud walls, the collapsed roofs of tile and thatch, at the creepers and weeds smothering everything. The village was a ruin - and they were now refugees, crammed into miserable huts on the sand dunes. His father, once the honoured headman, scorned and ignored. His body trembled with pent up anger and now even a stronger desire to avenge what had been done to him and his family.

Silently, the two men slid back down to the almond trees and planned their next movements. They couldn't use the village but they knew every fold of ground, every wadi, every bush in the fields around. Their pursuers would have a hard time finding them.

Despite their knowledge of the countryside though, it was a hazardous afternoon. As soon as they escaped from one patrol, another came from a different direction. The whole area was alive, forcing them further and further south, into the grey, featureless steppe of the Negev.

At last, the sun set, the sky turned deep violet, then finally darkened. And as they rested amongst the small trees of a young orange grove, gathering strength and checking their weapons, Ismail divided out the remaining ammunition and spelled out his plan.

'The Israelis will expect us to head due west for Gaza. But we shall follow the course of the Wadi Shelaleh. It will also give us cover.' The wadi divided and rejoined again and again in a number of channels, blocking all of them would be difficult. Ahmed listened carefully. *El Aaakil* had done it again. It was a long detour, but they would reduce the risk of ambush.

The bank of the dry riverbed was steep and often precariously undercut. To find a safe way down in the darkness, they split up and carefully explored the bank. Suddenly the ground gave way under Fais and he disappeared in a minor landslide. When the other three slid down the bank on their backsides, he was half buried by a mound of soil, gasping as he tried to stop himself crying out in pain. His left leg had been twisted in the fall. When the dug him out, his trousers were soaked in blood. His shin bone had broken and pierced the skin.

As they laid him out flat, Mohammed found a piece of driftwood and they bandaged the leg and tied it in a splint. Ahmed pulled out a dressing pad and stuffed in Fais's mouth to stifle any scream. Then they sat round and drew breath. From now on, they would have to help him along. Leaving him was out of the question.

'It will slow us down,' said Ismail. 'But with luck, in four or five hours we shall reach the border..

Half-carrying and half-supporting him, they covered a good distance down the wadi, Ismail out in front, looking out and listening. But as he glanced at the luminous dial on his watch whenever the others caught up with him, Ahmed sensed his anxiety. And for the second time, a twinge of doubt crossed his mind. But still they trusted to Ismail's skill - and to his legendary luck.

By the end of the next hour, Fais had lost consciousness and they took it in turn to carry him. Fortunately, he was short and lightly built. Ahmed remembered the thin, shy boy who stood on the side when they played sports. Fais, the *miskeen*, they called him, the weakling. But he'd grown into a wiry figure with tremendous stamina. And when he volunteered for the Fedayeen, no one laughed anymore.

By around four o'clock, Ismail passed the word. Only another mile or so. They had almost done it. But as Mohammed took his turn and humped Fais across his shoulders, a loose pebble skittered across the dry stones, sounding like a thunder-clap in the silence.

From the bank above, a voice barked in Hebrew.

'*Atzor! Mi Shum?*' Halt. Who goes there? A moment later, the voice shouted again, this time in Arabic, '*Min hada?*' They hurried on but then shots rang out and bullets cracked above their heads and snapped on the pebbles beside them. They had been discovered.

Mohammed was soon out of breath carrying Fais and Ahmed took over. But in having to keep tight against the banks, their progress was gradually slowed down. In addition, Fais had begun to be delirious.

'Quick,' hissed Ismail, 'those bushes. In that bend. In there. Quickly.'

As they parted the branches and slipped into the thicket, a green Very light arched into the sky, followed by a red one. For a moment, everything went quiet. Suddenly a flare exploded high above them, making it seem like day and gunfire raked the riverbed. Crouching motionless in the shadows, they waited until it burned out, leaving the darkness and silence to hide them once more. They were trapped.

Now, as the sun continued to rise higher, Ahmed moistened Fais's lips again. The prostrate figure mumbled softly, more delirious. If only he would last until help came. But from where? If the Egyptians didn't intervene, they could leave him here and make a dash for the border and some of them might make it. Much as he hated the Israelis, they didn't usually kill prisoners. They were much more valuable alive. But Ismail would decide. And they would accept his decision.

Ismail was silent, his mind racing to find a way out. But all the possible scenarios had already passed through his mind a dozen times. If the Egyptians didn't come in, they were doomed. And it was his fault. His responsibility. He had insisted on the lorry ambush and also the long way back. His stomach clenched as he accepted that through his decision, they could probably all die. But then whenever he'd made a judgement, he had always stuck to it. Hard. Like his father, they said.

Ismail too remembered clearly their expulsion, but unlike Ahmed, he wasn't so bewildered that day. Ever since he could remember, he'd heard his father bitterly complaining at the way Jews were buying up land and settling – arguing with Ibrahim that in the end, they would take their land too and leave them destitute. Yet despite their fathers' never ending feuding, he and Ahmed had tried to remain friends

While Ahmed was filled with rage for what had happened, he was fuelled by hatred – for every one of them. It wasn't his people's fault what Hitler had done. The Arabs hadn't made concentration camps or slaughtered them. It was Europe's crime and they should resolve it there – not come to his land and steal it, just like his father had prophesied.

Ismail thought of his family's almond grove, the beautiful pink and white flowers each year that told them the winter was over, the mad scramble before the autumn rains to pick and collect up those on the ground, then his fingers stripping off the velvety hulls and tying up the almonds in small sacks to be sent to market. He could still picture clearly the track through the prickly pear hedges where he and Ahmed led the village goats and sheep to pasture in the spring. And what were they now? Miserable refugees living on handouts from UNWRRA and the Red Cross.

Yes. All that had been taken away from them. And as soon as he'd turned eighteen, he'd joined the Fedayeen. Every day he'd dreamed of how to regain his family's honour and their house and land, for a chance to fight to throw the Jews into the sea and back to Europe. No, they couldn't raise an army like the Israelis – the Egyptians controlled the Gaza Strip and would never allow it. But at least the Fedayeen would begin the process.

As he thought again of their hopeless situation, Ismail accepted that he had always known that he might die in the attempt. But his and their fight would inspire others to carry on the struggle – even for a hundred years like the Arabs had done with the Crusaders – and eventually, they would win.

Ismail turned and nodded to Ahmed. Despite their desperate predicament or what would be the outcome, the blows they had struck these last two nights would reverberate through Gaza – and ensure that others would continue the struggle.

The sunlight slanted through the thin branches. Ahmed leaned back against the reeds and looked up. A lone buzzard wheeled in the cloudless sky, rising on the first thermals of the new day. He followed the flight, jealous of its freedom to slip and wheel in any direction it chose. Unlike the bird, his fate would be sealed down here, in the shadows of the riverbed.

The buzzard circled above him, taunting, lazily angling its wings. Soon the breeze would blow from the sea beyond Gaza and a fine dust would rise over the plain. But for the moment, all was still and the tamarisk fronds hung motionless. Ahmed glanced up again at the bird and wondered. Had it sensed a smell of death?

8.

Rising on the warming air, the buzzard rose and wheeled in the sky with imperceptible movements of its broad wings. The slightest upturn of a wingtip, the minutest inclination of two or three feathers took it in any direction or to any height it desired.

The bird sideslipped effortlessly, seeking carrion for its young and rising from one thermal to the next. Recognising neither border nor boundary, it flew across the grey desert, away from the grim anticipation in the wadi and towards the unsuspecting calm of the kibbutz.

Circling the bright green of the irrigated pasture, it hovered over the grey corrugated roofs of the cowshed where, in the shade beneath Harold strove to banish the traumas of the night.

It was time to give out the morning ration of meal but the trolley was nowhere to be seen. Clomping to the end of the central ramp, he found it tilted in the mud at the end of the incline. A careless tractor driver must have nudged it aside the evening before as he unloaded bales of straw. Harold cursed. In a community so interdependent and mutually accountable, so many cared only for their own work.

Extricating it from the mud, he trundled the trolley along the centre ramp to the tall, steel storage hopper, sneezing as a fine spray of meal shot from the chute. Picking up the old pickled-cucumber tin, he pushed the trolley slowly along the ramp, doling out a canful to each yoke.

As if having waved a magic wand, the yard suddenly came to life. Cows rose from the deep straw litter and cantered up to the yokes, the older ones thrusting their heads through to lap up the meal while the younger and weaker ones galloped back and forth along the row of rumps, desperately searching for a vacant place, humping and pushing to squeeze their way in.

Despite what Itzik maintained, Harold had a dim view of bovine intelligence. Day after day, he witnessed the same circus, the same frenetic struggle when all along there were always sufficient places for each cow.

Waiting until the shuffling had subsided and all the heads were through and slurping up the meal, Harold swung down a lever on each side. The yokes slid closed to lock them in, and there the beasts would remain until the vet came for his inspection.

Leaning against the end post, Harold wiped his face with the front tails of his shirt. Breathing deeply after the exertion, he looked around then glanced at his watch. It was almost eight o'clock, he was well on schedule. And with that, the black mood of early morning began to clear - even the red-oxide paint on the stanchions still looked bright and fresh.

The new cowshed, along with the milking parlour had only been finished five months before. And what a battle it had been. Every year, arguments raged over investment plans as each branch of the economy and services fought its corner, first at the farm committee and then at the general meeting. Usually three or four meetings were required as patriotic passions of each branch threatened to tear the kibbutz into component parts.

Last year, Avram insisted on a D6 caterpillar tractor for the new arable fields in the Negev, Yael threatened to return all the washing dirty unless she got a new machine for the laundry and Peretz had dragged a whole length of battered aluminium pipe into the dining room to show how much the new irrigation pipes were needed for the orange groves. But in the end it had been the dairy versus the rest.

At the time, the cows were milked on a concrete hard-stand, the cowmen running to and fro with portable machines and pouring the milk into churns then dropping them into a cooled-water tank. Every morning the churns had to be pulled out and loaded by hand onto the kibbutz van to be driven to the local dairy. After milking finished, dung had to be loaded and carted out by wheelbarrow to a nearby dungheap.

The dairy herd continued to grow however and had become successful, bringing in almost a third of the settlement's income. So Itzik and the cowmen decided on a frontal assault: either the kibbutz built a new milking parlour and adjacent deep-litter cowshed, or they might as well sell the herd. He was like that, Itzik. *Dughri.* No bullshit. And everyone knew that he meant it. The arguments were sound, but such a huge investment would rule out nearly all other demands. But the threat was akin to blackmail and Harold told him so at the time.

The arguments raged over three general meetings, late into the night and the early hours. Aviva held out for a new battery unit for the poultry, which was even more profitable than the cowshed. Harold remembered his joking that it was 'either all the eggs in one basket or all the bottles in one crate.' No one saw the joke - apart from Stan.

Chains and metal tags clinking on the metal bars of the yokes brought him back to the present as the cows licked the troughs clean. Even in the shade it was now growing warmer. Harold wiped his face again, remembering the argument with Itzik after the cowmen had won the vote.

'The trouble is Itzik' he said, 'is that you and a lot of your Sabra mates view the kibbutz merely as a large, modern farm - not as a new kind of society.'

Itzik though had remained cool.

'Look, Harold. You can't live on ideals alone. If the kibbutz doesn't succeed economically, then even with all your principles, it won't exist at all.'

Harold did realise the importance of a sound economy, and Itzik did have principles or he wouldn't be here. But it was a never-ending argument: efficiency and expediency versus lifestyle and principles. And forever compromising either one or the other to survive and have the strength to continue. Would it ever be resolved, he wondered?

Harold took off his woollen hat and stuffed it into his pocket. Whatever the arguments, work in the cowsheds certainly was much easier now, even though the herd had grown and milk production had almost doubled. A tanker lorry arrived every morning from the *'Tnuva'* co-operative to draw off thousands of litres of milk from the huge refrigerated tank. And instead of mucking out each day with shovels and forks, every few months a mechanical digger removed the sodden deep-litter in a matter of hours and loaded it directly onto a fleet of tipper trucks to be dumped out in the fields where it was needed. 'Untouched by human hand,' he'd joked to Ella.

As he came down the ramp into the open, the bright sunlight reflecting from the whitewashed walls of the dairy seemed to banish the memories of the night, he felt able to face the others.

About a dozen cows of the second group lingered in the collecting yard. If he gave Ella and Gavriel a hand to finish milking, they could all go up to breakfast together and be down again in time for the vet. And he knew that he desperately needed their company to face the dining hall this morning.

Ella came out to bring in the stragglers just as Harold ducked through the rails. She smiled, as though it was any other morning.

'Hi. All finished in the sheds?' she said in English, the familiarity of the language making him feel even more at ease.

'Sure. All done,' he said. ' I'll come in and give you a hand.'

The final batch went well and as the last three cows clattered out and down the ramp, Gavriel rolled up his sleeves.

'Right. I'm starving,' he puffed. 'We can wash down after breakfast.'

In the small office, they pulled off their rubber boots. The kibbutz had recently decided in the general meeting that the cowmen couldn't come into the dining hall in their working boots. Itzik and Gavriel had taken it personally: 'We're a farm,' they complained, 'Not a damn boutique!' But the decision was ratified. Even their clothes smelled bad enough, everyone else maintained. Ella, who always changed out of her trousers and boots anyway, abstained in the vote. They cowmen still chafed her over the 'betrayal'.

The three sauntered out but just as they crossed the sand towards the trees, a light-grey estate car hurtled down the track from the road and braked in a cloud of dust. Gavriel glanced at his watch and frowned. Menasheh, the vet wasn't due for at least another hour, they hadn't yet yoked in the last group of cows.

Surprised, they stood and waited. But before any of them could utter a word, the door of the car flew open and a short, wiry man shot out, his bald pate glistening with sweat and heavy, horn rimmed glasses slipping to the tip of his nose.

Slapping a khaki cloth hat on his head, the vet glared from one to the other.

'Yes. You may well ask what I'm doing here so early,' he barked, then pointing one arm back down the road continued, 'well you can thank your idiot neighbours, that's what.' He turned and picked up his briefcase from the passenger seat. Gavriel scratched his head. The neighbouring kibbutz, Tel Kerem, had a much smaller herd but he couldn't believe that they had no problems for the vet.

'What. No cows to inseminate, back there?'

Menasheh thrust out his battered, old brown leather briefcase, the one he'd used ever since he'd been a doctor in Frankfurt in the Thirties.

'Cows? Nutrition?' he growled, 'all they talk about is the Revolution, Lysenko's genetics, Imperialist domination.' He jabbed a finger at Gavriel's stomach. 'You go and teach them. I've had enough!'

Tel Kerem had been founded only two years before by a group of French Jews. Hailing mainly from Paris, they were still full of Left Bank ideas, spouting Marx and Sartre and looking to the Soviet Union as a bulwark of Socialism, despite Krushchev's recent revelations. They even had a greenhouse full of 'Michurian' plant experiments. 'A living example of what Lenin called "An Infantile Disorder"', Harold once said to Ella.

Although Menasheh was deeply religious and orthodox, he suffered the radical views of the kibbutzim in admiring their idealism and proficiency. 'You're all doing God's work, whether you believe it or not', he would say.' Now, as the vet fumed, Gavriel couldn't help but smile, their neighbours must have really overstepped the mark to make the man vary his routine.

Menasheh scowled then thumped his case on the sand.

'Go one. Laugh. You may think it funny. I don't.' He took out a large handkerchief, removed his glasses and wiped them. 'Look. I don't care about their ideas, their prattling on about Lysenko. Who wants early winter wheat anyway?' He put back his glasses. 'I can even suffer their calling a new calf Rosa after Luxembourg, or Krupskaya, Lenin's wife. But today, they present me with a Stalina. Stalina! After what that butcher did? Wiping out an entire generation of Jewish writers. After the doctors' plot?

'*Nu*. I thought you were used to those kids by now,

Menasheh. Give them year or two. They'll grow out of it.'

Menasheh looked towards Ella and Harold, then back to Gavriel.

'Pah. The cows are just a hobby with them. Anyway. I've had it up to here. You can get Krushchev to send them a vet from a *kholkoz*!'

For half a minute, all four stood in the burning sun, the three not knowing what to say while the vet looked from one to the other.

Menasheh had been a consultant gynaecologist but had left Germany after Kristalnacht. Arriving in Palestine penniless and finding too many doctors, he'd re-trained as an agricultural instructor and vet. But like most of the German Jewish immigrants, nicknamed *Yeckers*, a sense of humour wasn't one of his strong points. Respect for professional authority and discipline was more to their way of thinking.

Every morning, he would breeze in at the same time, change into his high boots and, before they could say *'boker tov'*, launch straight into questions about the herd, pregnancies, calvings, infections and so on. Then he would take up the record cards and march straight over to the cowsheds to begin his inspections.

Pulling on a long rubber sleeve-glove - Menasheh's condom they called it - he would insert his arm into the cow's rear, checking the position of the unborn calf, muttering comments for the cowmen to record on the cards. If a cow was on heat, he took out a long glass tube, charged it with semen from a thermos flask and inseminate, making sure everything was noted accurately, bull, batch, time, date, all accompanied by short, gruff phrases. Then, when he was absolutely satisfied that everything was in order he would depart. Professional, cool and competent, that was Menasheh. Which was what made this morning's outburst so unusual.

Eventually the vet broke the silence. He stepped back and looked straight into Gavriel's face.

'And if all that wasn't enough, some idiot starts to tell me how Nasser's Russian weapons will take the revolution and progress through the Middle East - in Israel as well.' He looked down. 'And with my son in the army? And you people here manning the border, I have to hear such rubbish, eh?'

Suddenly, he stopped, then shrugged, looking at Harold and then Ella then back to Gavriel again.

'All right, *kinderlekh*. We have work to do.' He picked up his briefcase, 'Thank God there are still a few sane ones about.'

Harold pointed the hill.

'Why don't you come up and have breakfast with us, Menasheh?' knowing that Menasheh would only eat strictly Kosher food but feeling obliged to offer, especially this morning.

The vet brushed a fly from his face.

'No. No thanks. My wife makes wonderful sandwiches.' He pulled a linen-wrapped package from his briefcase, 'Anyway, who knows what goes through your kitchens?' He slammed the door of his car. 'No. You go up and eat. We can start when you get down.' And walking over to the shade of the dairy, he sat down on an upturned orange box.

Gavriel looked at Ella and Harold, then shrugged.

'*Nu*. A *Yecker* is a *Yecker*,' he murmured, then more sharply, 'come on. I'm starving,' and the three of them walked up through the trees which, in the space of a few hours, had turned into a tracery of red branches and drooping the grey green foliage, the dry leaves crackling beneath their feet.

As they reached the road, a tractor and trailer happened to come in from the fields. They jumped on, their feet dangling over the sides as it grated into first gear to grind up the hill.

'Breakfast,' Gavriel grinned at Ella. 'That idiot Uri waking me early has given me a real appetite.' Ella winked at Harold. Gavriel's legendary appetite.

9

The Farmall tractor, its original bright red now faded to a dusty pink, swung in a wide circle and pulled up at the far side of the courtyard. Everyone slid off the trailer and headed for the dining hall.

Gavriel cursed as his feet touched the sand, it was red hot. He joined Harold, hopping from one tuft of grass or wild lupins to the next, both gasping with relief as they reached the shade of the young Casuarinas trees, their characteristically contorted branches as if from a Chinese painted scroll.

Gavriel envied the Sabras, they had soles like tanned leather through running around barefooted since they were kids. Itzik would walk straight across the hottest sand - even through thorns - in his bare feet. Ella smiled as she walked across, combing out her hair trying to get rid of the smell of cowhide. Men. Just plumb lazy, she always changed into sandals.

As she watched Gavriel hopping across the sand, Ella suddenly remembered the first time he'd invited her over for coffee with his wife that afternoon, discovering that despite the camaraderie of the cowshed, how little she really knew him. And in chatting to him and his wife Rivka, becoming aware of a world she hardly knew existed

It was the first time she was invited to one of the 'old timers' rooms. Also the first time anyone opened up about their painful war experiences. Yes, she had become accepted into the cowshed fraternity - and it was a 'fraternity' until she joined, but this invitation was a sign of acceptance, symbolic of being part of the community.

When they both finished the afternoon shift that day, Ella had taken her time to shower and change and to rest. Gavriel would have to hurry to be showered and changed for when his son came home from the children's house. Woe betides the father who was still in his sweaty working clothes, when the kids came to the room. *'Fooyah!'* they would snap, 'you're all dirty,' as though it were a personal affront.

Knowing that the children came home at around four each day, she waited until after five to give them time to be alone for a while with their son. Then slipping on her sandals, she set off to the far side of the kibbutz where the 'old timers' lived. 'Old timers', she smiled to herself, the oldest was barely over thirty.

Parents and children were strolling along the pathways and playing, some fathers had toddlers perched on their shoulders, there was no money for prams or pushchairs. The kids seemed to like it that way, to be higher than everyone else for a change. Lucky us, we single people, Ella thought as she passed between them. For the next three hours, the children would be the priority. 'Three hours hard labour,' Harold joked. Most of the parents' *Shabbat* rest-day would be similar.

Gavriel and Rivka's room was one of four in a new, single-storied concrete house - bullet and shrapnel proof, stifling in summer and with only a small paraffin stove, taking ages to heat up in winter. But they had the 'luxury' of a small, enclosed porch with a separate shower and toilet.

Gavriel was sitting on the tiled floor, playing with his son Udi, a little blond terror of about three when she knocked on the open door.

'*Shalom*, Ella.' Rivka waved her in. She had just showered after working until four in the children's house and wore a shapeless, printed-cotton housecoat. 'Take a seat.' His wife was a nursery school teacher, wavy, brown hair and a smooth, olive skin with crows' feet just beginning to show at the corners of her black eyes. Eyes unusually deep set, thought Ella.

Ella chose to sit on the double bed that was against the side wall. Her own room had only one chair that often doubled as a low table or temporary bookshelf, so everyone got used to sitting on the beds.

Along the wall opposite, rows of bookshelves made with deal planks and building blocks, were filled with books. Many were in French.

'It was our second language,' Rivka explained after Ella had queried. 'Most of the Balkans use Slavic tongues but Rumanian has a Latin root.' She had a similar accent to Gavriel, substituting 'B' for the Hebrew 'V' and also dropping the initial 'H's, reminding Ella of the immigrant Cockney Poms in Sydney. But Rivka's command of Hebrew appeared much more polished than Gavriel's, one word flowing smoothly into the next, at times so soft as to be almost inaudible.

'French.' Ella smiled, 'I learned for five years in high school and still couldn't buy a postage stamp when I was in Paris!'

Rivka smiled back, a gold tooth showing on one side.

'Ah, yes. But you have the whole of English and American culture in your own language. In Rumanian, there were only a few translations. French, for us, opened up a whole world.'

Gavriel was building a tower with Udi's toy bricks. He stopped, gripping a red cube in his fist.

'Huh. Rumania,' he scoffed, looking from Ella to Rivka, then back again, 'What a waste!' His face suddenly grew animated and his forehead furrowed. 'A marvellous country,' he continued, 'Rich soil. As much as you want. Rivers. Mountains. Oil and Minerals. Everything.' He wagged his finger, 'and what do they do with it? Nothing!'

He paused and added the brick to the tower.

'Nothing,' he repeated, 'except make one gigantic mess. And you know why?' He looked at Ella, tapping the side of his head with his forefinger, 'because they have none of this. That's why.'

Gavriel set up two more bricks. The boy leaned closer, fingers twitching. 'If we had a country like that,' Gavriel added, his hand circling in the air, 'we'd be one of the Great Powers. Them. All they can make, is chaos!'

As he was talking, Udi reached out and with a single swipe, knocked the tower all across the tiles, laughing and clapping. Gavriel swivelled round and hugged the boy against his chest.

'*Mazik!*' he grinned, playfully tweaking the boy's ear, 'you little menace.'

Udi broke away and scuttled around the room, collecting up the bricks. Gavriel ran his fingers through his hair. Ella recognised the movement. He did that whenever he was embarrassed.

'Sorry,' he said sheepishly, I got carried away. Can't stand waste, Ella. Especially of people. Of human effort.' He stood up and let out a deep breath. 'I'll go and make the coffee.'

Rivka took his place on the floor, playing with the boy.

'Gavriel didn't mean to be rude,' she said softly, 'Just that… Well, he had great hopes for the new Communist regime back there, after the war. I didn't. Perhaps that is why it doesn't affect me like that.' She paused, slightly embarrassed. 'He always gets upset when he talks about it.'

Ella raised her hand and smiled.

'Oh Please. Don't apologise. I'd like to know more sometime.'

The two women continued talking. About the new house. About Ella's family in Australia. Having picked up odd hints at work, Ella was careful not to ask about Rivka's past. And as the chatted, the boy nestled into his mother's lap, sucking his thumb and gripping a green brick in the other hand.

On the porch, Gavriel plugged in the electric kettle, then settled back against the wall, biting his lip. He shouldn't have sounded off like that. Not with a guest in the room. And not with Udi. The boy hated loud voices.

Ella probably wasn't offended, he consoled himself. Yet what could she understand? What could anyone who hadn't experienced the war, understand? The long columns of steel-helmeted automatons driving east, the even longer lines of Russian prisoners, whipped and beaten westwards to starvation and death. The shots in the night. Home grown fascists, the Iron Guard let loose to terrorise the Jews. The pogrom in his home town, Jassy. Hunger. His father deported, his mother dying of grief.

He took three mugs down from a shelf. No. This girl from the other end of the world could never really understand it at all.

He remembered the liberation, the Red Army marching west, marching and singing the whole time, all through the long nights, a lone voice in the darkness: *'Ni Pastoi, pastoi, pastoi...'* 'Sing. Sing or you run at the double!' a commanding voice would ring out and soon came the answering chorus echoing, hoarse and weary, fading gradually into the distance, all the way from Stalingrad. All the way to Berlin.

Gavriel closed his eyes for a moment. Even now. After all they and their Rumanian stooges had done, all they were doing to ingratiate themselves with Nasser using huge supplies of weapons, the tune of a Russian folksong still brought a catch to his throat. Yes. Even now.

He remembered the brief period of hope and promise, free education and hospitals for all, workers control in the factories, land to the peasants – and the outlawing of anti-Semitism. How they'd all rushed to join the Young Communist League! He recalled his studies at the university in Bucharest, discussions late into the night, singing, hiking in the mountains. Rumanians, Jews, Transylvanians. Who cared? Everyone did seem equal.

The kettle began to hiss. Gavriel glanced through the doorway. Ella was now on the floor with Udi. How quickly children respond to openness. The girl had a trusting, open face, a face that had never known the emptiness of disillusion, the betrayal of an ideal. Of shattered dreams.

Almost every morning before lectures, they would gather in a cafe on the square, drinking Georgiu's bitter coffee, talking of the night before in a fug of Turkish cigarette smoke.

One morning, the cafe was empty. As Gavriel came in, Georgiu threw a towel over his shoulder.

'Make yourself scarce, Gabi *nu*.' He wiped his walrus moustache and nodded towards the door. 'Two of your crowd were arrested last night.' The old man's eyes were half-closed and sad. He'd seen it all before. The Iron Guard. The Gestapo. Now the Securitate. Nothing changed. Gavriel didn't wait to ask more, perhaps the man had told him too much already.

Dawn arrests had taken leading communists into detention, most of them appeared to be Jewish. At first, he thought it merely a coincidence. Then Jewish community heads were arrested and, soon after, leaders of the Socialist Zionist Youth. All were charged with agents of Imperialism and the CIA.

Gavriel couldn't believe it. All of the accused were staunch supporters of the regime. Many had suffered under the occupation. It was surely a mistake? They would all be released he was certain. But instead, an atmosphere of suspicion and silence closed in on the city. The newly formed Securitate were everywhere. No one spoke without checking who was in earshot. Despite the summer, everything felt cold and damp.

The kettle began to boil, the simmering growing louder and louder, and in the confines of the small porch, Gavriel heard the roar in the square outside the courtroom where crowds of workers bussed in from the factories in the suburbs were shouting and jeering as the prison vans drew up: 'Death to the traitors. Kill the Jewish scum,' and the crowd taking up the cry, shaking their fists, faces red with hysteria. Above, a bright red banner screamed: 'Hang All Zionist Imperialist Saboteurs!'

The courtroom was no better. He remembered the trial as if he were there today. Secret police everywhere. Public galleries packed. The judge - the same one who had served under the hated Antonescu regime, the chief prosecutor who had worked under the Gestapo. He saw the accused, young, idealistic people Gavriel knew and trusted, people who had given everything to the new society, who couldn't even have imagined the crimes with which they were charged.

He could still see them now, standing in the dock. Hunched, ashen faced, rumours of torture and beatings, of starvation to make them confess. Only one refused - a young Socialist Zionist.

Looking straight at the judge, he shouted:

'Who are you to pass judgement on us? There is more Marxism in my little finger, than you will ever have in your whole body.'

Amidst uproar and counter cheers, the court was cleared. More arrests followed. Then the terrible waiting. Hoping for death sentences to be commuted to imprisonment. But by then, Gavriel had made his decision. Rumania was no country for a Jew. Not even a socialist one.

The kettle boiled. Steam filled the porch. Gavriel pulled out the plug and spooned coffee into each of the mugs. As he poured in the boiling water and the coffee frothed, again he regretted losing his self-control. One day, perhaps, he could tell Ella why. When he was sure she might understand - if she was still interested.

He didn't yet know what had brought her here, what she was looking for. Perhaps Harold did. He wondered whether she could comprehend that this tiny patch of scorched desert was his only homeland. His country. He had, nor wanted no other. Here, he would build his socialist dreams into a reality. Amongst his own people. And if someone hadn't been through all the ignorance, the brutality, the betrayal, the waste of so much human spirit and resources - and of lives, perhaps they would never fully understand.

As he placed the mugs on a tray, with some biscuits from their weekly ration, Gavriel felt that there had been another reason for his exploding like that. Something sub-conscious. Perhaps a wish to let Ella know that he wasn't just the good old placid Gavriel. That he too had a temperament, strong feelings. Maybe? Still, he shouldn't have lost control like that. Picking up the tray, he opened the door and went in.

As Gavriel hopped onto the porch and paused to get back his breath, Ella remembered his coming back in with the tea tray, looking sheepish.

'Sorry I got annoyed Ella.' He smiled. 'I'll explain one day.'

'Please don't apologise,' she'd said. 'And yes. I would like to now more.' Then Udi had nudged her to carry on playing memory game, pointing at the cards. Yes. One day she must prompt him to tell her more.

10

The dining hall was a long, wooden hut, painted light green at the top of the slope. The dirt track from the road led up to the rear end for deliveries to the kitchen. Roads cost money and the first one was built to where it was most needed for heavy traffic, to the cowshed and the grain stores, and the kitchen. So the inevitable first view of the kibbutz for any visitor, was the pile of boxes and crates by the dustbins.

On one side of the dining hall, the ground fell away towards the road and the cowsheds. On the other was an open, sandy space they called the courtyard at the far edge of which was the showers' bloc, a low gleaming white building only just completed. Beyond that were the children's houses and to the right of them, the new houses. Along the other side of the courtyard, were the office and reading-room huts and behind them, most of the dwelling huts.

From the showers, the ground rose to a narrow summit on which stood the concrete water tower, the first solid building they had erected when the kibbutz was settled seven years previously. From here, beyond the barbed wire perimeter fence, a sparse scrubland undulated for about a mile and a half up to the sandstone hills that marked the border.

At one end of the dining hall, was a covered porch with two hand-basins and a large notice board. Panting after their scramble across the hot sand, Gavriel and Harold strolled across the cool, newly washed-down tiles of the porch and peered at the work roster on the board.

'Who's down for afternoon shift,' asked Ella.

'Nahum,' murmured Harold. 'Glad we've got someone reliable to help with the fodder beet.'

Every evening, the work organiser pinned up the large, white sheet listing the work places down the right hand side and opposite each branch, names of people allocated to each one. All writen down – but in pencil. By the time supper was over, many names would have been rubbed out and transferred to different places as demands changed or someone fell ill.

Work organisers were elected – often kicking and screaming - into the job and rarely lasted more than six months. It was a thankless task and no one ever volunteered. 'Trying to cover an ever expanding bed with a tiny sheet,' quipped Harold, 'always having to leave somewhere – or someone - out in the cold.'

Ella glanced at the kindergarten space. Hedva was sick and Sarah had been plucked away from the orchards to replace her. The children's houses, kitchens and livestock had to have their full quotas whatever happened and the fields and the workshops were usually the losers. There must have been a fierce argument last night between Ami, the head of the orchards and Yosef the work organiser. Poor Yosef, Ella mused, wondering how he survived.

Harold was looking in the cowsheds' space where Yaacov's name was written in. Taking the rubber tipped pencil tied alongside, he rubbed out the name and substituted his own. Then, removing his name from the 'Sick' space, he wrote Yaacov's name where it had been the evening before: *'Shabbat'* - day off -and felt better. Now he existed! He turned and noticed Ella observing.

'All plans are a basis for change,' he winked. She nodded and smiled back

As he waited for the other two, Gavriel glanced towards the border and again he was wondering, were those really shots in the night – or just his dreams? In the warm glare of the morning sun, everything looked so peaceful. Yet for all he knew, at that very moment, some Egyptian lookout might be focussing his binoculars directly at them.

What did they make of this patch of green in the grey, barren desert, these sons of the Nile, he wondered? Didn't they have enough to do in their own impoverished, disease ridden country, instead of maintaining a huge, standing army?

Inside the hall, the tables were arranged in two rows, one along either wall, each with three places along either side. Harold and Ella sat opposite one another, nearest the window. He was glad they had come up early for breakfast, before the mad rush when the field workers came in at half past eight. Gavriel hovered, undecided and Harold looked up and touched his glasses, grinning.

'Still making up your mind?'

Gavriel ran his fingers through his hair.

'Never simple,' he winced. 'If I sit in the centre, I can reach everything by myself, but I won't be able to eat in peace because people at each end will keep asking me to pass jugs and dishes.'

'So sit at one end, like I do,' said Ella.

'Maybe,' Gavriel sighed, 'but then I have to ask others to pass things to me all the time.'

Harold smiled. Seven years hadn't been sufficient for Gavriel to reach a final decision. Wearily, Gavriel eased himself in beside Harold.

'Just a concrete illustration of dialectics,' said Harold, 'unless we get square tables for four into this year's budget.'

'Pigs will fly,' said Ella.

At the far end of the hall, a double door led into the kitchens. Music blared from a transistor radio tied above the sinks to overcome the boredom of washing up. It added to the general cacophony of clattering dishes and animated conversation in which the Sabras seemed to revel.

This morning, Harold felt he couldn't take it. He rose and went to ask them to turn it down a bit. They did, but by the time he had seated himself again, everything seemed just as raucous. This general noise level, together with the speed with which everyone ate were, in Harold's opinion, the main drawback to communal eating. Added to this was the fact that their dining hall could only accommodate half of the kibbutz population at one time. So the servers and cleaners were forever waiting to clear tables and re-lay them for the next sitting as soon as they could, working clockwise around the hall.

Harold however, liked to take his time.

'Decent, quiet eating, is a sign of civilised society,' he would moan to Ella, whenever the cleaning trolley stood poised at their supper table. Ella agreed. But she also liked the feeling of community that the hubbub of conversation over the day's affairs gave to the dining room.

At breakfast, Harold contented himself with a large plate of semolina porridge into which he dropped two spoonfuls of jam. This, a slice or two of bread and a cup of chicory coffee was usually enough for him. Gavriel and Ella though began slicing up vegetables from a large bowl in the middle of the table - cucumbers, huge tomatoes, radishes, olives, green peppers, Ella preparing hers as though for marquetry.

Harold never failed to be fascinated by this procedure. It took the best part of the half an hour breakfast time, leaving them just a few minutes to eat it all. But like most, they did it every day.

The next problem to resolve was that of the soft boiled egg as the server came round with the two wire baskets full of eggs. Choosing a hard one was simple. They had been allowed to boil and bubble to overkill, rock hard. But choosing a soft one was inevitably a lottery.

Just before breakfast time, the cooks plunged about two-dozen eggs into a huge aluminium pot of boiling water. The water would obviously then go off the boil. By the time it boiled again and the three-minute timer pinged, those at the bottom would be hard while those at the top had barely gelled. Somewhere in the middle, would be real soft-boiled eggs.

Ella smiled across the table

'Great decisions time for you too, eh?'

Harold wrinkled his nose.

'And never were there greater ones.'

Like Gavriel's, his problem had to be faced every day. Right now, deciding that he couldn't face the chance of a runny egg, Harold opted for the certainty of a hard boiled one.

As he peeled the egg, Harold looked around the hall, the beige coloured walls, the brown woodwork and the fly spotted, cream ceiling and everything around him in perpetual motion, eating, talking, yawning, laughing. At every table, arms stretching out, shoulders bumping, food bowls and plates passing to and fro.

'People watching, again?' Ella's brown eyes looking at him across the table. Harold jumped, then smiled.

'Oh well. Harmless enough. But the noise. The noise...'

Ella chewed on a slice of green pepper.

'You're just too sensitive Harold. You ought to have joined the Trappist monks at Latrun. Take a vow of silence?'

Harold winced.

'It's in Jordan,' he muttered. And anyway. All men!'

The two of them often indulged in this kind of banter, but this morning Harold's nerves were too frayed to put up with the general noise. After gulping down the last of his coffee, he stood up.

'I'll wait outside,' he said softly and slowly sauntered out through the double swing doors onto the porch. Ella watched him go then glanced at Gavriel.

'Cross fingers,' she murmured and they continued to eat in silence.

In the shade of the trees and porch roof, it was relatively cool. Harold eased himself down onto the tiles and leaned back against the low, concrete block balustrade. He looked at his bare feet and rubbed between his toes. White loess dust filled the grooves and outlined each toe nail. So different from the rich brown soil of his first kibbutz. In this amazing land, every twenty of thirty miles, north to south threw up a different kind of soil, from the Terra Rosa of Galilee through every shade of brown, grey and yellow, to the brilliant white of the salt-laden chalk around the Dead Sea.

As he rested back, Harold began to feel the tiredness coming on again. His eyes closed and his mind drifted back to his family, back to Manchester.

As a teenager, being a Jew was something he'd come to see as irrelevant. The more he progressed through Grammar school, the more his studies became the only important thing in his life. He wanted to be a marine biologist. His family's Jewishness seemed hypocritical, synagogue only on High Holidays a few times a year, or for weddings, *matzos* at Passover, not eating bacon or shellfish and a grandfather who spoke mainly Yiddish - which he couldn't understand anyway.

It had come to a head one day when the collector came to empty the little blue box of the Jewish National Fund which always stood on their sideboard. The money went to buy land for Jewish settlement in Palestine, said his mother. It was almost empty

'Never mind,' his father said, 'Here. Take a few pounds.'

'Many thanks,' said the little, bearded old man, wrote a receipt and with a *'Sholem Aleikhem,'* backed away from the door and walked away to the next house. In Prestwich, many streets were entirely Jewish.

Harold had been watching from the front window. As his father came in, he swung round.

'If you believe in all that, why don't we put money in the box every day?'

'Never mind,' said his mother, 'it's more than he'll get from most houses.'

'It's like you pray each Passover, "Next Year in Jerusalem", but never intend going there,' persisted Harold.

'The money is to settle refugees. From the camps after the war,' his father grunted. 'They need our money.'

Harold was sickened. If that was the extent of their Zionism, their lip service to Jewishness, he wanted no part of it. Anyway, it was society as whole that required changing, not splitting it apart with petty nationalisms he maintained, as his views drifted steadily, through the Statesman and Nation and over to the Left.

But if he wanted to forget his Jewishness, others didn't. There were the snide remarks about Jews and money, the relish with which the boys took to baiting Shylock in their school's reading of 'The Merchant of Venice', all of which changed to open hostility, when the Jewish 'Irgun' hanged three British sergeants in Palestine in retaliation for killing one of their leaders. He remembered the picture on the front page of the 'Daily Express' and boys chasing him down Cheetham Hill, throwing stones and shouting: 'Bloody Jew murderers'.

He'd taken refuge in Ronnie Cohen's house in Hightown, in the shadow of the red brick walls of Strangeways prison. Two up, two down with washing hanging in the kitchen. 'Jewish millionaires'? The anti-Semites should have seen this. And they weren't the only Jews living like that. But logic didn't seem to count.

Harold's daydreaming was interrupted as a tractor came in from the fields followed by boots clattering on the porch and a hubbub of voices slowly disappearing into the dining hall. Then, as it grew quiet again, Harold remembered the Christmas holiday during his final year at school.

Ronnie had invited him to go for a weekend visit to some training farm in Bedfordshire. Said there were young people living there as a commune and preparing to go out to live on something called a *Kibbutz,* in Palestine. Harold feared it would be like the mumbo jumbo of the synagogue, but not having any other plans, trusted Ronnie and agreed to go.

It was Hanukah, the Feast of Lights. About forty young people were gathered in the large room of the old manor house, reading passages from the Book of the Maccabees, but also readings from Howard Fast, Gorky, Shalom Asch and other writers, all interspersed with songs as well as mime on a makeshift stage.

He remembered asking: "Are these really Jews?" And Ronnie laughing, "Of course. But its not only Jewish freedom in ancient times we're celebrating. It's for our liberation now, and for other peoples' struggles for freedom." And on that evening, in the light of the eight-branched candelabra and struck by these young Jewish farmers with their political awareness, their pride and their culture, Harold was as Saul on the road to Damascus.

By chance, it was about this time, he had his first attacks, just brief fainting fits at first. The doctor had reassured his parents: 'Just part of growing up. It will pass.' But it hadn't and just before his exams, several fits had occurred within a short time, keeping him away from school for over three weeks.

Poor Mum. She was devastated. And his father. Would Harold ever be able to go to University? To be 'somebody', as he put it? The doctor now admitted that it was epilepsy. Said Harold's brain was overworked, that he should do simple manual work for a while. And it was then that Harold remembered the training farm.

Looking back, it had been the happiest time of his life, working with the poultry, salvaging something of the ornamental gardens that had once graced the manor house, discussing art and politics until the early hours - even coming to appreciate Shostakhovich. But above all, he became enthused with their social life and their idealism – and especially their purpose.

Breaking his parents' hearts, Harold decided to give up further studies and join them. And in the following year, after the State of Israel was born, he had sailed with the group on an Israeli ship from Marseilles to Haifa. His ship. His country.

For a while, he'd lived on a kibbutz in Galilee. But it was too staid, almost everyone was married with children. A community of families in which he felt an outsider. So Stan, Judy and himself had come down here, to this younger kibbutz in the Negev.

Harold opened his eyes and flicked up the leather flap on his watch-strap. It was nearly half past eight. The sun was beginning to penetrate the young trees, casting patches of light on the porch tiles. Home. His home. His homeland, despite the odd feeling of Englishness.

No one here would ever question his loyalties, expect him to cling on to trappings of religion to prove his Jewishness. And no one would call him a bloody Jew again. Here, he was at peace. Harold rubbed his forehead, feeling the slight bump from the night before. Yes, As at peace as he would ever be.

Raising himself, he sat on the concrete balustrade, waiting for Ella and Gavriel to come out. His head throbbed. He knew they would willingly have let him go and lie down for a bit. But he wouldn't ask, he wouldn't give in. He would last out the whole shift.

Glancing up at the work rota, he felt pleased that he had altered it. But the memory of last night was still there to haunt him and he grew angry - angry with his own stupidity. If only he had listened to Ella and gone to his room to sleep.

11.

Now, sitting on the concrete wall, much as he tried not to, Harold's mind again switched back to the previous evening.

After the soldiers had driven away with the Arab boy, he came back up with Ella to the dining hall. He felt drained, and in the light of the porch must have looked it.

'You're dead beat, Harold,' said Ella. 'Best to have an early night, don't you think. You're on early shift tomorrow.'

'Sure,' he nodded, 'You're right. See you tomorrow.'

Ella went in to take the cup and plate back and Harold continued down the path, his mind still churning from the confrontation. What future was there for the country - for the whole area - if a majority came to think like that soldier? His feet dragged on the path and he felt despondent.

As he crossed the courtyard, a yellow light shone from the windows of the reading-room hut. It beckoned. A beacon of culture and sanity, tempting him - newspapers and magazines from all over the world. Harold glanced at his watch - it was nine thirty – not that late. 'Need an early night,' Ella had said. But what future was there for him if life had to stop before ten in the evening. Just work and sleep? Sleep and work? And he felt even worse.

Above, stars shone from a clear sky and to the south the half moon glowed. Leaves hung listless from the Judas tree and a scent of Jasmine drifted across from the creeper by the showers. And the lighted window still beckoned - the devil taunting him.

Harold stopped for a moment, swaying to and fro as he deliberated. Ella was right, he should go straight to bed. His head ached and his eyes smarted, but it was still so early... Perhaps just a short browse through the newspapers, that wouldn't hurt. And it would take his mind off the argument. Slowly, he turned and ambled across to the hut.

The fly-mesh screen swung closed behind him, bringing a puff of cooler air into the close atmosphere still warmed from the wooden walls. Three people sitting in easy chairs looked up as he entered, nodded then carried on reading. Harold crossed to the wide shelves at the rear. And couldn't believe his luck. The latest 'New Statesman & Nation' lay there. Still in its wrapper! It must have just arrived.

As if guilty, Harold glanced over his shoulder, then snatching up the magazine he sank into a nearby chair. Slowly, with the deliberate movements of one who is about to savour a great delicacy, he eased off the brown paper sleeve.

Although he had a good working knowledge of Hebrew, like most of the English speaking members, Harold indulged in old habits, smiling at the 'This England' column, struggling with the Weekend Competition, and avidly devouring the book and film reviews.

'The whole problem with learning a new language,' he consoled Ella as she struggled with Hebrew grammar, 'is that you are reduced to talking like a five-year-old, until you have mastered it.' He hadn't completely mastered it himself and still required these frequent transfusions of foreign affairs, news of concerts he would never go to, plays he would never see, but which he just had to know about. To be involved. To feel alive.

Harold turned to the pages at the back, scanning the notices of political meetings. The Young Communists were there of course. The Commonwealth party? Was that still kicking? The regular meeting protesting about Franco. Betty Ambateilos pleading for support for her husband imprisoned in Greece.

Nothing seemed to have changed.

Just as he turned to the book reviews, Stan bowled in. Pipe in mouth, ginger moustache and bright red face that would never become accustomed to the burning sun, his faded khaki shorts looking forever as though he'd just crossed Cyrenaica with the Eighth Army – which he had.

'Trust you to get it first, you jammy bugger.' Stan grinned. 'Won't be any print on the page by the time you've finished!'

Harold lowered the magazine and looked over the top of his glasses.

'All in good time,' he drawled, 'all in good time. I'm having an early night.'

'Right then.' Stan sauntered across to the shelves, 'I'll hang about then, else some anti-social bastard will whip it away to his room.'

About ten minutes later, the screen door clunked again. It was Ella. She stopped and frowned to see Harold there, but said nothing as she walked across and picked up a copy of 'Newsweek'.

'Bloody Imperialist trash,' Stan snorted, nodding at the magazine. "Why does the kibbutz pay for that rubbish, anyway?'

'It doesn't,' Ella muttered. 'Comes free, from the U.S. library in Tel Aviv.'

'Typical,' said Stan, 'More C.I.A. propaganda. Can't see why you bother.'

Ella sat on a bench by the wall and thumbed through the pages. She'd heard it all before.

' Propaganda it may be,' she murmured, 'but they seem to know more about our politics, than we do. Look at this Israeli spy business in Cairo. Our newspapers don't mention a word.'

The discussion made the others readers restless. One or two coughed. Harold looked up and adjusted his glasses.

'Will you two put a sock in it, please?' But as he looked down at the magazine again, suddenly the print began to swim in front of his eyes and lights flashed way in the back of his head. He had to get to his room. And quickly.

Slowly, as if nothing was happening, he got up and handed the 'Statesman' to Stan. It was the last thing he remembered. Everything went dark and he felt himself sucked into a whirlpool. Down and down. His knees buckled and he slumped to the floor, unconscious.

Everyone stood up, reaching out their hands, helpless. Stan threw down the magazine and went towards him.

'Wait,' called Ella. 'Wait. Don't move him!' She knelt beside Harold's prostrate figure. 'Here, Stan. Just raise his head a little.' Pulling a small cushion from one of the chairs she slipped it gently under his head. 'And take his glasses,' she added softly.

Gingerly, Stan unhooked the glasses and laid them on a low table. A thin line of froth laced Harold's lips. Taking out a large handkerchief, Stan handed it to Ella. She wiped the mouth then folding it neatly, wiped his forehead. Sitting back on her heels, she looked down at the pale, thin face.

'Just leave him like that,' she whispered. 'He'll come out of it on his own.'

They stood up, Stan tugging at his moustache.

'Hasn't happened for quite while,' he murmured.

'Who knows?' said Ella. 'Maybe we just haven't been there.'

They waited, silent, for what seemed hours. Others in the room sat down again and turned away, half looking from the corners of their eyes.

After about ten minutes, Harold opened his eyes. Slowly he sat up, rubbing the back of his neck as if waking from a spell.

'Thanks Stan,' he murmured as he took his glasses. Looking up at Ella, he half smiled. 'Thank you too,' as if knowing that it was she who would have known what to do.

As he stood up, Stan stepped forward.

'Here. I'll help you to your room.'

Harold waved him away.

'No. No need. Thanks. I'm fine.'

'Sure?'

'Quite sure.' Harold walked to the door, then stopped and half turned, 'Oh. Look after the 'Statesman'. I'll finish it tomorrow.' The screen door clunked. And he was outside.

Stan eased his lanky frame back into the easy chair and took up the magazine. But he couldn't read. He'd lived near Harold in Cheetham Hill. Knew him from well before 'all that' had happened. He sat with closed eyes. Why Harold? Why did things like this happen to such good people. People who gave so much of themselves whilst the evil buggers seemed to live ripe and healthy into old age?

Stan had lost faith, along with his best friend at Benghazi in '41. If there was a God, he was a right mean bastard. He opened his eyes and stared at the unfocussed print, and a deep sadness spread through his whole body. Ella stood for a while, undecided, then quickly opened the door and went out.

Harold was standing in front of his veranda, hands in pockets and head sunk into shoulders.

'Sure you're okay,' she called softly as she came along the path. Harold glanced over his shoulder.

'As good as,' he replied

'Shall I change you over to the late shift?' she asked, coming up to him.

'No. No.' Harold's words spilled anxiously into the night air. 'No. Don't. Leave it as it is, Ella. Please.'

'Right. See you in the morning then,' adding as she turned, *'Layla Tov.'* She had no hesitation in using the more colloquial form of 'good night', with its *double entendre* of 'have a good night'. Harold stepped onto the veranda and responded with the more poetic form.

'Leyl Menucha,' adding, 'see you tomorrow.'

That brief exchange embodied the essence of their friendship. Ella offered neither sympathy nor advice, just understanding and respect for his wish to be independent. Harold in return treated her as a whole person – mind as well as body. He never imposed nor threatened like many men did. Like Itzik…

As she walked away, recalling the way he'd calmly yet firmly held his ground in the argument with the soldier, Ella felt an affinity with to him and that it wasn't just on the intellectual level – though as yet she didn't know exactly what. More concerning at that moment, was whether she should have tried to persuade him to sleep late and work the afternoon shift. Even more, she wondered what Itzik would decide when he came up from evening shift. He was bound to hear.

Harold stood for a moment, listening to her footsteps disappearing into the darkness. He breathed deeply on the cool, night air, looking out over the fence lights. From the dark dunes beyond, a little owl screeched from its stump. In the distance, a jackal wailed. The scent of oleander drifted across from the bushes by the babies' house. Life could be so beautiful. Turning to his door, his head still heavy, he opened it and went in.

Harold's room was one of four in a long, wooden hut. The window was opposite the door and along the left-hand wall, was his bed and a small wardrobe. Under the window, a small lamp on the table-cum-desk was half buried in a pile of books and papers. On the right hand wall, a bookcase of deal planks supported on concrete blocks was crammed to overflowing. Above it, hung two framed lino cuts by Franz Masarel, a parting gift from his friends at the training farm. 'Nothing like a bit of

Social Realism,' Issy had said, 'remind you of Salford, mate.'

Harold undressed as in a trance and slipped quickly into bed. Automatically, he reached out to switch on the small wall light beside the Turner print he'd bought at the National Gallery, usually he read late into the night. But not tonight. He dropped his hand, he must try to sleep.

Closing his eyes, he tried to do just that but his mind was spinning from the events of the evening. The room felt stuffy and he swung out of bed to open the shutters. The moonlight spilled in with the night air casting a white rhombus on the tiled floor and as he got back into bed and turned on his side, the moonlit splash on the floor reminded him of the light through the porthole. Of his traumatic voyage on the immigrant ship, to Haifa.

After a sleepless night on the wooden seats of the train from the Gare de Lyons, his small group of from the training farm waited on the quayside in Marseilles, creaking corduroy trousers and scuffed leather jackets. Despite the weariness, they couldn't hide their excitement as they stared through the port fence. A Jewish ship with a Star of David flag and Herzl's seven stars on the funnel symbolising the man's dream of a seven hour working day - when even kids still worked twelve or fourteen hours in the mills.

A group of affluent Jewish tourists also waited to board and one called over to them:

'Hey, *Chalutzim*. Have some Bananas you pioneers. Best we can do.'

Harold remembered the mutterings, they didn't want charity from the bourgeoisie of Golders Green. But they hadn't eaten since Paris and hunger forced its own compromise. With grateful thanks, they took them. Later, in bright sunshine and an almost delirious feeling, they sailed out and past the Chateau d'If on an azure sea. They were on their way.

After the straits of Messina though, storm clouds gathered and amidst the lashing rain and howling wind of a sudden Mediterranean storm, waves almost stood the old Rangoon river-steamer on end. Every few hours, they rushed to the side and let go any food they had managed to get down. Except Moshe from Dublin. Frequent crossings of the Irish Sea had given him a cast-iron stomach. He ate for them all.

As the storm continued and grew even more violent, a stench of vomit rose from deep in the bowels of the ship and every so often, white eyed figures burst up the stairs to retch over the sides. Curious, Harold went down to the holds - and saw a scene he would never forget.

A mass of dark skinned people from Morocco and Algeria lay on the floor, surrounded by bundles of clothing, blankets, cooking pots and jars of all description. Women and old men wailed and moaned, children ran around crying and screaming in turn. Harold felt it was like something from Dante's Inferno. It was the time of wholesale immigration from the Arab countries. Shaken, he crept back to his own cabin where ten of them were crammed into bunk beds, thinking they were overcrowded. Suddenly it seemed like a luxury berth.

As he remembered that scene, Harold suddenly thought the young soldier down by the silo. He could easily have been one of those very kids down in the hold.

At Haifa, there were equally unforgettable scenes. Bearded Moroccan Jews throwing themselves prostrate to kiss the concrete of the Holy Land for which they had prayed for so long. But also the two Polish women who'd been moaning about not having a cent to buy food, flaunting expensive woollen cardigans they'd bought with smuggled dollars in Naples. And the burly man carrying a heavy sack that split on the gangway, scattering onions all over the quay, screeching as he ran about collecting them. He'd heard that there was a shortage in Israel at the time and he said they would keep him for a month at least.

He recalled thinking at the time: Yes, these kinds of Jews were coming too. And the young state needed them like a plague. But who was he to decide? To pass judgement? But all had been forgotten as they themselves celebrated by dancing a noisy *Horra*, all the way to the customs shed.

Harold began to think over his time on this kibbutz. More and more of his friends had now married. Many had kids. He was now part of the ever-dwindling band of bachelors in a pioneering society where there was always a shortage of girls. 'And even if there were enough,' he often thought, 'who would want to marry someone with my complaint?'

Sure, he enjoyed the friendship with Ella. He might even have his fantasies, but he was too much of a realist to take them further. Would she even suspect him of having such thoughts? An attractive girl like Ella could choose anyone - like Itzik, say, though he couldn't quite fathom out what was going on there.

Harold was still daydreaming on the porch with his eyes half closed when boots clattered on the tiles nearby, people were coming out of the dining hall. Ella and Gabriel would soon be out too. His eyes were so heavy and his body weary. Would it always be the same? Just take the pills, heed the warning signs and take it easy, said the doctors. And above all, don't think so much! Harold's chin sunk onto his chest again and his eyes closed for a moment. Like that, was life worth living?

12.

Lost in his reveries and with his eyes still half-closed, Harold felt a tap on his bare foot and a voice seemed to come from high above him.

'Wish we all had time to snooze.' It was Ella. 'Never mind the cows, eh?'

Harold opened his eyes and squinted up at her.

'Can't a bloke enjoy a minute's peace from that din in there?' He slapped one hand on the concrete and creaked to his feet. 'How long do I have to wait for you two, anyway?' he grinned, jamming his hat on his head.

'Bloody *khutzpah*,' said Gavriel. 'Let's go.'

As they stepped off the porch. Ella hesitated.

'Er. See you down below,' she called, turning away. 'First things first,' and hurried away towards the new shower bloc.

Gavriel and Harold continued down the path towards the road but as they reached the eucalyptus trees, an army command-car raced in through the gates and braked beside them in a cloud of dust. A young officer leaned from the passenger seat.

'Where's your telephone. Our radio's playing up.'

'In the office.' Gavriel pointed up the hill. 'Why? Trouble?'

The officer shook his head.

'Not yet!' But as the truck drew away, Gavriel noticed the soldiers in the rear in full battle order. He looked at Harold. They both shrugged, then continued their way through the trees to the cowsheds.

Hurrying across the courtyard from the dining hall, Ella shielded her eyes from the glare of the sun on the sand and was glad to reach the shade of the shower block.

She often took advantage of coming up to eat to use the toilets there. Those in the dairy weren't that rough and in her travels all over the world she'd used every possible - and impossible - place. But here it mattered, it was her home. This morning though, it wasn't just the hygiene. Much more, she sought the quiet and the calm.

The tiles were still cool and fresh smelling from their daily wash-down. Sitting on the slatted wooden bench, Ella leaned back against the damp, tiled wall. Everything still smelled of fresh paint, the new showers had only been completed the previous month.

The showers were an integral part of their communal life. Everyone showered straight after work, the hot water washing away the tiredness, renewing spirits and preparing for the evening, separating toil from leisure. 'Or,' Harold joked, 'as old man Marx would say, "separating the structure of society from the superstructure."'

The old corrugated iron shed had long passed its time and a new shower bloc had been agreed in principle. But year after year, more pressing investments had pushed it to the back of the queue. The showers were the village pump. On the men's side, news of the farm was exchanged and discussed, new political twists argued over and the latest scandal spread about. On the women's side, it was similar but with more attention being paid to the reported pregnancies - or denials.

Often, parallel discussions were taking place at the same time and would be shared and shouted through the iron sheet partition. Then some joker would hurl a *kafkaf*, a wooden shower-sandal, against the tin, shouting,

'Away with all these artificial divisions. We are all equal!' The resounding thud would bring high pitched responses and an answering thud, with shouts of:

'Vandals' or 'Go to hell!'

Everyone clunked around on these sandal-shaped slabs of wood held on by strips of old inner-tube. With use, the strips often broke leaving the wearers hopping around like a lame frog to avoid dirtying their feet. At busy times, there was always a queue for *kafakfim* in the muddy changing area. From Itzik she'd learned that in Sabra slang, calling someone a *kafkaf* implied that they were as thick as two short planks.

Ella stretched out her legs and closed her eyes. She ought to do what she had come in for then hurry back down to work. But it was so peaceful and right now, she needed the short respite. Especially after last night.

To reassure herself that Harold really had gone to bed this time, she had waited in the shadow of the acacia bushes until his light went out – and found herself thinking about their friendship, how easy it was to be with him, how she admired his trying to live a full life despite his disability – and how the kibbutz gossips were always looking for something deeper between them.

After a few minutes, in the light of the half moon, she made her way back to her hut. But, as she passed Miriam's room, raucous laughter and snatches of song came through the open doorway and someone was fingering an accordion. The Sabras were like that, bowling into each other's rooms without plan or reason and when more than four or five got together, out came the *finjan* to brew up coffee, someone started up a song and before you knew it, they had a *kumsitz,* another party.

Ella tried to creep past, she was too tired. But just then, Uri came out to fill the *kumkum* at the veranda tap and spotted her.

'Hey, Miriam,' he called through the doorway, grinning as he wiped his moustache, 'another cup, for your intellectual friend.' He meant no offence. Just that he found girls with brains unnerving.

Ella made to walk on, but Miriam ran out and caught her.

'Take no notice of that *muzhik*, Ella. For the first time in two thousand years, the good for nothing is actually making the coffee.' 'For two thousand years', was the standing joke of the new State, the Israeli establishment forever recording some event or other taking place in the Holy Land - 'for the first time, since the expulsion by the Romans.'

Ella stepped onto the veranda then turned to Uri.

'Hang on. I thought you were on guard duty?' she said smiling.

'I am,' he grinned. 'I'm guarding the maximum number of people at one time,' and took the *kumkum* back into the room.

For Ella, Uri was the archetypal Sabra - though she admitted it was wrong to stereotype. He worked in the *Falkha*, the cereal crops where most of the Sabras wanted to work. Diesel oil flowed in their veins, said Harold, alluding to their obsession with the huge tractors. In the two main seasons, ploughing and sowing in the autumn and the harvest in late spring, they worked long, long days and into the nights, coming back and crashing through the doors to the dining hall, red eyes peering from blackened faces, goggles perched on their heads, clothes covered in white dust, wanting to give the impression that they were the 'real farmers'.

Harold resented their attitude that they were the 'bread-winners' of the kibbutz. All the grain produced was subsidised by the government and anyway, one in every three harvests was a dead loss through drought.

Now, with the wheat and barley harvest over, the *falkha* workers were making up their quotas of hours in the kitchen and on guard duty. And making everyone feel that they were doing great favours.

For Ella, their main characteristic was an intense dislike for 'isms', ideologies, principles and the like. They had a deep mistrust of 'intellectuals', as though all that precluded 'real work' and interfered with the 'realities' of everyday life. Again, she knew that this was generalising and probably unfair. The kibbutz did need people who were crazy about their work and strove for efficiency, part of the synthesis, as Harold would say. But did it need to be so polarised?

Having been dragged into the *kumsitz*, Ella became involved chatting with Miriam and Hava, and it was almost midnight when she left to go to her room. By the time she reached her door, the moon had almost set over the sand-hills to the west.

Ella's room was similar in shape and size to those of Harold or Uri, but there, the similarity ended. Print curtains were drawn across the window and on the blue bedspread lay a brown and white sheepskin she'd bought at the Bedouin market in Beer Sheba. She loved to lie there in the cool and silence of a morning off, face pressed against the fleece and her fingers playing with the curly wool.

On the wall opposite the bed, hung a woven *dhurri*, memento of her journey through India. In the corner, a black pottery jug held a collection of convoluted dried thorns with large, spiny pods and around the other walls, small shelves with neatly arranged paper-backs, small ornaments and pieces of coral from the Barrier Reef.

Ella sat on a stool by the small table and flicked aimlessly through a neat pile of letters. Where on earth would she find time to answer them all? The framed photograph of her mother and father stood by a small vase of orange Gerberas. Home. Mum with her hennaed, ginger hair, Dad with his long pale face and balding head. They'd worked from morning to night in their milk bar in St. Kilda's, no holidays, just work, work, work ever since they'd arrived in Melbourne just before the war.

She remembered how her mother had sulked when she brought Roger home one day.

'Why can't you find a nice Jewish boy like your friends?' They'd argued. Mum had cried. Dad tried to calm things down.

'Easy for you,' he said, 'you were born here, not like us. But we are different. Sure. Roger is a nice boy. But his family won't let you forget what you are.'

Poor Dad. She could always talk things over with him. Mind full of useless information. Always reading, whenever he could snatch a few spare moments. She'd inherited his love of learning, perhaps why she so admired Harold.

Roger had come and gone. And yes, his family were a bit awkward. But she felt that had more to do with their not wanting to lose him from the farm. No. At that time, her Jewishness didn't seem to count. It was the boys who worried her. Never wanting anything other than that. And if they did start by admitting that she had a head as well, it was only a prelude to getting below the neck.

After Roger, came Tony, combining Marxism-Leninism at the university with sweaty hands after lectures. She too became enthused with Socialism but was sickened at Kruschev's revelations about Stalin - and even more by Tony's trying to justify it all. His political means were just to an end with her too. Treating her like just another brainless Sheila.

The Trotskyites were no better, the boys never making the coffee, the leader always accompanied by blonde acolytes, typing his speeches and warming his bed. So after a degree in sociology, Ella had seen enough. Perhaps out there, was another world and she joined the steady stream of Antipodeans, trekking through Nepal, backpacking across Turkey and Greece and 'doing Europe'. 'Culture with a capital K,' said Mike whom she met at the Acropolis.

With him, she hung around the Left Bank in Paris, coming and going as they each wished. At least he had no pretensions. Sex was sex and no illusions. They took the ferry and joined fellow expatriates in Kangaroo Alley at Earl's Court, but it was too much like home and she left him there. But when she got back to Melbourne, it was stifling. Parochial.

Home. Ella tried to rearrange the letters on the table but was too tired to make much order. She did want to keep contact. Especially with Dad and the one or two friends she really did miss. And with Jeffrey, who'd wanted to come out here with her, but never did. Too soft. Staying to care for his senile mother. But she had liked him - and could have liked him much more.

Ella stood up and started to undress for bed, hanging her shirt on a hanger in the small cupboard, thinking about him. Jeffrey. Tall and wispy, horn rimmed glasses and spiritual. Should have been a monk. Or a Rabbi, rather. It was he that gave her the idea of kibbutz. He was going one day, he'd said. When his mother... Well, maybe.

Ella once stopped off on a kibbutz, between Afghanistan and Turkey. Worked for a week weeding onions. Boring work. Too closed. Too isolated. But at her loose end in Melbourne, Jeffrey's suggestion seemed to click.

Firstly, there was the outdoor life. Ever since going with Roger, she loved the outback, but found it too Redneck for her to settle there. Secondly, she never abandoned her Socialist ideals. And here, they were living them weren't they? And above all, there was equality. Men and women. So all in all, kibbutz seemed tailor-made for her – if she didn't have to weed onions all the time.

Ella glanced at a print of Van Gogh's olive trees on the wall. 'A fellow neurotic', Jeffrey laughed as he gave it to her, a goodbye present. The olive trees in Galilee looked just like that, contorted and anguished. Jeffrey's last letter was on the table too. 'Had she found what she was looking for?' he'd asked.

Ella felt that she had, the work, the camaraderie, creating a new society. On the other hand, she'd been surprised by the number of those just there for the ride, *nochshlappers*, her father would have called them. Physically they might be here but spiritually, still in the world outside, contributing little except their labour before moving on. It was one of her recurring discussions with Harold.

Ella finished undressing and put on her nightshirt. But with her windows still closed to keep out the day's heat, the room suddenly felt stuffy. She switched out the light before opening them. 'Never open the shutters at night before dousing the light,' Stan had cautioned when she'd first arrived, 'or the room will fill with mosquitoes.' He'd grinned. 'Sad when your only company for the night is a load of bites!' Later she'd learned the real reason - not to present a silhouetted target for an infiltrator just beyond the fence.

With the windows open, but leaving the shutters closed, Ella switched on the light again and took the rug from her bed. But just as she pulled back the sheets, there was a tap on the door. She started and glanced at her watch. It was nearly midnight.

'Who is it?' she asked, her words thin and choked.

'It's me,' came a deep voice through the plywood. 'Me, Itzik.'

Ella clutched a hand to her throat. Oh. God. Not now, she panicked as the voice continued, 'I'm making coffee. Saw your light and thought you might like to join me?'

Outside the door, Itzik waited, a towel draped round his neck. He'd just come up from evening shift in the dairy. Like a moth, he'd been drawn towards the light shining through the slats of Ella's shutters. Perhaps, using Harold's collapse as an excuse he could get to talk to her. Try again, despite the rebuffs.

Ella clutched the sheepskin close against her breast. Oh God! It was the last thing she wanted tonight. Why couldn't the man accept that it was all a mistake, all finished. After weeks of awkwardness from that last clinch, they'd managed to resume normal conversation again. If she had to tell him tonight, he would go back to his sulking self. And all because of one stupid incident – no, two really - but finished all the same.

Following that first incident in the dairy, she'd been careful not to give out any mixed messages. She'd learned since that he had also a steady girlfriend Shosh so she'd been more relaxed. Too relaxed. Otherwise how could she explain how stupid she was to allow it a second time, stupid and weak? Maybe because it had been a while that... well...

She and Itzik had both been out on horseback with the herd in the wadi. It was how she'd always imagined, the wide open spaces, a dry sunny day and the herd moving gently through the last long grass of the river bed before the summer's heat scorched it dry. Suddenly two buzzards, disturbed from a jackal carcass flew up and part of the herd began to bolt towards the border. In a mad chase, the two of them managed to head them off and shepherd the herd back to the cowsheds.

Tired and still a little breathless, they returned with the horses to the stable. As they unsaddled them, suddenly she felt the exhaustion from the tension and the mad gallop and must have shown it. Itzik laughed and flung an arm around her shoulder then somehow, still breathing heavily she found herself sinking down onto the straw and lying on her back and Itzik beside her, one leg across her thighs and all as if it wasn't her - in a kind of dream.

She felt his fingers opening her shirt buttons. Her mind told her it had to stop but her reactions were sluggish as his hands began stroking her breasts, his fingers tickling her nipples and despite herself she began to be aroused. Soon he was kissing her breasts too and still she was still letting it happen, conflicting emotions charging through her head. But as his hand slipped into the waistband of her jeans, alarm bells started to ring.

'No Itzik Please,' her lazy voice echoed in her head.

'It's okay, Ella. It's okay,' came his voice as though from high above, but at the sound of her zip being opened, she tensed her head began to clear. What the hell was she doing letting this happen. She didn't want it. She didn't want him, she didn't...

'No. Itzik. No. Stop. I don't . . .' she heard herself saying as he rolled on top of her and she felt she couldn't move. But as his hand slipped under the elastic, suddenly her head cleared. She convulsed and twisted sideways. 'No. No.' she snapped again and with a huge effort, jerked herself free and pulled her shirt closed.

Itzik was propped up on one elbow, his face flushed and pained.

'What's up?' he murmured. 'Why not, Ella . . ?' as if he too didn't know what to say.

Feeling more composed, Ella got up on her knees, pulled up her zip and buttoned her shirt.

'I was just dead beat, Itzik. Didn't know what... All a mistake... That's all.' She stood up. 'I want us to forget about it. That's all. Forget about it completely. Please. Okay?'

Standing up, she brushed herself down and now completely in control, splashed her face and neck in the half-drum water trough then hurried away down to the dairy to shower, leaving him sitting on the straw, his face still puzzled.

That was three weeks ago and she made it absolutely clear

since then that there was nothing doing. But here he was, outside her room.

Ella stared at the door. Was the handle turning? Holding the rug tighter against her, she stepped forward and, placing her toe about two inches back, opened it.

'Thanks for the offer, Itzik.' She looked down to avoid his eyes, 'but I'm dead beat. I just came back from Harold. You know... he had... well, a bad one.'

Itzik leaned close to the narrow opening. Very close.

'I know. That's why I came. Thought you could do with a cup of good coffee. You must have been really shaken.'

'Yes. A bit. But I'm already half asleep.' Ella tried to steady her voice, 'Some other time perhaps.'

Itzik leaned away and dropped his hand from the handle.

'Okay. *Maalesh*. Anyway. *Layla Tov*, Ella.'

'*Leyl Menucha*,' restful night, she replied, leaving no room for misunderstandings.

As he turned away, Ella looked up. His fair, curly hair was still damp from the shower and hung over his face. Like a little boy. She closed the door and turned the key, his crestfallen face nagging at her conscience.

Ella sat on the bed, waiting for her heart to stop racing and her breathing to return to normal. She had to get the message across, that she didn't want to fool around, that she felt he was only interested in her body. That she wanted someone who would love her for her mind as well, for her ideas - for her whole self. And anyway, he already had a steady girlfriend.

Standing up again, she pulled back the covers and slipped into bed. Staring at the dark ceiling, she tried to decide how she would play it the next day. To hell with it. She wouldn't play it at all. She would tell him, *Dughri,* straight out, as he was fond of saying. Repeat that anything that had happened was just a mistake. She was sorry, but there was nothing in it. Nothing at all. Somehow, she must find the opportunity. And the nerve. Yes. She must do it tomorrow, whatever. Or was it already, today. ?

13.

As he stepped off Ella's veranda and crossed the lawn back to his own room, Itzik glanced over his shoulder. The moon had set, leaving the night to the stars.

He felt empty, puzzled and empty. It was a new experience for him to be rebuffed. With Shosh as with all the others, it had always gone his way. Now, the more Ella rejected him, the more he wanted to know why and impelled to try again. He wanted her to know that he wasn't playing about, that he was in earnest. He was determined to let her know that - and that in itself was becoming an obsession.

Back in his room, Itzik sat on his bed and lit a cigarette, a cheap Degel, from the green paper packet. The sharp smell of Turkish tobacco filled the room and made him feel more awake. Not that he could sleep anyway.

He left the door stood ajar, wanting to hear the footfalls of the night guard, to catch Uri and tell him to replace Harold with Yaacov on the early call list. He drew deeply on the cigarette and blew a cloud of smoke from his nostrils. Harold. Yes. He had to give some thought to that as well.

Itzik stared at the green distempered wall opposite, thinking of that time in the dairy. Ella's slim body against him, her breasts pressing into his stomach, her tiny fists on his shoulders. Then that time in the stables, his hand on her breast, their kissing... Why had she suddenly changed? She was no kid, had travelled the world! Must have known what she was doing. Why?

He'd been attracted to her almost as soon as she started working with the herd. It wasn't only that she was attractive, she had real character. True, her being Australian added spice – someone from the big, wide world out there. But Ella was a girl he could settle down with. Never boring, like Shoshanah would be eventually.

Itzik lay back on the bed, watching the smoke drift up to the light bulb. Suddenly he jumped. *'In al abuk,'* he cursed - the best curses were in Arabic - the cigarette had burned down to his fingers. He swung his legs off the bed and stubbed out the butt in the old two-inch mortar-bomb cap that served as his ashtray.

Itzik's room was similar to Harold's or Ella's, but appeared larger for its emptiness. The walls were almost bare, apart from one framed print of the modern Israeli artist, Shraga Weil's "Harvest". Shosh had worked hard to introduce him to 'culture'.

On the adjacent wall was a large photograph in a clip frame, him and five others on a burned out Egyptian tank. Underneath, the caption: 'Abu Agheila - 1948'. Itzik closed his eyes for a moment. Only he and Dudik were still around. Two were still wandering the globe somewhere, and Heskel and Eitan had left it forever.

By the window, hung his old Sten gun complete with empty magazine. Like so many other weapons, it had never been handed in at the end of the War of Independence. At the bottom of his wardrobe, lay a small cardboard box of nine-millimetre ammunition.

Still restless, he stood and went out to the veranda. Lighting another cigarette, stared into the darkness. In three weeks time, it would be his stint of reserves' duty, which he always viewed with mixed feelings. Yes, he would meet up with old comrades and learn the latest news on this one or that. On the other hand, he felt he'd had enough of the army.

Like most of his generation, Itzik had seen fighting in one form or another for as long as he could remember. Even as a kid in the world war, he'd run messages for the *Haganah* intelligence, avoiding Palestine Police roadblocks, joking with the Australian soldiers in their floppy hats. They also spoke English but were so different from the hard-faced British paratroopers. *Kalaniot,* poppies, they called the red-berets. But no one joked when they turned over houses and rounded up Jewish suspects.

He was a still young teenager when uncle Simkha came home from serving with the Jewish Brigade in Italy. With him came the stories of the Holocaust. Itzik drew on his cigarette, remembering the fierce arguments with his parents, he and his friends would never had gone like lambs to the slaughter! He'd also said so to Gavriel, when they talked about it one day. Gavriel had just nodded and quoted the old Sages: 'Never judge others until you find yourself in the their place'. Maybe. But he would have fought. Like they did in the Warsaw Ghetto.

His thoughts were interrupted by footsteps along the path. Stepping off the veranda, he called out.

'Hey. Uri. Have you got the waking up list?' Uri hitched up his Sten and ambled towards him.

'I always knew you cowmen never sleep. No. I'll pick it up when I go to eat.'

'Good,' said Itzik. 'Well cross out Harold and wake Yaacov instead. Okay?'.

'No problem.' Uri nodded and grinned. 'But get some sleep sometime eh, cowman?'

Uri walked away into the darkness, shaking his head. A wonderful girl like Shosh and that idiot was chucking it in. Uri would have gone for her like a shot, tall, slim, long blond hair and enormous grey eyes that could make you weep. How could a man ditch a girl like that? And all because of his infatuation with the Australian? Crazy. Such a solid bloke, acting like a school-kid on his first crush. Uri shook his head again. Crazy.

Itzik closed the door behind him and stubbed out the cigarette. He looked around the room. The table was piled high with magazines and papers. More were on the chair by the bed. There was hardly a dairyman's journal - in Hebrew or English - that he didn't receive. And read. Two visits to Holland had given him valuable insights into their Friesian herd. Now, they, the *kibbutzniks*, were teaching the teachers.

He picked up the latest edition of the Israeli Dairy Farmers' Magazine. Under it were the last ten issues with which he used to compare statistics. In the latest 'league table', his own herd was now second in yield per cow and third in buttermilk percentage. Top were Beth Alpha, the *kulak's* from up north. By the next few issues, he hoped to overtake them.

Aimlessly, he flicked over the pages, he'd read it through a few days ago, but he couldn't settle. He sat on the bed and looked down the columns of figures again. Everyone sat on their beds out of habit. Harold always joked that it was a waste of money for the kibbutz to buy chairs...

Harold. Itzik looked up from the page. What about Harold? What if the next attack came whilst he was at work? He might slam his head against the steel yokes, collapse and be trampled by the cattle as they scrambled through the gates, anything. And it would be his, Itzik's fault for letting him continue to work there.

It seemed that the fits always came in the evening - in his own room generally. And after each one Harold reassured him that he'd be okay when engrossed in the routine at work. No mental exertion, he smiled. And because he was such a conscientious worker, with a great sense of humour - though his jokes were difficult to appreciate at times - Itzik agreed that he could carry on. At the same time, he still couldn't understand how could anyone be cheerful when at any moment he could be just a limp body stretched out on the floor? How?

Itzik was no stranger to disability, seen more than enough during the War of Independence. A shell landed, a man lay shattered and bleeding - and would spend the rest of his life in a wheelchair. But that was final. No illusions of a return to normality. But with what Harold had, the normality was an illusion. Like living balanced on a tightrope - and a deep void beneath.

He remembered how helpless he the first time he saw Harold laid out on his veranda. Angry that he could do nothing, he, Itzik who had carried wounded men for miles on a stretcher, just had to stand by and watch as Ella sorted it out. A shiver ran through him as he thought of it. God! If he had an affliction like that, he'd have ended it long ago with a nine-millimetre bullet.

Lighting up another cigarette, Itzik began to wonder about Harold and Ella, the way she laughed so much at his jokes, her round, open mouth and tiny teeth, the smooth neck diving into the vee of her shirt. What did such an attractive girl see in him? Yet women were strange.

He recalled beautiful girls who could have had any man, hitching themselves to boys hopelessly crippled whom they'd nursed through hospital - even men with faces half burned away. But still. Ella with Harold? It didn't seem to add up.

Itzik felt his forehead growing hot. He threw the journal on the chair and stood up, looking down at his toes on the black and white calf-hide that served as a carpet, the broad feet and thick calf muscles. The light glinted on the brass *finjan* and coffee cups in the corner, a present from the Bedouin whose flocks grazed the stubble in their fields after the harvest. The *finjan* must have come from Hebron. He didn't ask. The Bedouin had always survived by ignoring borders.

The sheikh had been so grateful it was embarrassing. The fields would lie fallow until the autumn ploughing, so why not let them graze it? It was this live and let live that made him unable to comprehend the viciousness of the Fedayeen attacks.

Itzik had a simple logic. The Jews hadn't started the war in '48. The Arabs had. They'd lost and many of them had fled. If they'd have won, he and his family would be six feet under and there would be no state of Israel. Not even the tiny one the U.N. had agreed upon.

No. He couldn't see any large-scale repatriation of the refugees, like those from Gaza. At least until the surrounding Arab states - and the *Fatah* gave up trying to destroy Israel. Perhaps, when a peace treaty was signed, some could return. The rest would have to settle in the Arab countries, there was so much empty land, so much oil money. Why couldn't they settle their Arab brothers like Israel had with the hundreds of thousands of refugees fleeing from the Moslem countries?

Itzik undressed and pulled on a pair of pyjama shorts. It was too hot for a jacket. He switched off the light and lay back, remembering when they came to settle here in '49. The long convoy of some thirty trucks across the bare plain and up to the deserted hilltop. The only green in the entire area was the thin line in the bed of the wadi.

His first job had been to plough a deep furrow beside their fields. The United Nations officers had planted a line of staves to mark the 'Green Line' of the Gaza border.

As his huge D8 Caterpillar tractor approached a clump of dried up trees, an old Arab ran in front, long *galabaya* flapping and waving his arms, tears streaming from his eyes. Itzik disengaged gear and jumped down, and with his armed escort ran up to shoo the man away. He might have been ground into the sand.

The man clutched at his wrists, pleading and pointing. This was his almond grove. There had been a drought for two years, but *Insh'allah*, when the rains returned, they would bloom and give fruit. Itzik looked at the stunted trees, then at the line of sticks. Green lines on maps take no account of trees.

He glanced at the soldier, then at the old man, then at the trees again, shrugged and climbed back into the driving seat. Engaging gears, he pulled on the left-hand clutch and steered the tractor in a semi-circle around the grove. About thirty metres on, he returned to the line.

When he'd glanced over his shoulder, the *fellakh* was kissing his fingertips and waving, before being lost to sight in the cloud of dust as the tractor carried on south. The state of Israel had lost half a dunam. *Maalesh*. So what? That was how he saw it. Life was give and take. But of one thing he was sure, this tiny strip of land along the Mediterranean Sea was his country. No oil, no minerals, dry and dusty and half its area just bare sand and rocks. But it was his. He had no other. And no one was ever going to take it from him.

At times, he wearied of the discussions with Harold and Gavriel. Their constantly seeing everything in terms of Big Powers involvement, of the 'refugee problem', of Ben Gurion's megalomania. All he wanted was to be left in peace, build up the kibbutz and make this corner of the desert bloom. And to be able to defend it.

Harold said that was too simplistic. Maybe. But it was good enough for him.

Itzik closed his eyes, but he couldn't sleep, his mind still bubbling from the encounter with Ella. He consoled himself that he was on afternoon shift and could sleep late - but it was small consolation to the emptiness in his stomach. He guessed that Ella would be asleep by now. If only he could be with her now, to hold her small breast in his hand and feel her soft skin against his – and like that, fall asleep beside her.

Ella wasn't asleep. She'd given up trying and lay on her side, staring into the darkness, knowing that she would be hopelessly tired for work the next day. Today. She lay, wondering how to tell him. Again and again, she tried to visualise the situation, when to say what. How to finish off so that it would still leave them on speaking terms.

Finally, it crystallised in her mind. At last she knew what and how to do it - and quite suddenly, she relaxed and fell into a deep sleep.

14.

Ella suddenly sat up and blinked, the cold and damp of the wall-tiles had begun to seep into her back. She had no idea how long had she been sitting in the showers, daydreaming. Glancing at her watch, she jumped up, splashed cold water on her face and hurried into a toilet cubicle.

Emerging into the brilliant sunshine of the courtyard, Ella shaded her eyes and looked around. Stretching away to the east and the south, the vast plain of the Negev shimmered and merged with the hazy horizon. To the north, were the gullies and clefts of the badlands and the great wadi. Nearby to the east, was the belt of trees along the main road. Even closer, but to the west, the glaring white sandhills along the border.

The border. She'd crossed more frontiers than she could count on her way around the world. Seen so many countries and different peoples across thousands of miles. Yet here, less than two miles away, was a country about which she knew nothing, people she could not even go and see.

Ella wondered about those 'on the far side' - Gaza. She often talked about it with Harold. And now she thought of that young boy those soldiers had caught the previous evening. His father had escaped, they said. How did they live? Was there a mother? Brothers, sisters? And what made them so heartless and callous as to murder school-kids, like those in the boarding school at Shomera the other night?

Even if she had been driven from her home - lost everything - she could never bring herself to commit such an act. Perhaps women wouldn't do those things? Or was she being too ration-al? If she'd seen her home destroyed, her family suffering and starving, she might feel different. If only she could meet them. Talk with them. If...

At that moment, an army truck swung round the rear of the dining hall and braked, raising a cloud of dust. Two soldiers leaped from the front and ran over to the office hut. Ella watched for a moment, then sensing the eyes of the soldiers in the rear staring at her, pulled out her headscarf, tied it round her hair and hurried past down to the cowshed

Gavriel was coming out of the dairy with the vet as Ella ran down from the eucalyptus trees.

'See that command car,' she puffed. 'Soldiers. Looked in a real hurry.'

Gavriel shrugged.

'Just a routine patrol. Said they wanted to use our telephone.' He was more concerned about the heifers at that moment. One hadn't come into calf for a second time and he wanted Menasheh and his A.I. kit over to her as soon as possible. 'And Ella,' he continued, 'could you give Harold a hand to wash down before you feed the calves?'

His casual manner reassured Ella and without more thought she hurried round to the office to change into her boots. From the milking parlour came the distorted blare of the *Symphonie Fantastique*. Harold had turned up the volume on their small transistor to overcome the noise of the vacuum.

In the cowshed, Menasheh pulled on his long rubber glove. Gavriel buckled the strap around the vet's shoulder and looked at the four cows that had been yoked in. Perhaps Yardena would be more co-operative this time. The vet pushed and eased his hand and arm into the rear of the cow. She humped her back and stamped. When he drew it out, Gavriel held up the tail whilst he inserted the long glass tube. And the job was done.

After each of the cows was inseminated, the vet hosed down the glove and noted the details: time, day, bull, batch number, all in his meticulous handwriting.

'Any other problems,' he asked as they stood at the end of the ramp. Gavriel wiped his face with his blue cloth hat.

'Just one calf, lame. Over in the calf shed. Oh. And two with a touch of mastitis, I think.' He pointed to the second shed. 'They're yoked in at the far end.'

'Good,' muttered Menasheh, 'I can go and see to them myself. You've enough to do.'

Gavriel didn't argue. He took the thermos box and the equipment back to the vet's car. So lucky to have someone like him, he mused as he crossed the yard. Pity he won't ever come on Saturdays.

Menasheh, being strictly religious would not travel on the Sabbath. If a cow came on heat on Friday afternoon, they lost the chance of a calf and another month's milk yield as well. 'God intended his animals to rest as well on Shabbat,' the vet would grunt.

To overcome the problem, Itzik had reared their own bull. '*Kfir*', he named it, 'lion cub'.

'Some cows just recognise the real thing and won't settle for less,' Harold had joked with Ella. The young bull had already sired five calves and with any luck would enter the attested bulls' register next year. That would be a real achievement.

The bull lived a life of comparative luxury in his own pen built of six-inch steel tubing. At one end, was a yoke arrangement for the cow. 'Never on a Sunday,' joked Harold after the Greek film had come and gone, 'But always on a Saturday.' Adding a pun on the rabbinical quotation, 'For Kfir "The Sabbath is truly a joy"'.

Whenever a cow was led across the yard, the bull would paw

at the sand, snorting and tossing his head. Any kibbutz kids in the vicinity would immediately rush to climb the nearest haystack shouting: 'Hey. Come and see. Kfir is going to stick his in!' while the more prudish amongst the mothers would blush and turn away.

On occasions, the bull missed his aim and one of cowmen had to guide it in, encouraged by the kids jumping and shouting from the haystack. Then, with a short stab or two, it was over.

Gavriel half-smiled as he remembered those weekend visitors from Tel Aviv who came that time with their American tourist friends.

'Is that all?' asked the lady in a broad-brimmed sun hat as Harold brought the cow back to its shed.

'That's all, folks,' Harold said, unable to resist adding, 'our bull hasn't read up on Henry Miller yet.'

Having completed his inspections and medications, the Menasheh wrote out his report and with a wave, drove up onto the road. As he drew level with the trees, the army truck roared down from the dining hall and out towards the main road, enveloping him in a cloud of dust.

'Army drivers!' yelled the vet, shaking his fist as he braked, then slowly drove off again. Gavriel stood for a moment, staring after the command car and wondering, then turned away and hurried across to the calf shed. Time was creeping on.

In the milking parlour, Ella and Harold finished washing down and plunged the rubber hoses deep into the large, stainless steel, sterilising sinks. Beside them the refrigerators throbbed and a huge paddle slowly stirred the milk in the cooling tank. Harold rinsed his hands, took a mug and opening the lid, skimmed off a mug full of creamy milk from the side of the tank.

'Nothing like it,' he sighed after the ice-cold liquid trickled down his throat. 'How's the time?'

Ella glanced at her watch.

'Ten o'clock. Not bad going, eh?' She took off the watch and went to hang it in the office before it made her wrist sweaty.

Inside the dairy, it was still cool and damp. Outside, the glaring sun climbed higher into a clear sky. Down in the wadi where the shadows had shortened back against the overhanging bank, the air was still. With the heat growing more oppressive, Fais was becoming more and more restless, groaning with pain and his hands clutching at the sand.

Ahmed peered through the tamarisk fronds but kept well in the shade. It was the best camouflage, those looking from outside had to squint against the bright sunlight. He guessed that the patrols were biding their time until the trap was closed from all directions. Then they would move in.

Sitting back on his haunches, he rested the automatic in the crook of his hip. It seemed as though they had been in this accursed wadi for weeks. Was it only three days ago, that they left their base at Beit Hanun?

He glanced at his watch, then stared aimlessly at the far bank remembering the first time he came home from his Fedayeen training. In his olive green fatigues, he swung proudly through the huts at Shati, no longer a miserable refugee but a warrior, fighting for his village, his father's honour and for his people.

Young boys ran alongside, whooping and wanting to hold his hands. Girls peeped from the small windows, white headscarves fluttering and Ismail's father Abu Salah ran up and slapped him on the back. His father hugged him too but his eyes were sad. And that evening, the two old men argued again.

As a stone rattled upstream in the wadi, a light touch on his elbow made him jump. Ismail had crept up unheard.

'They're coming,' Ahmed whispered.

'Yes. And taking their time,' hissed Ismail. 'They don't like taking casualties, the Israeli's.'

'Yes. Plenty of time,' said Ahmed, 'All day to flush us out, if they want.'

Ismail tapped his arm again.

'The local Egyptian command may not know we are coming back this way. But they must be able to see what's going on. If only they could create a diversion?'

Less than a mile to the west, the wadi cleaved through the sand-hills in a deep chasm. On either side were extensive Egyptian positions. It was the first time the commander had mentioned the Egyptians. For Ahmed it was an admission, without their intervention, they had little chance of escaping.

'*Insha'llah*,' Ahmed murmured, glancing downstream, 'but they've never helped us before.'

'Who knows?' Ismail shrugged. 'Anyway, I'll go and see Mahmud. He's keeping an eye on the upstream bend.'

As he crawled back, Ahmed turned to watch him, wondering whether they would ever get through this together. Ismail. They'd been with each other ever since they were kids in the village. '*Sumsum*,' it was called, Sesame seed, dusty tracks winding between hedges of prickly pear and a smell of dried dung, two hours walk to the nearest road and a day's journey to Beer Sheva or Gaza.

As young boys, the two of them had helped to look after the goats and sheep and water the vegetables in the long, hot summers. Most of the houses were of mud brick and thatch, but a few, like his father's, were of stone.

Although his father Ibrahim was the *mukhtar*, they never had a lot, but when the winter rains came on time, they ate well.

When they didn't, it was hard. But most years left some wheat over and almonds that his father took to market on a hired tender. It was the only time Ahmed ever saw a town, buying sticky *halkum* with the few mils his father could spare.

Ahmed remembered how he and Ismail played the fool with old Abu Araf, the *mu'allam*. He taught Koran to the village children as well as their first lessons in reading. The old teacher had tried to keep the peace between his father and Ismail's fiery father, Abu Salah. The two had been quarrelling ever since Ahmed could remember, like that time in the World War when the great sheikh of Beit Jibrin sold land to the Jews.

'It's our land, he's selling to the Yahud,' Abu Salah was shouting, his face like a beetroot. 'We should keep Arab land for the Arabs, like Haj Amin, the Mufti says. Drive them away.' And his father shaking his head and sighing.

'*Ya* Abu Salah. The land belongs to the sheikh's family. It's all thorns and gullies. They can have it. There's enough barren land like that around for anyone.' The arguments continued for weeks and weeks, but he and Ismail carried on being firm friends.

Ahmed remembered the great desert war. Stories of German armies at the Nile. English soldiers on manoeuvres in the nearby hills, red faces, ginger hair sticking up out of the Bren-gun carriers. And the Jews settling a new village about seven miles away.

'Locusts. They're like locusts!' screamed Abu Salah, 'Soon, they will have it all. Ours as well.'

'It's poor, dry land,' came his father's calm voice. 'Even the Bedouin hardly use it.' But Abu Salah was incensed and, for the very first time, forbade Ismail to come to Ahmed's house.

Ahmed looked upstream, then down towards the border again. No sign. No sound. But out there, the Israeli patrols would be closing in and he tried to picture their faces.

The first Jews he ever saw were the two horsemen who came over from the new village. They rode into the small square one afternoon and remained in the saddle, glancing nervously about them until his father came out and welcomed them into the courtyard of their house.

He remembered his mother brewing strong Turkish coffee served with small cubes of halvah and the strangers handing over presents wrapped in coloured paper, talking in a mixture of Arabic and English. One, named Daud, was their *mukhta*r. He invited his father back. Said they would be good neighbours and had a nurse who would come over if they wanted, a garage that could repair their tools and carts.

When they took their leave, everyone shook hands and smiled.

'Honest men,' said his father. 'You can see it by their eyes.' But as they rode away, Abu Salah ran out and shook his fist after them.

'You will live to regret it, *Ya* Ibrahim. You will see!'

Ahmed crept gingerly up to the fringe of the bushes again. Tamarisk fronds brushed his cheek, the sea breeze was beginning to make its way up the wadi. Soon, it would be midday. And by then they would come. And it would be over. But he would make them pay dearly, though nothing could pay enough. Nothing. For what they had done.

It was springtime. 1948. Pink almond blossom in the fields, red anemones and yellow sulphur bells in the crevices. Long lines of Egyptian army lorries whined along the road from Gaza to Beer Sheba. He'd never seen so many people at one time.

'*Ya* Ibrahim,' roared Abu Salah, 'soon they will capture Al Quds. Drive out the infidel from the Holy City. And we shall drive them away from here.' And about ten villagers went with him to join the attack on a Jewish settlement near Iraq Sweidan. 'We shall bring back their heads on bayonets. Like they did last week in Majdal,' he screamed, but Ahmed's father and most of the village, stayed to look after their fields and flocks.

The attack failed. So did that of the Egyptian army at Jerusalem and on their retreat, they were surrounded at Faluja, about fifteen miles from the village.

All that summer, hordes of villagers from the hills and the surrounding countryside, streamed west along the roads and through their fields towards Gaza. Some carried heavy bundles, others pushed handcarts, women weeping, babies crying.

'What are you waiting for?' screamed an old man as he passed them on a donkey. 'The Jews are coming. They will slaughter everyone.' He drew a hand across his throat, 'like they did at Deir Yassin.'

'He's right,' said Abu Salah, the white moustache he had grown especially for the fighting, bristling. 'The Egyptians are preparing a huge offensive. We should get behind their lines or we shall be caught up in the fighting.'

Ahmed remembered how frightened he had been. How he and Ismail searched out a cave in which they could hide. But his father had remained calm.

'We are going nowhere,' he said, gripping Ahmed's hand, 'We have harmed no one. This is our land. Our village. No one will harm us.'

The Egyptian attack never materialised. After a United Nations' truce, they retreated to Gaza, the war ended and everything appeared to return to normal. Abu Daud came over in a jeep with three others, one of them a woman. They brought a small black and white calf and everyone shook hands and smiled again. Except Abu Salah. He stayed inside, sulking. But Ismail was allowed to come to the house again.

Ahmed remembered how proud he had been of his father. Even now, with all their differences and arguments, he still respected and loved him as much as ever...

Suddenly he stiffened, the sound of an engine. The Israeli half-track was on the move again, closer, though still some distance away. The throbbing of the engine reverberating through his head, reminding him of the roar of that convoy of Israeli army lorries. The day he would never forget.

It was autumn, a year after the war. Grey clouds were scudding across the sky and a chill wind followed Ismail and him through the wicker gates as they brought in the flocks. Just then, a huge cloud of dust blew down the track and with it, came the noise of heavy lorries.

The two boys ran to see, perhaps the Egyptians were coming back again? But the lorries were painted brown, with large white six-pointed stars on the sides and high ladders fixed to the back, like those they used to take melons to market.

Holding their hands to their ears, the boys followed the convoy into the square then watched, trembling as soldiers jumped from the first two trucks. Pushing open the doors of the nearby houses, they called out everyone who was inside.

Other soldiers ran through the village, pushing open doors and shouting. Soon, lines of villagers were making their way to the square, men waving their arms, women hugging babies and bundles, young children clinging to their skirts and crying.

Suddenly he saw his father in the square, arguing with a short, fat army officer. The man was waving his stick and pointing to a sheet of paper.

'Security reasons,' he snapped in Arabic. 'Government orders. Security reasons.' Then, turning towards the crowd gathering in the square, he shouted, *'Yalla. Udrub. Yalla.* Get a move on. Security reasons.' Those seemed to be the only words of Arabic he knew.

Spotting Ahmed by the well, Ibrahim ran over to his son.

'Quick. Ahmed. Take Abu Jasser's mare and get Daud. Quickly.' One glance at his father's face told him all he needed to know.

Half way to the Jews' settlement, he met Daud with three others racing towards his village in a jeep. By the time he turned the horse and galloped back to the square, Daud was arguing with the officer, shaking his fist, his face flushed and angry. Ahmed thought they were going to fight until two soldiers came between them.

Daud's wife had also come in the jeep and was speaking to his mother. The two women hugged each other, tears streaming down their faces. Ahmed felt tears in his own eyes and turned away to stand by his father who was still protesting to the officer. Meanwhile the square became more and more packed with villagers, screaming and crying, chickens squawking and scuttling between their feet. Ismail ran up and tugged his arm. What was happening? Ahmed remembered that he couldn't even reply, his throat so choked with tears and dust...

The engine of the half-track stopped. High on the far bank, tufts of grass quivered. Someone was observing the thicket. Then everything was still again and in the silence, his mind switched back again to that terrible day.

All his father's protests and Daud's arguments didn't help. Gradually, the villagers were herded onto the trucks. The tailboards slammed and the officer got into his command-car and lit a cigarette. With a wave of his stick, the trucks moved off one by one, up the track to the main road. Men cursed and shook their fists, women cried and children peered bewildered through the wooden slats, whilst Daud's wife sank to the ground, head in hands, sobbing.

As the lorries passed by Ibrahim who was still pleading with Daud, Abu Salah leaned out of one.

'Honest eyes, eh, *Ya* Ibrahim?' he shouted. 'Honest eyes, you said. Well never mind the eyes,' he sneered, quoting the old Arab proverb. 'Just look at their hands!'

As Ibrahim and Ahmed were forced onto the last truck, Daud ran up to them.

'Listen. It must be a terrible mistake. We're driving straight away to Tel Aviv. Now. We'll sort it out. I promise you. You will all be back. I promise.'

Ibrahim just nodded. He didn't know what to believe any more.

Ahmed sometimes wondered whether Daud had ever gone to Tel Aviv or whether they had tried. His father was sure they had. It wouldn't have mattered, he said afterwards. Jews like Daud and his wife don't make Israeli government policy.

A few hours later, they were dumped at a roadblock on the Green Line, beside a Red Cross tent. Heads bent and weary, they shuffled past the Egyptian sentries towards Gaza. Destitute and homeless. Refugees in their own land.

The sea breeze was strengthening, the tamarisks swayed and the smell of dry loëss dust tickled Ahmed's nostrils. The half-track was moving again to his left, towards the west to cut them off from the border. Then the patrols in the wadi would move in. Ahmed closed his eyes for a moment, wondering whether it was true that all your life flashed before you in your last moments. Were these his last moments?

At that moment, a sudden flash of light caught his eye. He glanced up towards the sand-hills along the border. Again a glint of reflected sunlight. Someone was observing the wadi through binoculars. The Egyptians. They must be taking an interest? And if they were, would they intervene?

The engine noise of the half-track moved closer. Ismail came forward again to crouch by him. Ahmed told him what he had seen then gripped the trigger guard. And together, they waited

15

Raising his binoculars again, Major Mustafa Salah Salim peered out from his outpost up on the sandstone ridge. The sun shone directly into his eyes and they ached under the strain of his weariness, he'd been awake since shortly before dawn.

Below him, the yellow and grey expanse of the rolling plain stretched away to the east like a gigantic sand table at his military academy in Cairo. To his rear, between the ridge and the sea were the scattered villages and orange groves of the Gaza strip.

The Major was searching the area for signs of movement, traversing the folds in the ground, patches of scrub and the odd acacia tree. Somewhere out there - so intelligence had reported - a Fedayeen group was holed up on its way back. If he didn't locate them soon, the Israelis certainly would.

A few hours previously, Sergeant Mohammed had woken him, gently shaking his shoulder, as if apprehensive to do so. It was still night-time but if the Sergeant had taken the trouble, Major Salim knew it must be important.

'A flare, sir. A star shell. And shooting,' the Sergeant said softly. 'I thought you'd want to know, sir.'

The Major had waited until he went out, then swung his legs off the bed. As he washed in the small basin, he glanced in the mirror. Was his hair getting thinner? And those lines on his forehead. Were they always that deep?

He felt the folds of his stomach as he tightened his belt and wondered whether he was putting on weight. He always kept himself fit, no one would guess he was approaching forty-five. But, as he laced his boots and stood up to buckle on his Sam Brown. At this hour, he felt his age.

He hurried out and up to the lookout post. The sky was dark and everywhere, silent.

'Over there, sir.' The Sergeant pointed to the north-east. Major Salim squinted into the night, seeing nothing. But he never doubted the Sergeant's judgement.

'Send a message to Captain Farhi at Intelligence,' he grunted. 'Tell him it's from me, personal. If anyone knows something, it will be him.'

The Sergeant saluted and hurried off to the signals' post and the Major waited a while, wondering whether to go back to his quarters. But he wasn't sleepy and soon found himself pacing the vehicle park.

A sentry leaning on a Russian-made personnel carrier jumped to attention and challenged him.

'Next time,' snapped the Major, 'don't wait until I'm so close. The Israeli's won't give you that much warning!'

At that moment, a jeep careered into the square and screeched to a halt. Three officers clambered out and staggered away to their quarters, laughing at the sentry's challenge. The Major clenched his fists. Drunk! Straight from the brothels in Gaza. No wonder the ordinary soldiers had no fighting spirit. His forehead grew hot and for a while the Major stood, pensive, before going up to the post again.

Now, in the daylight, focussing the glasses he searched the area, looking intensely into the great wadi that snaked across the plain to his left. No movement there either. As he lowered the glasses and leaned back against the trench wall, the Major remembered the drunken laughter last night. No. Nothing had changed in the army.

After finishing military academy, he'd been posted to Kantara on the Suez canal. Here, he found common ground with younger officers, all enthusiastic in creating Colonel

Nasser's new democratic army, an army of the people bringing in a new social order for Egypt. Everything would be different.

But after only a few months he realised that little was changing. All around him in the higher ranks, the tone was set by officers of the old regime, sons of effendis and soft bellied merchants for whom the army was just a stepping-stone in their careers. They paid lip service to Nasser's revolution, but at the same time made sure that nothing would upset their precious regime.

The Major thought again of those drunken officers, spending money like water - money from corruption rackets and smuggling, run by the army here in Gaza. And not only here. At Kantara, covered lorries coming in from the Sinai desert, crossing the canal into Egypt proper and no questions asked.

Now he had seen the source. Every week, boxes and crates unloaded onto the strand at Gaza from ships lying offshore. Boxes with Japanese and Hong Kong lettering and multiple 'Fragile' labels, television sets, cameras, radios, plastic toys, ivory ornaments, luxury goods, all in short supply in Egypt but smuggled in with army help by agents from Beirut and Cyprus.

At each stage of transit, wads of notes passed from hand to hand, enough to keep a whole peasant family for months. And all around, Palestinian refugees and local *felakhin* alike were sunk in abject poverty. Was this what they called the new peoples' army? Officers who pretended to lead the struggle against Zionism and Imperialism? No wonder young Palestinians took it into their own hands to go out and fight.

Major Salim pulled a thin slip of paper from his breast pocket. An 'off record' note from Farhi in response to his message. Israeli patrols had been pursuing a Fedayeen group for the last two days. It was believed to making its way back by the great wadi. Headquarters had been kept posted but had not responded.

Major Salim wasn't surprised. It might affect 'normal business' or provoke an Israeli reprisal raid. He tore the note into tiny fragments and threw them up into the faint breeze coming from the sea. They fluttered high into the air, drifting towards the small hill that rose from the plain, about a mile away.

Raising his binoculars, he peered at the red roofed houses that straddled the hilltop. It was a Jewish settlement, a '*Kombaniyeh*', the locals called it. Something like a Russian Kholkoz, but more collective. Sharing everything - even wives - they said. In the fields below, men moved long irrigation pipes across a brilliant green patch. Further away, a caterpillar tractor pulled a disc harrow, raising a plume of dust.

The Major breathed out. Idealists? Maybe. But their ideals were irrelevant to him. First and foremost, they were military out-posts, spearheads of Zionist expansionism. And if he didn't stop them here, they could end up at the Nile!

He looked at the tractors in the fields again, then lowered the glasses and closed his eyes against the glare. He remembered his own village in the Delta, the reed-lined muddy ditches and tiny plots of land from which they barely eked out an existence. His father working every hour of daylight, then paying most of it back to the effendi who owned the land. He could still feel the beating his father gave him when he wanted to leave school. Did he want to end up a miserable peasant too?

Then came the war in the Western Desert. British soldiers in khaki shorts and high socks, heading out to fight Rommel. The mixed feelings when they drove him back to Libya. Many of the Egyptian nationalists, like Neguib had hoped for a German victory to remove British imperialism and the humiliation of being treated like ignorant colonials.

He remembered too, the British being forced to leave. Then the revolution of Nasser and Neguib that removed king Farouk and given people like himself, the son of a poor peasant, the chance to become an officer.

Yes, the new army. So much talk, so little to show. Being an honest man, Major Salim knew himself, accepted that his anger against the Zionists was fuelled as much by the corruption of his fellow officers, as by the Jewish State. Yet despite all that, he was instilling the new spirit into the men under his command. When the time came, they would fight like lions and drive the Zionists from this land. Then Egypt, with all the Arab peoples, would remove the disgrace of '48.

Raising the binoculars, he looked out again. The wadi. Farhi had mentioned the wadi. He focussed to where it cleaved through the hills to his left then worked slowly upstream. Suddenly, a sharp movement caught his eye.

About a mile away, a group of khaki-clad figures was working its way through one of the channels. A few yards in front, a Bedouin tracker was bent double, scanning the gravel, pointing out tell-tale signs then moving on and the soldiers following. The Major had no doubt. The Israeli patrol had picked up a definite trail, probably that of the Fedayeen. He raised his head and called along the trench.

'Sergeant Mohammed!'

The tall, moustached figure hurried up and saluted.

'See there,' the Major pointed to a bend in the dry river bed, 'Keep that patrol under constant observation. Oh, and get the machine gun-crew to cover it as well.'

According to protocol, he should have delegated these commands to a junior officer. But they were new and he didn't yet trust them. 'And send a runner to lieutenants Nazim and Faras to take up action stations. Israelis are approaching the border.'

The Sergeant hurried away. He'd been on this border for three years, but it was the first time they had ever initiated any action and he was concerned. The last time there was a flare up, it ended with heavy guns on both sides. But he recognised the Major as a new type of commander, strict and professional. He must know what he was doing.

As the Major continued to scan the area by the wadi, a brown half-track emerged from a gulley and edged towards the bank of the wadi. He could clearly discern the white star on its side and had never seen one so close to the border before. There was no doubt in his mind now. It must be in pursuit of the Fedayeen. But where were they? Where?

Being a decisive man, Major Salim had already decided what to do, and he would pursue it to the end. He would rescue those men if at all possible. But first, to find them.

Focussing and re-focussing, he traversed up the wadi, then back again. Suddenly he stopped. That patch of green in the bend. Bushes. The only real hiding place. And the Israeli patrol in the wadi wouldn't see it until they rounded the sweep of the bank.

As he focussed the glasses, the top of a reed quivered, for just one second, then was still again. He waited. No more movement. A breath of wind would have rustled it again. Now he was sure. Someone was inside there. But equally as sure, the Israelis would reach that conclusion too. He had to act. And quickly. Taking a notebook from his pocket, he scribbled three short sentences, then called for the Sergeant again.

'Sergeant Mohammed. Get this through to headquarters. Immediately.' As the man ran away along the trench, he called after him, 'and wait for a reply.'

He looked back into the wadi. Unless they acted soon, the Palestinians would be annihilated. And the longer they delayed, the more certain it would be.

The sun continued to rise into the sky. It grew hotter, the sea breeze still too faint to bring relief. But it wasn't the heat that made the Major boil, it was the answer from area headquarters that Sergeant Mohammed thrust into his hand ten minutes later.

'Message received,' it read. 'Keep us informed.'

'Nothing else?' snapped the Major. The Sergeant shook his head. The area commander wasn't there and they were trying to contact him, he said. Major Salim turned away and gripped the trench parapet. Of course he was away. Probably still with his mistress having a late breakfast, whilst the Israelis had their way and the army sat by. His head throbbed with the frustrations of the past months. No, this time, it would be different.

'Sergeant Mohammed,' he said softly, but firmly, 'repeat the message. And add: 'Demand immediate authorisation of necessary action.' He was overstepping the mark. And he knew it. But someone's hand had to be forced at headquarters. This would not be like Khan Yunis when they were caught with their trousers down. No. This time, the Egyptian army would take the initiative, he would avenge that disgrace.

The Major sent for his junior officers. On Faras, he could rely implicitly. He sensed that they had similar views on the army. Nazim, he suspected, had been planted by high command.

'Your sector, Faras, will keep the half-track in their sights. ' Sergeant Mohammed will deal with the patrol in the wadi.' Nazim's sector, he would keep in reserve. 'Everyone clear?' he asked, after he had outlined his plan of action, 'and wait for my command. Okay?' The three men nodded and disappeared along the trenches.

The Major watched as the Sergeant's machine gunners threaded the ammunition belts and everyone donned steel helmets. And as he observed the preparations, a strange calm replaced his anger. Yes. It was a gamble. But if he could pin down the Israelis long enough, the Fedayeen could sprint the last few hundred yards to safety. And if it succeeded, the world would know that the Egyptian army meant business.

Looking up, he noticed that the first buzzard he'd seen earlier had been joined by a second. Now the two circled high in the sky, wheeling on the rising thermals. Looking down again, he took up his binoculars again and studied the movements of the patrol and of the half-track. He wanted to pick his right moment...

16

Stones crunched in the silence. Someone was out there. Ahmed crept forward again and joined Ismail. They squinted along the sun-drenched riverbed and released their safety catches. Suddenly two khaki-clad figures sprinted across the gravel and flung themselves down behind a drift on the far side, facing them. A moment later, three more soldiers came slowly around the near side bend making straight for the thicket. Ismail touched Ahmed's knee and nodded. Together they opened fire.

Acrid smoke stung Ahmed's eyes as dust and stones spurted around the soldiers. One crumpled and fell while two others dodged back into the bank. At that moment, the blunt nose of the personnel carrier poked over the far rim. The two men withdrew into the bushes and as Mahmud came through to join them they crouched and watched - and waited...

When Itzik woke, it was already mid morning. The room was dark from the shutters closed to keep out the heat, but already it was warm. He lay back, thinking of Ella, wanting to reach out and feel her body beside him, of turning over and making love in the silence and intimacy of the dark room as he re-lived the incident in the stables, the softness of her breast, the erect nipple tickling his palm.

His crotch began to burn - everything suddenly felt too hot. Throwing off the sheet he reached out and lit a cigarette. The firefly tip glowed in the darkness and the fantasy faded. He wanted to think of something else but couldn't, she was still there in his head.

Ella, should he persist, make another approach? One way or the other, he had to be sure, the uncertainty was unsettling him. Last night she'd made it pretty obvious, yet it was worth another try. When she wasn't so tired, perhaps. Yes. He would try again. Today. Yes or no. He had to settle it today.

The cigarette burned down to his fingers. He stubbed it out and lay back again. He'd never had trouble with women before. Always the opposite. Like with Shosh. Everyone thought he was crazy to finish it. But he knew why. It had to end.

Shosh and he were young teenagers when they met. By chance, colliding with one another as he belted away from scrumping loquats in Avrameleh's orchard. It was a wonder they ever met again, coming as they did from such different backgrounds.

Itzik's father was a cobbler, his mother already ill and quite weak, a legacy of poverty in Pilsudski's Poland. They lived in a small bungalow in Rechovot at the southern end of the town where side-locked Yemenite Jews lived in their own community. In the Forties Rechovot was still like a frontier town. It was surrounded by orange groves and Arab villages from where the *felahin* brought vegetables and fruit to the open market.

Shoshanah lived in a large villa at the north end, near the Weizman Institute of Science. Her father, a bank manager had seen what was coming and left Germany in the early thirties. And while Shosh went to the Gymnasia high school, Itzik attended the local Trades Union's school.

'Landed gentry!' he scoffed, when they first met.

'Red menace,' she replied.

But at sixteen, by chance they found themselves in the same left-wing youth movement, she too now one of the 'red menace', much to her father's disgust, or perhaps because of it. By eighteen they'd became very close, she with her honey brown skin and long blond plait down to her waist, he with his unruly mop of hair and boundless energy.

Itzik stared at the faint outline of the ceiling, remembering her wet face smiling at him through the dripping ferns of the oasis at Ein Gedi. That same night, they'd made love for the first time on a stony hilltop opposite the ancient fortress of Massada. And from then on, it was Shosh and Itzik, Itzik and Shosh, as though they were Siamese twins - apart from his time in the army. Though she knew nothing about that...

But it had all become too staid, too pre-ordained. Many of their friends continued their teenage romances into marriage and now had children. He'd felt more restless as the years passed. Nothing new would develop in their relationship and they would eventually bore one another to death.

Itzik lit another cigarette. Shosh didn't see it that way, blamed the split on his infatuation with Ella. But it would have happened anyway. Perhaps it had needed someone like Ella. But he had no regrets. Shosh and he had been part of those heady days leading up to the establishment of the State, a period of tremendous hopes and expectations with the departure of the British and the desperate struggle against the invading Arab armies. And as he reflected on that now, he wondered whether the demise of their relationship was in a way symbolic of what was happening all around them.

He drew deeply on the cigarette. The wall beside him glowed orange for an instant. Yes. Great days. But then afterwards, the disappointments. Government bureaucracies springing up one after the other, new restrictive religious laws, the first Prime Minister, Ben Gurion, disbanding their elite Palmakh units to incorporate them into a regular army - an army of officers messes, insignia and all the rest.

He remembered how he and most of his comrades had pointedly handed in their commissions and left, some to study, some to kibbutzim, a few went abroad, others to slot into the system. Itzik closed his eyes for a moment. Whatever had happened to the spirit of '48? Was it so unrealistic to have expected it to survive? Even for a few years?

Opening his eyes, he swung his legs off the bed and sat up. Lying horizontal brought out his most pessimistic thoughts. He stubbed out the cigarette and glanced at the photograph of his unit in Sinai. At the rear, Shmuelik was waving a red flag. They were all socialists of one sort or another, then. But after Kruschev's revelations of Stalin's crimes, most had thrown out the socialist baby with the Stalinist bathwater.

Itzik slipped off his pyjamas. Some like Gabriel and Nahum and Harold still talked of class struggle. Of Marxism. Marched with the Trades Unions on May Day in Tel Aviv. Maybe. For him, the kibbutz itself expressed his socialist ideals. It was *takhlis*, something tangible.

Itzik didn't want to dwell on the past, wanted to think about something else. It wasn't difficult. His mind flipped back to work - as it often did. It had been a crazy month in the cowshed. Six calvings. And only the evening before last, they'd had to work all night, pulling a difficult one out with a rope round its forelegs. Ella had been so anxious, biting her lip almost to bleed. But it was a beauty. A heifer-calf too.

Glancing back towards the door, he wondered whether Uri had woken Yaacov. Perhaps Harold had got up and gone down too. It would be just like him to do that. Once again the morbid thought ran thought his mind that if he suffered from a disability like that, he would have put a bullet through his head long ago.

Grains of sand rubbed against the soles of his feet as he stood up on the tiled floor. Itzik couldn't abide sand in the room, it ended up in the bed and amongst his clothes. Opening the door, he took the broom from the veranda and swept a small heap of sand out and over the edge. Later, he must wash the floor.

Inside again, he shut the door, pulled on a pair of shorts and yawned and stretched. Being nearly six feet tall, his fingers brushed the whitewashed ceiling. Itzik was well built and still sported his mop of fair hair, the sunshine and freedom of his homeland bringing out genes long hidden in the dank and poverty of the Polish *shtetl* and making him tower over his father.

A quick wash and teeth-brushing under the veranda tap and he was ready to make coffee, a ritual in which he could indulge on mornings like this. No rush, no pressures, all the day ahead of him until the evening shift.

Half-filling the small electric *kum-kum*, he plugged it in and waited for the water to boil. Outside, a Bulbul was singing in the oleander bush and through the window came the tck-tck-tck of the sprinklers on the lawn behind his hut.

The water boiled. Itzik pulled out the plug, put in two heaped teaspoons of ground coffee, added a pod of cardamom and brought it to the boil again. Then, just as the brown foam threatened to spill over, he dripped in some cold water and, as if by magic, it immediately subsided. Unplugging the kettle, he waited for the grounds to settle.

This was the moment he relished most, the compensation for working late into the night. A chance to relax over a cup or two of hot strong coffee brewed as it should be, savouring the aroma of Turkish coffee and cardamom that filled the small room. Then in the cool and stillness of mid morning, to sit back and read through his magazines, undisturbed.

Itzik sank into his one easy chair, the nylon webbing tight

against his bare thighs. Warm sunlight played through the trees onto the veranda tiles. Somewhere, a dove cooed and from the laundry on the far side of the courtyard, came the muffled thump, thump of the washing machine. Stretching out his legs, he took a few sips of coffee.

As he pulled off the wrapper from the latest dairyman's journal, the short burst of gunfire sounded in the distance. Itzik sat up and tried to place it. Somewhere to the north? He took a few more sips, then stood up and went out through the doorway Still holding the cup he waited, puzzled, listening intently.

Up on the half track, lieutenant Dani peered through the slit into the wadi below. At dawn his Bedouin scout had picked up the tracks of three men and an occasional stain of blood in the river-bed. Another patrol was working its way along the bank to cut them off from the border and two more sections were out in the plain on either side.

For two days he had been following the Fedayeen, ever since they murdered those kids in the smallholders village, but now, it was personal too. These same bastards had ambushed his friend, Avi on his way back from Rechovot market.

Avi should have been with him now, on reserves' duty. They did it together year after year. But because of the new baby, Avi had postponed it for two months. Now it was ironic that he, Dani, was on active service and alive whilst Avi, still a civilian, was dead.

Suddenly, shots rang out. A man screamed down in the wadi. Edging the half-track closer, Dani saw smoke rising from a clump of bushes at the far side. Below him, one soldier lay sprawled on the stones.

'At the thicket,' he shouted to the machine gunner. 'forty metres. Open fire.' As the heavy gun clattered, spitting bullets into the bushes and across the riverbed two soldiers ran out and pulled the wounded man back behind the drift of gravel.

Local headquarters had placed this half-track at his disposal. It could cope with the rough ground and gullies and would be essential if the Egyptians decided to intervene. True, they had never before stuck out their necks for the Fedayeen. But nothing out here was certain. Ever.

Picking up the radio microphone, he talked rapidly to the patrols on either side. No need take no risks. They had all day yet. He thought again of Avi. Of Orna and the baby. And his eyes watered. And he would get them, the bastards!

In a small hollow within the bushes, Ahmed, Ismail and Mahmud lay flat on their stomachs. Bullets clipped through the reeds and thudded into the earth around them. Then the firing ceased.

'Listen,' muttered Ismail, 'there's no point in making plans. From now on, each must take his chances.' Instinctively, they all glanced at he prostrate figure of Fais. Ahmed shrugged.

'*Maalesh*. So be it.'

They shook hands, looking into each other's eyes.

'See you in Gaza,' Ahmed hissed as they separated and slithered away to the fringe of the bushes.

From the far bank, came the sound of the half-track. To the west, the sandstone hills shone white in the sunlight. The Egyptians up there must know by now, Ahmed was thinking. But would they care? Perhaps. Perhaps. *Insh'allah*. But there wasn't much time left...

17

As the first shots echoed from the wadi to break the morning stillness, hooded crows scavenging the fields rose in ungainly flight and circled, waiting. Up on the sandstone ridge, Major Salim scanned the bed of the dry watercourse. And stopped. Wisps of smoke rose from the reeds.

As more shots rang out, he re-focussed. The Israeli personnel carrier was firing as it tried to edge its way down a steep gulley. Soon, it would be in dead ground.

He cursed. Headquarters still hadn't answered his last message. Hadn't even bothered to say 'No', their usual reply. It would be only a matter of minutes before that half-track reached the bed of the wadi. If those fighters were to be saved, now was time to act.

The sea breeze had freshened and played on the back of his neck and as if to stress the urgency, the grass on the parapet of his trench quivered. The Major thought for a moment then slapped his fist into the palm of his other hand. If no one else could make a decision, he would.

'Sergeant Mohammed,' he called. The tall figure turned and stood to attention. 'At the half track,' the major shouted. 'Range six hundred. Rapid, fire.'

A fine dust rose and drifted along the trenches, mingling with the smell of cordite as the Browning chattered, joined by the other small arms. Major Salim leaned back against the trench parapet and folded his arms. That would shake them.

Lieutenant Dani could hardly believe it as bullets thudded against the armour plate. Tiny splinters of steel stung his arm.

Dust and stones spurted up around the personnel carrier, followed by the rattle of machine guns from the ridge to his right. Luckily, no one was hit but he was stunned, the Egyptians taking the initiative?

'Quick,' he barked at the driver. 'Down into the wadi. Find a way down. Any way!'

Tracks screeched against the wheel sprockets as the vehicle slewed round and tilted dangerously into the steep gulley, threatening to overturn. The lieutenant took up the microphone.

'Take cover. Everyone. Watch out for the Egyptian positions up on the ridge and wait for orders.' He knew that the patrols nearest the border were in a tight spot, but there was no way he was going to let those murderers escape. Not now. 'Omri,' he called to the squad in the wadi, 'keep those bushes covered. We're on our way.'

Ahmed heard the burst of gunfire in the distance. Carefully, he parted the reeds. Earth showered down from the top of the bank opposite and the blunt nose of the half-track disappeared from view. Blood raced through his head. It couldn't be? A miracle, Ismail had called it. But it was. The Egyptians had actually intervened!

Although they'd hoped against hope that they would, each in his heart didn't expect it. They never had in the past. But the dust and the gunfire were real enough. Suddenly he felt elated. Just when all seemed lost, it had happened. This was their opportunity. They were going to be saved!

Holding his automatic high in front of him, Ahmed burst from the bushes. As if by plan, the other two hurtled out of cover and all three of them sprinted down the wadi, zig-zagging and dodging the boulders, leaping over roots and dead branches in a mad dash towards the border.

A burst of fire came from the drift of gravel opposite the reeds. Mahmud swivelled round and fired back, but as he turned to run on, two bullets thudded into his body and he pitched forward onto the stones, lifeless.

At that moment, the half-track reached the river-bed and opened up with its Besa. Bullets ricocheted from the stones all around them as they ran. Ten yards on, Ismail was hit in the leg and fell. He reached round and fired back upstream. Ahmed hesitated for a moment, half stooping to help.

'*Rukh. Rukh*! Get out!' Ismail jerked his head downstream, '*Halas*. I've had it. Run. Run!' And a moment later, hit by a shower of bullets, the commander convulsed then lay still.

Ahmed didn't wait. Running into the bank, he dodged from one niche to the next in between bursts of gunfire from behind. Suddenly he felt a sharp pain in his shoulder, his arm went numb and the Carl Gustav fell from his grasp. With a final leap, he dived into a shallow depression, breathless and in agony, pressing his body into the ground. And he lay there motionless, waiting for the end.

Major Salim had seen the three figures sprint from the thicket and saw the first two fall. Cursing, he grabbed the field telephone.

'Lieutenant Faras. Direct your fire onto the half-track in the wadi. Pass the order to lieutenant Nazim as well. He felt like adding: 'and let them have it,' but was too much of a professional for that.

As the trenches echoed with the clatter of gunfire, he saw the third figure stumble and fall. When the dust cleared for a moment, it had gone and he supposed that he too had been killed. The blood rose to his head. If only those at headquarters had answered him, they could have pinned down the Israeli patrols earlier and those men could have been saved. His throat dried and he clenched his fists. How he despised the general staff in Gaza.

As he thought over his next move, the crack of bullets passed over his head and earth and dust spurted from the sandbags in front of him. The Israelis were firing back. Along with everyone else, Major Salim dived to the floor of the trench. Crawling along to the concrete gun emplacement he peered through the observation slit. Out in the plain, bluish smoke rose from at least three small knolls.

Just then, an orderly came up with a radio message from H.Q. asking what was happening? The major raged silently. To hell with them. Now, they want to know! Hurriedly, he scribbled a note: 'Under fire from Israeli forces. Request urgent artillery support. Major Salim. Position L52.'

As the orderly hurried away, a soft, crump, crump, crump came from his right. Plumes of smoke and dust rose from around one of the knolls followed by explosions sounding from the plain. Suddenly he felt elated. His friend Fawzi's positions to the south had opened up with three-inch mortars. A few minutes later, an Israeli command car raced over the parched ground to pick up the soldiers there, then sped off towards the village in front of him, dust billowing in its wake. The major stood up and called into the telephone mouthpiece.

'They're running, Faras. We've got them running this time!'

Hardly daring to breath, Ahmed slowly raised his head. The firing from behind him ceased and dust spurted from the tops of the high banks. Despite the acute pain in his shoulder, he felt light-headed. From the noise and dust, it was clear that Egyptian heavy machine guns must have opened up from the ridge. Ismail's miracle had really happened.

He looked down the wadi. About five yards away, was a tangle of flood-washed driftwood and dried grasses. Slowly and painfully he slithered towards it, every slight movement, excruciating every metre like a hundred, his right arm limp and useless and the midday sun merciless on his head. And with each movement, expecting the Israelis to start shooting again.

From the battle, the dust had began to swirl. Ahmed felt it drying in his nostrils as he painfully eased himself under the tangle of branches and curled up on the dried mud beneath. His head spun and tears came to his eyes from pain. Or was it from grief? Mahmud gone. Fais. Poor Fais. What would happen to him? And Ismail. His boyhood friend. *Ya* Ismail, You dead too?

The sea breeze crept up the wadi and rustled through the dried grasses above him. Through the branches, Ahmed saw the sky. Blue, a brilliant blue. Then exhausted from the long day and the night before, his eyes closed and he lay absolutely still. Waiting.

In the pause after the first burst of gunfire, Itzik had settled back to enjoy his coffee. Must have been a soldier trying out a new weapon, he conjectured. But as he raised the cup to his lips again, the gunfire was renewed, with other, heavier weapons joining in. No mistaking the clatter of the Besa.

Setting down the cup on the tiles, Itzik got up, buckled on his sandals and hurried out onto the veranda. The gunfire increased as he crossed the lawn and now he could place it, down by the wadi and out towards the border.

At that moment, explosions came from beyond the wadi. 'Mortars,' he muttered, breaking into a run, 'three inch mortars. What the hell is happening?' He'd always said that one day, the Egyptians would feel confident enough to take the initiative. Could this be that day?

Early diners up for lunch had spilled out of the dining hall, faces tense, looking towards the wadi and across to the border where smoke and dust were rising. Yoske, who'd been laying the tables, stood on the porch shielding his eyes, incongruous in his tiny blue apron. Itzik paused to catch his breath.

'Yoske. Get down to the cowshed and take the tractor and trailer from Gavriel. Bring everyone in from the orchards. Everyone, right?'

Yoske didn't question. Itzik was the elected commander in times of trouble and the expression on his face was enough. Untying the apron, he flung it on the first table inside the doors and took off down the hill as Itzik broke into a run again, heading for the telephone in the office.

Major Salim waited once again for an answer from headquarters. Return mortar fire had now landed on his trenches showering all and everything with fine dust. One bomb landed on the machine gun, wounding a gunner and a signalman. Dust and smoke were beginning to raise a haze over the plain, making it difficult to see exactly what was happening. But along the main road, even bigger clouds of dust were being churned up by heavy transport. 'Just as I thought,' he muttered, 'hurried reinforcements. We really caught them napping this time!'

He called for the wireless operator and sent yet another message to H.Q.: 'Israeli armour being unloaded along main road. Request intervention of heavy artillery. Urgent.' He closed his eyes for a brief moment, trying to envisage how the day would develop. Most likely was a direct frontal assault by the Israelis, expecting the Egyptians to panic and flee like last time. But now, it would be different. He'd discussed just such a scenario with Captain Fawzi only a month ago, one of the few likeminded officers in the sector.

'What is the use of keeping all those heavy guns and tanks out here. Just to polish them up for general's inspection each month?'

No. This time it would indeed be different. Their heavy artillery would catch the Israeli armour out in the open plain. Give them a real pasting. Show them that things had changed for good.

Major Salim looked up at the sun. Soon, it would past the zenith and begin to descend, shining directly into the Israeli's eyes.

'We are up here. And they are down there,' he muttered to the sergeant. 'Soon, the whole front will be alight.'

The Sergeant nodded but said nothing. Trained by the British in the last war, Sergeant Mohammed didn't express opinions, whether he had them or not. He just listened and carried out his orders. But trained to care for his men too.

Major Salim often thought of how he, with all his ideals of a people's army, could never achieve the rapport with the men that the sergeant could, despite his rigid ways. Did the sergeant wish to redeem the honour of the army, the major wondered. Or did he too, just want to complete his tour of duty without too much trouble? Of one thing he was certain, he would never know.

As more positions in the sector opened up, the major sent back a further signal: Israeli armour preparing to attack. 'That should make them sit up at headquarters,' he muttered, then turned to the signaller.

'Maintain contact with H.Q. whatever happens. Right?'

The signaller saluted and returned to the dugout.

'Sounds easy, when he says it like that, ' he murmured to his colleague as the major moved away. There was a dark, sticky patch on the leather battery case.

'Insh'allah,' said the other, who often wondered what they were doing out here when colonel Nasser said that their real struggle was inside Egypt, *'Insh'allah.'*

The exchange of fire had now become continuous and increasing in intensity with every minute, as new positions joined in on either side. Others, still further away, chose their own targets. Soon, the entire border was ablaze. No one was thinking now about the wadi, of pinning down the Israeli patrol – or of the Fedayeen. Much greater issues were now at stake.

18

Harold was throwing hay bales off the trailer as Gavriel eased the John Deere tractor along the central ramp of the new cowshed. The booming exhaust of the old two-cylinder, horizontal engine echoing from the roof left them completely oblivious to the sounds of gunfire outside. Even when they emerged into the sunlight, the engine still drowned every other sound. Only when he saw Yoske running down the slope towards them, waving his arms in a frantic semaphore, did Gavriel suspect that something was up.

He braked sharply, almost toppling Harold from the trailer.

'What's happening?' he shouted as Yoske jumped onto the drawbar.

'Itzik told me to take your tractor and trailer,' he puffed, 'bring all the workers in from the orchards.' Seeing that the other two knew nothing of what was happening, he added, 'trouble. Over by the wadi. Gunfire. Mortars. Sounds serious.'

Gavriel brought the tractor round to the Dutch barn, jumped down and called Harold off the trailer. Yoske engaged gear, pulled out the throttle and chugged out onto the roadway, leaving behind a cloud of oily smoke.

For a few seconds, it was strangely quiet. Then the sounds of gunfire and explosions reached them. They looked at each other and Gavriel told him what he had heard.

'Look, Harold. You give Ella a hand to wash down. I'll go up top and see what's happening.'

Ella was squirting water onto the concrete stalls to the beat of the Israeli Top Twenty from *Galei Tzahal*, the army's popular radio station. The brief rest in the shower bloc had revived her spirits. She'd even framed what she would say to Itzik when he came down after lunch to check the vet's records. That would put an end to it - though she knew that for a while, the image of the pained expression in his face in the stables would still haunt her.

Overhead, the vacuum lines hissed and pulsed, circulating pink cleaning-fluid through the glass containers while the black rubber hoses quivered and jerked to the throb of the compressors outside. Soon she would finish the washing down, then go and feed the young calves.

Apart from riding out to pasture, this was the job she liked best, taking pails of warm milk to the stalls, letting the tiny creatures suck her fingers and leading their muzzles down into the milk. Maternal instincts and all that, Harold joked. And suddenly, there he was, standing in the centre doorway, his face almost as white as it had been early that morning.

Ella shut off the spray and gripped the steel rail.

'What's up, Harold?'

'Don't know for sure.' Harold paused, breathless. 'You can't hear a thing in here, Ella, but there's some battle going on down by the wadi. Machine guns. Mortars. God knows what else.'

He jumped down into the pit and took up the other hose.

'Gavriel says I should help you finish the washing down. We may have to get up top.'

Ella raised her hands.

'We can't. Not yet. I haven't fed the new calves.'

Harold squirted water on the tiled wall.

'Maybe. Let's see what Gavriel says when he gets back.' He shrugged, but Ella saw how tense his face was and her stomach began to clench as she took up the spray again.

Itzik was opening the door of the office as Gavriel hurtled around the corner of the hut.

'*Le'at, le'at*,' said Itzik. 'We'll have casualties even before anything happens.' But he wasn't smiling. Gavriel stood by the telephone as Itzik dialled a reserved military number. A girl's voice answered and he asked for and extension. It was engaged.

'Then keep trying,' Itzik snapped into the mouthpiece. He wiped a hand across his face and breathed out. Wasn't the telephonist's fault, everyone must be trying to contact local command.

A series of clicks was followed by a man's voice, questioning.

'Two, five, seven,' said Itzik, 'and I want Dudik. Okay?'

'He's engaged,' came the voice, but just as Itzik's face reddened, the voice came again. 'Moment. He's just come off the other line.'

Itzik had been Dudik's company officer in '48. When Ben Gurion had created a professional army and the majority of the elite troops had quit, Dudik was one of those who stayed on. 'Someone has to keep the old spirit alive,' he'd said, 'try to influence the way things will go.' Itzik remembered the heated discussions. The arguments. Now, Dudik was the sector commander in the old, brown stucco Palestine Police fortress at Magen, on the only real hill in the area.

'Listen. Dudik. What's up?' Itzik snapped, then without waiting, continued, 'Why have the Egyptians opened up? What's going on?' Itzik pictured Dudik's face as they conversed, the curly brown hair had gone but the Zapata moustache still flourished on his upper lip.

Gavriel overheard the low gruff voice at the other end, but not the words. And when Itzik put down the 'phone, his face said it all.

'Serious. Headquarters are as puzzled as we are. A patrol clashed with a Fedayeen group in the wadi. It's happened before. But this time the Egyptian army has joined in. Anything could happen. They'll keep us informed.'

Khaim, the bookkeeper stood up behind his desk, face questioning. Itzik nodded.

'You stay here, Khaim. Keep the 'phone free. No calls out. No one. Okay?' Khaim nodded. Just then the 'phone rang again. It was Dudik. Kibbutz Nachal Oz, some ten miles away had come under fire. A state of emergency had been declared along the whole length of the Gaza border.

Gavriel's stomach turned as he heard those last words. Everyone knew what that meant. From now on, Itzik their elected military commander was completely in charge. Gone were general meetings, committees, arguments over decisions, all the tools of their democracy they had carefully forged and cherished. From now on, Itzik's word was law. For everyone, a new experience - and for Itzik, a terrible responsibility.

Khaim took the telephone over to his desk and sat down again. Like Gavriel and Itzik, he too had seen enough of war, fighting with the Red Army right through to the liberation of Prague. His commanding officer had turned a blind eye when he deserted to make his way illegally to Palestine, they had both seen Terezinstadt. Now, blinking through his horn-rimmed glasses, he wondered whether there ever would be an end to fighting...

Outside the hut, Itzik stood with Gavriel for a moment on the path.

'Listen, Gabi,' he said, 'those mortar bombs are a bad sign. Someone high-up over there is making that kind of decision. I don't like it. Don't like it at all.' His mind was whirring as he spoke, forming a plan of action. 'Look. Get everyone up from the cowsheds. Then run to the garage and tell Meir to take the jeep and bring in the *felakhim*. They're in the winter wheat. To tell them to leave the crawler tractor where it is. The rest of the workshop and garage to report to the armoury. I'll meet you there too.'

Gavriel's rubber boots chafed as he ran down the short cut through the trees, cursing as he ran. In another half an hour, they would have completely finished the morning's milking. Then he thought about the people at Nachal Oz, a new kibbutz astride the Gaza road.

It stood at the foot of the Ali Muntar hill, where in the First World War, General Allenby had lost thousands of men trying to take it from The Turks. Now, it had been honey-combed and reinforced by the Egyptians who could pour fire straight down into the kibutz courtyard.

Itzik tried to console himself that their own location was much better. The kibbutz was over a mile from the border and there were no strategic roads. But they were still well within range. They'd practiced what to do in the event of... but this time, it wouldn't be just manoeuvres.

From the office, Itzik went through the dining hall and into the kitchens. Apart from Yael, all the cooks had gone.

'Doesn't look like we'll be needing this for lunch,' she said, putting trays of food into the refrigerators.

'Where is everyone?' asked Itzik, surprised, 'I wanted them to get down to the children's houses.'

Yael put her hands on her hips.

'And what makes you think they haven't gone already?' She half smiled. 'We heard the guns. Saw you running. That was enough.'

Itzik stood for a moment, thinking. Feminine intuition or whatever, he had to hand it to them.

'Look, Yael. Could you look in at the laundry on your way over. Make sure they've wrapped up and switched off. Those machines make one hell of a racket.' As Itzik ran off towards the armoury, Yael finished locking up the refrigerators, then pulling off her headscarf, hurried out.

Despite all their principles of sex equality, whilst the men worked in the fields or workshops, all the services around the courtyard were run by women, the kitchens, clinic, clothes store, children's houses, laundry. All of them.

Yael remembered that when they first came here, many women worked in the fields. Some drove tractors, others even managed whole branches like market gardens and orchards. But, as time passed, despite endless discussions, they had been drawn back into traditional areas of work, driven out by the increasing mechanisation in agriculture with its heavy machinery and bulk packaging, and pulled in by increasing demands for children's nurses as more babies came along.

Yael pushed open the door to the laundry. As she had expected it was empty, the machine idle and precious boiling water draining into the floor gullies - as if a motion picture had been frozen on one frame. Itzik ought to have trusted their judgement. Hannah and Tzipora had gone to the children's houses too.

Heading towards the kindergarten, Yael's thoughts continued in the same vein. Ostensibly, all work in the kibbutz had an equal value. But in reality, those branches earning the money had assumed greater importance both in labour allocation and investments. And in those branches, the men worked. The hard struggle for survival in the dry plain of the Negev laid down its own rules, exacted its own compromises. Sex equality in work had been one of them.

At that moment, two more explosions came from the north, followed by gunfire and Yael began to think instead of the children. She hurried down the path towards the white building beyond the babies' house, the kindergarten.

The overhead sprinklers were still spraying the collecting yard as Gavriel ran across the sand track, the cleaning up must almost be finished. He stopped by the rails, hesitating. Ten minutes more and they would finish completely. Turning aside, he knew he had to get down to the workshops first, he'd collect Harold and Ella on the way back.

On his way down, he ran past the tall, red-roofed silage tower. Only three weeks ago, it had been filled with cut maize, blown in through the top. To get the best silage they had to expel as much air as possible, the more they could tramp it down and compact it, the more nutritious feedstuff it would be.

The kitchen organised biscuits and lemonade, and after work, everyone came, mums, dads, kids and harvest-camp youngsters, all climbing the long steel ladder and tramping round and round, backs to the circular walls, singing and laughing, and the kids jumping and bouncing, the blown cuttings absorbing their wild somersaults like the softest of mattresses. People joined and left as the evening wore on, new voices taking over to sing as others grew hoarse and all the time tramping round and round and pressing it down.

For Gavriel, it was a true expression of community. Of togetherness. Now it stood outlined against the sky and as he knew from his mortar squad training, the perfect sighting target for some trigger-happy gunner. All their efforts and half a year's silage could be blown to smithereens in a few seconds. Trying to blot the possibility from his mind, Gavriel ran on down towards the garages.

Meir was repairing the broken drawbar of a trailer, welding-hood over his head and the blinding white arc casting grotesque shadows on the walls. Over by the double doors, Yankeleh was hammering out a huge dent out of the wing of a Ferguson tractor, creating a deafening din. The workshop was a world of its own, a cocoon - just like the milking parlour in its own way, though Gavriel preferred the warmth of his cows to this cold, black metal.

Both men were so used to the noise and flashes that they didn't notice him coming in and as Gavriel tapped Yankeleh on the shoulder, the metalworker spun round, hammer in the air.

'Oh, no,' he groaned, 'Not another *puncture* in the cow-shed.' The word puncture was used for any breakage or mishap, and as far a Yankeleh was concerned, the dairymen were the world's worst in looking after mechanical equipment. He was constantly having to reschedule work to deal with them.

Meir stopped welding, raised his visor and came towards them. He was a stocky man with a black, walrus moustache, one of Gavriel's friends from Rumania and the champion chess player of the kibbutz. A game with Meir rarely finished in one evening, exhausting even the kibbitzers as he sucked on an empty pipe.

What's up, Gabi?' said Meir, sensing that it was no routine call.

'Listen,' Gavriel gushed, 'you two can't hear down here. There's a battle over by the wadi and spreading. State of emergency has been declared along the border. Itzik sent me down to get everyone up to the armoury.'

Without waiting, Meir strode across to the far wall, threw down his helmet and switched off the welding machine. As the whine of the motor died away, two explosions echoed through the corrugated iron walls.

'See what you mean,' he muttered.

'Itzik says to take the jeep and bring the boys back from the winter wheat. Leave the crawler tractor in a gully somewhere.'

Yankeleh hurried out to unload the mobile welding gear from the back of the battered '45 jeep. Meir jumped into the seat, engaged the four-wheel drive and set out along the track towards the arable fields some three miles away. Like Gavriel, Meir was no stranger to war.

After Itzik, he was second-in-command. Immediately he recognised from the heavy machine guns and the crump of three-inch mortars that it was no local incident. Someone, somewhere over there had taken a major decision. God knows what a real artillery barrage would do to the kibbutz.

Changing gears, he sped out, leaving a cloud of dust billowing in his wake.

19

Rivka was a light sleeper. Despite the weariness from her spell of night duty, she woke at the sound of the first explosions. By the next shell-bursts, she was up and getting dressed. Taking her brown working jacket from the cupboard and tying on a headscarf, she hurried from the room. Outside, the sky was blue and clear and the morning hot, but in the shelters, it would be quite cold. Rivka was no stranger to underground bunkers.

Along the path, she was joined by other women, anxious lines furrowing their faces, all hurrying in the direction of the children's houses. No one had given orders, each had drawn her own conclusions from the sounds of battle.

As she hurried along, Rivka recalled the manoeuvres last year, rehearsing taking the children down the shelters. Daliah had collided with one of the visiting officers, spilling orange juice all down his battle-dress. How they'd all laughed. There wouldn't be much joking now.

Rivka wouldn't be with her own son. Her job was to help with the young babies and their mothers. She placed her hand on her stomach for a moment, thank God the next one was still inside her.

Avram, the carpenter, was waiting by the babies' house, he'd been checking out the shelters.

'What's happening?' asked Rivka as they met. Avram shrugged.

'No one knows for sure. Fighting, down by the wadi. Itzik's been in touch with Magen. They've declared an area emergency.'

Ruth, in charge of the babies' house, came out with the mothers each carrying her tiny bundle and a small bag with napkins, warm clothing and a bottle of sugar water. Some of the babies were still asleep. Others, rudely awakened were leaving no doubt as to what they thought of it all. One after the other, they followed Avram along the short length of trench, out of the sunlight and down the gloomy, concrete steps of the new, deep shelter, built at enormous cost the year before. At the general meeting, no one had dissented and no expense had been spared to make it safe even from a direct hit.

Avram had already been down once but at the bottom, again he checked everything, water in the tanks, paraffin in the lamps and oil heaters, spare bulbs, three powerful torches, first aid box. Everything. Rivka passed by, carrying one of Rachel's twins.' Avram smiled at the baby as she sat down on one of the narrow bunks. It was still fast asleep.

'Lucky chap 'By the time he's old enough, all this will be in the past.'

Rivka smiled weakly, her face still taut.

'*Hallevai,*' she murmured, 'who knows?'

Avram sensed the apprehension in her voice. Like most of the women, she seemed always more tense and aware of living on the border. While the men seemed to grow accustomed to the constant tension, as time passed the women seemed to become even more worried. He wondered whether it was due to their having a more passive role in security affairs. Or was it something innate? Either way, it was there.

Gradually, the babies were settled into the tiny bunks along the wall and the mothers sat on the benches opposite talking in low tones. Feeling that there nothing more he could do, Avram waved *shalom* and went up the steps to check the other shelters.

When he emerged, excited children were running across the

lawns, shouting and laughing, treating it as just another rehearsal like the last manoeuvres, a break in their daily routine. Soon the tiny heads bobbed above the parapets of the deeper trenches, before disappearing into the dark maws of the older shelters, which gave protection mainly against shrapnel and bullets. There was no way the kibbutz could have afforded deep shelters for everyone.

As one class entered, another came along, the younger children holding onto their teachers, the more anxious kids sucking thumbs, forefingers curled around their noses and each teacher wishing she had a dozen hands. For about ten minutes, the whole courtyard hummed with activity. Then, just as suddenly, it ceased and an eerie silence took over punctuated only by distant gunfire and explosions.

Breathless from running down and back again from the garages, Gavriel helped Harold and Ella to stow away the milking equipment. After checking the yards to make sure that all the bolts were shot home, they made their way up the hill, Ella continuing to complain that the young calves hadn't been fed.

'They'll get frantic with hunger,' she moaned, 'and run around the pens and bruise themselves against the rails.'

Harold and Gavriel nodded but said nothing, each preoccupied. Despite what was happening, neither wanted to believe that it would develop into anything more serious.

'I don't envy Itzik's job right now,' puffed Gavriel as they climbed the hill. 'That last 'phone call from Magen had him really worried.'

'Still could be making more of it than need be,' muttered Harold, conscious that each skirmish and every encounter also postponed 'the day peace would break out' as he joked. He'd had more than one argument with Itzik, 'Thinks you can solve the Arab problem through the sights of a rifle,' he said to

Gavriel one day as they drank coffee in the dairy office. Gavriel had countered that Harold shouldn't lump all the Sabras together politically. 'You can say that about people like Uri and Shumikeh. But not about Itzik.'

Ella was only half listening to the two of them. She was still thinking of the poor, defenceless creatures she'd abandoned below. Pausing for a moment, she looked down past the eucalyptus trees. What would happen to them in a real battle? Unable to bear the thought, she turned back and ran to catch them up.

They were joining the crowd gathering outside the armoury when Itzik hurried out - and almost ran into Ella. She blushed as he stood hesitant for a second, arms hanging by his sides and thinking how so much he'd wanted to speak to her today - had even phrased how to begin. But now all this... Quickly recovering, he turned to Gavriel.

'All buttoned up down below?' Gavriel nodded. 'Good.' He glanced back through the doorway. 'Uri,' he shouted to the armourer, who had been woken from his deep sleep by the mortar fire, 'you take over here and carry one. I'll go and check out the first-aid bunker.'

Itzik hurried past the dining hall. It was lunchtime but instead of the bustle and hum, it was eerily silent, just the breeze hissing through the young Casuarina trees. He continued up the track, to collect the emergency medical supplies from the clinic.

The squat, white stucco building stood just below the crest of the hill. Built in the very first days after they'd settled, they had worked three shifts without stop, everyone, girls too - pouring wet concrete as fast as the four skilled carpenters from Rishon had erected the shuttering. Until it was finished.

Itzik paused to catch his breath. Yes, the blockhouse, reinforced concrete walls thirty centimetres thick, their first refuge in a hostile landscape. It had been their original dining hall, then the first nursery and now their clinic.

On the concrete roof, stood the steel-plated watchtower with its powerful searchlight, the door swinging in the breeze where the lazy night guard had left it unlatched. For a split second he recalled the night Uri's beam had by chance picked out Stan with Avram's wife - and how the dining hall had buzzed the next day.

Outside the clinic he stopped abruptly, his sandals scuffing on the gravel. The emergency supplies were inside, but also, he suddenly remembered, would be the nurse, Shoshanah. As he hovered, a command car shot out from behind the building and sped down towards the road. In the back crouched two blood-spattered soldiers. A third was strapped to a stretcher. When the dust cleared, Shosh was standing there holding a stainless steel tray of bottles and dressings, her long fair hair wound up in a tight bun on the top of her head.

For one brief moment, their eyes met and Itzik's neck burned, they'd not stood so close for some while.

'They just came in from the wadi,' she softly said in her beautiful, clipped Hebrew. 'One of them will be lucky even to make it to hospital.'

Itzik fingered a shirt button, embarrassed, almost as if it were that first day they'd collided near Avremeleh's orchard.

'Messy business,' he replied, 'and it's not over by a long shot.'

They stood for what seemed to him ages, he staring straight past her at the white wall opposite, Shosh trying to look into his face.

The sudden crump of explosions in the distance and machine-gun fire echoing from the dunes, made them both start.

'Dangerous to stand here like this,' said Itzik. 'Best be taking the gear down to the bunker.'

'There's another box just inside the doorway,' she called over her shoulder as she started to walk away. Itzik went inside and waited a few seconds before picking it up, allowing the distance between them to widen.

Shosh trod carefully down the narrow, winding path. As she stepped down into the corrugated-iron sheeted trench, she couldn't stop thinking of Itzik, of him and that Australian girl. It was obvious to everyone, everyone except Itzik that she had no time for him. Had she found a more attractive man than Harold, she was thinking, he would have seen it. And despite the anger, she was sad to see him make a fool of himself like this.

Despite all the hurt he'd caused her, she still loved him. What had she done wrong, she kept asking herself? What Dybbuk had made him change so suddenly? But she would wait. Let things run their course. In time, she was sure he would come back. But for now, it was painful, so very painful.

As she reached the mouth of the bunker Reuven, the army-trained paramedic hurried across the lawn towards her, humping a huge canvas bag. Yes. She would need him if, God forbid, they had casualties. And she was also glad to have someone else around to distract her from her preoccupation with Itzik.

Itzik too was glad to find Reuven there when he arrived with the box of field dressings. He didn't stay long.

'I'm going back to the office,' he called as he hurried out. 'I'll send Khaim over as a runner and switch the 'phone through to here.'

'Okay,' said Reuven, 'We'll keep you in touch.'

'*Shalom* Itzik,' said Shosh, trying to smile, adding almost inaudibly, 'take care,' as she watched him climb out of the trench and run away across the lawn. Despite his tough façade and self-confidence, to her he was still the little urchin who had once ran into her by the orange grove.

Back in the armoury, Itzik joined Uri again in allocating the weapons.

'Moshe,' he called, 'you take your section to the trenches behind the childrens' houses. Itcho,' he called to another, 'take the Besa and your unit up to the spur on the hill, same position as in the last manoeuvres. Okay?'

One by one, people filed into the dark interior of the small concrete building, took their weapons and ammunition belts and dispersed to their allotted positions. No talking. No panic. All too preoccupied with what might, or might not, happen.

Itzik began to jot down notes in the armoury notebook, one ear finely tuned to the sounds of the explosions. He noted the directions, the frequencies, identified the different weapons and had no doubts, it was the most serious situation in all the seven years they had been here.

Just then Gavriel came through the door with Ella beside him.

'I haven't yet fed the young calves,' she was protesting. Itzik stopped writing, his chest tingling as she stood near him.

'Well. Can't be helped now, Ella. I... Er,' then stopped, trying to collect his thoughts. First the encounter with Shosh, now Ella... What the hell - any minute they could be under bombardment. He turned to Gavriel.

'Take your mortar crew up to the pits. And don't forget to put the spare bombs in the rear pit.'

Yaacov backed the small, grey Ferguson and two-wheeled trailer up to the door. Ella felt superfluous and squeezed past and out onto the lawn as the two men loaded first the heavy steel base, then the barrel, while Stan, the third member of the team brought out six cases of mortar bombs, one by one from the rear store. She stood and watched as the tractor slowly bumped away over the lawn with its cargo of death, up the track past the dining hall.

Up in the sandbagged pits they'd prepared last year, Gavriel supervised the work, first a cushion of hay, covered by an old groundsheet under the baseplate. Then setting up the barrel and pointing it towards the west, with the sight rods stuck in the sand about five yards away. Finally, they offloaded the cases of bombs into a pit some ten yards back, connected by a zig-zag trench. When all was prepared, Yaacov engaged gear and took the tractor down to hide it amongst the trees.

The sound of the engine died away and as other two sat back on the circle of sandbags, the sun began to dip from its zenith. Gavriel looked across to the border where dust and smoke rose above the low ridge, trying to fathom out what the Egyptians hoped to gain. They'd been so decisively hammered at Khan Yunis last spring but perhaps Nasser's latest pact with the Soviets had suddenly made them more confident? Still, what would they achieve? But as Harold often said, no point in searching for logic in the Middle East.

Yes. It was the irrationality that made him anxious, any minor incident could suddenly turn into a major war. Involve the major powers, nuclear weapons. Anything. Despite the midday heat, Gavriel shivered. War. It made him think of Rivka. They hadn't seen each other since five that morning. It seemed now such a long time ago.

He guessed she would already be with the babies in the shelter, below ground. Bunkers. It would revive old memories and fears and he wanted so much to be with her, reassure her. For a moment, he closed his eyes and saw her face as he had first seen it, sad and pale, standing by the open grave.

It had been during the occupation. The Rumanian fascists, The Iron Guard were running wild, beating and killing whenever they felt like it. Children were sent down to cellars or up to lofts so they would be safe and wouldn't see. But they could hear. The shots. The terrible cries of the maimed and the bereaved.

Rivka had been in the loft with her brothers when shouts and screams came from below – and she recognised one voice - her mother. Squeezing against the shutters, she peered through the cracks. A group of Jews had been pushed against a wall opposite, amongst them her father. Shots rang out. He fell. Her mother ran forward, arms outstretched, still screaming. They opened fire again. And she fell beside him.

Rivka had banged on the shutter, shrieking and crying. Two men turned and aimed up at the window, bullets thudding against the wooden walls as her brother threw himself upon her and dragged her away, smothering her screams in an old blanket, whilst the shutter splintered into fragments.

At the funeral a few days later was when Gavriel first met her. Rivka was standing between two aunts, long brown coat, tears streaming down her pale face. But still so pretty in her long black plaits. And as they left the cemetery, he went over and tried to console her, to give her courage to continue. News of the Red Army's offensive in the Ukraine had begun to filter through. He put his hand on her arm and she'd leaned against him, saying nothing. Just crying and crying all the way back into town.

She was fourteen at the time. He was two years older. From that time they'd become close friends, loaned each other the few books that were still around and gradually grew closer. Together, they rejoiced at the liberation – and together they had become disillusioned with the new communist regime.

In the autumn of 1947, with about fifty others, they managed to reach Istanbul on an old diesel barge. There they'd been transferred to a rickety river steamer with hundreds of would-be immigrants to Palestine, nearly sinking before being boarded by a British destroyer within sight of Haifa.

Even though it was the last days of the Mandate and despite all that had happened in Europe, the White Paper regulations limiting Jewish entry were still being applied to the letter. They were deported to Cyprus.

Pained by the reminiscences, Gavriel stood up and looked over the chicken houses below, to the barbed wire perimeter fence. Barbed wire, the British prison camp in Cyprus.

Gavriel had considered themselves lucky. Thousands of others had been shipped back to Hamburg, to the very charnel house from which they had just fled. But for Rivka, the wire around the camp, the armed British soldiers and the confinement had all reminded her of the occupation, plunging her into bouts of depression against which he felt powerless.

Six months later, the State had been declared and they were released. And when they came down here to build their new home, Rivka had smiled and laughed again, then Udi arrived and everything seemed to be fine. But every so often at night, she would lie still and cry softly, silently, and Gavriel would hold her tight against him, waiting for those terrible memories to fade.

Sitting on the sandbags, Gavriel wished so much that he could hold her close now. To comfort her that this too would pass, as he was sure it would.

The gunfire grew louder and more incessant. He looked across at Stan, he was smoking his pipe. Stan shrugged, then looked away. Nothing could match Alam Halfa... Gavriel went over to the mortar and checked the spirit level again. Nothing more to do now other than wait. Wait for what though, he wondered?

In the shelters, at one end Yael was reading a story to the toddlers, at the other, the kindergarten children drew pictures for the harvest festival in two weeks time. And in the babies' shelter, shielded by thick concrete walls from the noise of battle, Rivka waited and wondered. Would there ever would be peace?

In the emplacement up the hill, Dov and the machine gunners on the Besa threaded ammunition belts through the breech. Those with rifles, loaded clips of bullets, all ready for whatever might happen.

By the armoury, as she waited with a few others to be detailed to one of the trenches, Ella looked out towards the wadi. Where a few weeks ago they'd taken the cattle for the last grazing before the summer drought, a dust haze hung in the air. To the west, the border ridge was almost obscured by a cloud of smoke and dust that was drifting across the plain. It was the first time she'd ever experienced the sounds of battle and with her stomach turning, she was trying hard to hide that fact that she was absolutely scared stiff.

20.

Major Salim was following events through the slits of the concrete observation post, his eyes bloodshot. Dust clung to his eyebrows and moustache, turning them prematurely grey. The fine loess soil stirred up by the battle was beginning to obscure the whole area.

Lieutenant Faras came along the communicating trench.

'The Israelis are returning heavy fire,' muttered the Lieutenant. 'We'll need more support, sir, don't you think?'

The major nodded then grunted but said nothing as together they turned to look out again over the plain. He had given up on headquarters.

Suddenly the major nudged Faras's elbow.

'There. See there.' He pointed to the long plume of dust left by Meir's jeep, as it sped out to the fields. 'An army jeep. From that village.' A few minutes later as the command car carrying the wounded soldiers drove out of the kibbutz gate towards the main road, the lieutenant pointed.

'Isn't that another military vehicle?' said Faras .

'The second one,' snapped major Salim. 'Farmers. Communes. Maybe. But first and foremost, they are military outposts, Faras. Mark my words.'

Refocussing their binoculars, they followed the truck out to the main road about five miles away. It turned north and was lost to sight between the belts of eucalyptus trees along the roadside.

Sharaj Yahud, the Jews' Tree, the local Arabs had named the eucalyptus, after first settlers had planted them to dry out the swamps of Hadera. Here, struggling to survive in the arid south they were a faint shadow of the mighty trees up north but still provided welcome shade and cover.

The lieutenant lowered his glasses and leaned back.

'Lots of movement along that road. Could be reinforcements.'

The Major turned to face him.

'Sure. But more important. what have they concealed in those villages? Ample cover in those orange groves and trees, eh. Could be artillery. Even tanks - where we'd least expect them, eh, Faras ?' And for a moment, both men were silent. Pensive.

Major Salim knew his recent history. Comunal villages like these had held back massive Egyptian forces during the '48 war. Hadn't Presiden Nasser himself – then a colonel - been wounded in the attack on that one near Iraq Sweidan, Negbah, it was called?

For a moment the two were silent, listening to the gunfire and ducking down very time a mortar bomb landed nearby.

'Have headquarters answered your messages, Major?' asked the Lieutenant.

'Damn headquarters,' the major snorted. 'They've had long enough and still they won't make a decision.'

They looked out again, each with their own thoughts. Both despised the men at the top and were disgusted with the corruption they witnessed daily. Both wanted a revitalised army and had spoken about it obliquely at various times. Yet each was wary of revealing too much, especially with lieutenant Nazim snooping about.

Of the two, Major Salim was the more cautious in what he said. Short and stocky, betraying his peasant origins, the Major had come up the hard way. Faras would never fully understand the major's feelings of insecurity, his innate suspicions. He had so much more to loose than Faras, the tall, slim officer with his sharp, aristocratic features.

The Lieutenant came from a wealthy family in Alexandria. It was even rumoured that his brother was married to a Jewess. Major Salim didn't give it much significance. They were all mixed like that in Alexandria, had been for centuries, Greeks, Copts, Egyptians, Jews, Russians.

The Major felt no resentment at the easy way promotion had come to Faras. The man had courage - and the right ideas, which were the most important thing in the army at this time.

As the two men stared over the plain, a distant whistling grew suddenly louder. Instinctively, they threw themselves down on the floor, covering their heads with their arms. A moment later, a salvo of eighty millimetre shells landed about fifty yards away, followed by two more. They sat up, coughing and spitting as dust and fumes filled the dugout. Israeli artillery was beginning to find its targets.

The major sat back on his heels. Through the observation slit, the white house on the hill in that village opposite glowed through the haze. He leaned forward and peered at the trees and orchards.

'We must find out what they have hidden in there, Faras ,' he muttered, 'even if it means lobbing in a few rounds.' The lieutenant tensed but merely nodded. He knew the Israeli mentality. If a civilian target were attacked, they would throw everything they had back at them.

Much as he admired and respected the major, he recognised an obsession when he saw one. And the major was obsessed with the notion that heavy armour was hidden in that village. Faras was much more worried about the increasing traffic along the main road. That was where a counter attack would come from. But he had no intention of disputing the major's words.

By now, the exchange of gunfire and artillery had intensified and with every minute passing, more and more of the major's own positions were being put out of action. But as a forward observation post however, it was still invaluable. Again and again, he sent back reports to headquarters requesting intervention of heavy artillery.

'We must keep the initiative, Faras. Not allow ourselves to dragged into the enemy's strategies.'

The minutes turned into an hour. The Major despaired. Dust clogged his nostrils and lined his throat. And still no response. Then, without warning, came the rumble of loud gunfire from the rear. The major clenched his fists.

'At last, Faras. At last!' Major Salim wanted to cheer, 'our own heavy guns. Now we'll show them!'

Lieutenant Faras peered through his glasses. Although their heavy mortars could reach the main road, someone was taking the major's suspicions seriously. Two shells landed just to the south of the village, raising a huge cloud of dust and smoke that blotted it from view, except for the white house which seemed to hang in the air above the trees.

As the dust cleared, two more shells fell way beyond the village, followed by a pause. As the two men looked out together and waited, the Lieutenant knew that their gunners would be making their calculations.

After Gavriel's mortar section had gone, Ella stood with Harold as he waited with the dwindling group by the armoury to collect his rifle and ammunition. Just then, the first explosions came from beyond the cowsheds. As they reverberated through the ground Itzik, who had come back, hurtled out of the narrow doorway closely followed by Uri. Everyone turned to stare at the thick grey pall of dust and smoke that rose into the sky from beyond the orange groves, mesmerised as though not able to believe it was really happening.

'In'al abuk,' cursed Uri, 'that was close.'

Itzik flung out his arm.

'Quick. Everyone in the trenches. Ella, you take the nearest children's shelter.'

Jumping into the nearby, corrugated-iron sheeted trench, Ella squeezed past to head for the shelter entrance. Just then, a second salvo fell somewhere beyond the main gate. Itzik clenched his hands, looking from one cloud of dust to the other.

'Elohim!. One behind. One in front. Getting the range!' He clenched his fists and his face turned pale. 'The bastards. They trying to get the range. On us. On the kibbutz!'

For a few seconds, no one moved, frozen in the strange silence that followed the explosions. Itzik though was thinking, fast. The herd, all cooped up. One salvo and it could be completely wiped out. They had to act now - but he had to stay in the command post and Gavriel was up with the mortars.

'Ella. Wait,' he called. You and Harold. We have to disperse the herd. Quickly. The next load could land right on the cowsheds!' His whole body was shaking. 'We must get them out to the fields. Now!' Itzik's head raced. It was his herd. He couldn't leave it just to them. 'Uri,' he called, 'until Meir gets back, you take command up here. I won't be long.'

Ella climbed out of the trench, her head churning. The nightmare she had imagined, was becoming a reality.

'Harold.' Itzik pointed down to the stables. 'You and Ella take two horses and join me at number three. I'll get down and open the gates. But quickly. Quickly,' his voice rose to a shout. 'There's no time. No time!'

Ella had never seen him like this, so wound up and emotional, almost as if he had lost control. But she had no opportunity to think further as she joined Harold in a headlong rush through down the young pine trees. Then as they ran along the road, suddenly she remembered the young calves. Oh God. What would happen to them now?

In the stable, the horses were stamping and pulling at their chains and whinnying, eyes white and bulging. Ella managed to calm and saddle the chestnut mare whilst Harold held the bridle. Saddling the black colt proved more problematic. It turned into an uneven wrestling match as she strove to slip the bit into its mouth and twice it threw off the saddle as Harold tried to buckle the girth strap.

As they tried for the third time, two more shells fell, this time closer, in the orange groves just beyond the chicken houses. The colt bucked and reared as the shrieks and cackling of thousands of chickens followed the explosion. Ella stopped and stared.

'Never mind the damned saddle,' Harold shouted, 'we've got to get to the cowsheds. I'll ride bareback.'

'You can't' Ella said, 'It's got a backbone like a razor.'

'No time,' Harold snapped and with a leap, somehow seated himself on the colt's back and cantered out, just managing to stay there as Ella followed on the mare.

Itzik meanwhile was running through the eucalyptus trees. He broke off a long branch, and stripping the leaves as he went. In the yards, the cattle were milling around and bellowing, tails swishing the air. In the calf pens, tiny hooves clattered on the slats, thin bodies slamming against the rails in panic. In the yard of the first shed the cows were bunched at the far end.

Throwing open the gates, Itzik lashed out with the branch as he ran round and tried to get them to the gate.

'*Yallah. Yallah.* Out, you idiots. Out.' His head burned. His own cows and he was losing his self-control, panicking at what could happen if they didn't get them out. '*Yallah, yallah,*' he shouted, again and again, desperately swishing and striking out with the stick.

At last, the leading cows made for the open gate and the others followed creating a humping, heaving mass, all trying to get through at once. He ran across and opened the second yard gate. They too streamed out, following the first group. By the time he opened the older calves and heifers' pens, they needed no encouragement.

Leaning back against the rails, Itzik caught his breath. Sweat soaked his body and his lungs seemed on fire, but the cattle were out. Away. He threw down the branch and waited for the blood to cease pounding in his forehead. Suddenly, the leaders began to bunch up along the track.

'Idiot,' he cursed, 'what an idiot I am!' In his excitement, he had forgotten that the fences had been set to direct them to the nearby, irrigated pastures for that afternoon. They would be no better off there if the shelling continued.

Just then, the shells fell behind the chicken houses and the cows began to panic even more, heaving and pushing along the narrow track. In a wild leap, Itzik scrambled over the perimeter fence, ripping his trousers and lacerating one shin. With every ounce of breath left in him, he ran round to the front of the herd.

'*Akhora. Akhora.* Back. Back,' he yelled, waving his arms in a crazy semaphore. With their innate wariness of a two-legged animal, the front ranks halted, swinging their massive heads from side to side. But the rest came on, clashing and crushing against them in a gigantic pile-up. Some reared, others kneeled in an attempt to escape the crush, a mass of arching necks, twisting horns and lashing tails.

For a moment Itzik turned his head away, unable to look on the agony. Every one of those poor creatures, he knew by name, had seen through illness and calvings, watched their milk yields climb. He felt sick, but all he could do was wait as the waves rippled back and forth, those at the rear pressing on, those in the centre backing away as the herd tried to sort itself out. It was touch and go.

Harold and Ella saw the crush as they came round the second shed.

'They've taken the wrong track!' shouted Ella.

'You give him a hand,' Harold shouted. 'I'll ride round and open the rear gates. They're probably closed.'

Tying the mare to a rail, Ella climbed gingerly over the fence, those barbs were sharp.

'Glad you got here,' puffed Itzik, sweating, his face flushed, 'any moment, they could have rushed me.'

Ella herself was almost panic stricken at the heaving mass still being pushed towards them but in front of Itzik, knew she had to show control. Slowly the two of them walked towards the cattle, hands outstretched, fingers almost touching and in all this chaos, Ella realised the irony of the situation. At last, they were alone - and in the safety of the open air. And this was the day she had planned to let him know once and for all, that it was over - if there ever had been anything to start with. But Oh God. Not now. Not with all this going on.

And strangely, in these few minutes of staying calm as they tried to turn the herd, she felt an admiration - even a warmth for him. Perhaps, if he hadn't been so pushing, so overbearing? If. . . God! What on earth was she thinking about at such a time?

Galloping down to the rear gateway, Harold jumped off and tied the reins to a nearby bush. One leaf of the steel gate swung open without any problem, but the other half was jammed by its bolt where it had been struck by a trailer of beet the week before. He tried to free it by rocking the gate leaf. It wouldn't budge. He pulled and jerked at it with both hands, kicked it with his boot but still it would come up. Just then he heard the rumble of hooves, Itzik and Ella must have turned them at last.

Sweat pouring down his face and neck, again and again Harold pulled and rocked the gate. The bolt rose from the ground socket by half an inch then seized again. The thunder grew louder and turning round, he saw the leaders, about fifty yards away. No time. With just a few seconds to spare, he ran to the colt, he untied the reins, heaved himself onto its back. He galloped into the track through the orange groves, just as the wave of cattle slammed against the gate and, with its bolt dragging in the sand, knocked it askew as they stampeded through.

While Itzik slowly brought up the rear, Ella ran back to open the young calves' pens. The half-crazed youngsters dashed out and were soon lost in the cloud of dust eddying around the cowsheds the gate. Chest heaving and head spinning, she hurried to untie her horse.

'Wait 'till Meir sees that gate,' said Ella, as she rode up to meet Itzik, trying to defuse the tension of being so close to him again, 'he repaired it only last month.'

Itzik didn't smile. He stood with his hands on his hips, his face flushed and breathing heavily

'I've just realised something,' he puffed, looking after the herd that had disappeared into the dust cloud, 'that track leads out to the barley, then to the sorghum fields along the border.'

Ella gripped the reins and thought for a moment, then leaned down.

'Look. I can skirt round the side of the trees and meet up with Harold. Together, I'm sure we can turn them towards the main road.'

Itzik looked up, and as if suddenly aware that it was her, Ella, his voice softened.

'Okay,' he said, 'but take care, Ella. Don't take risks. Never know what those idiots on the ridge will fire at. And get back up top and under cover as soon as you can. Okay?'

'Sure. Okay,' she replied. As her the horse started forwards, spontaneously she added, 'you take care too, Itzik.' Then embarrassed, dug in her knees and quickly trotted off.

Itzik watched as she rode off along the cypress trees wind-break, her slim figure hunched over the mare's brown back, her light blue shirt sweat-stuck to her back. So much he wanted to be alone with her, so much to say to her. To explain. Yes. He must find the opportunity later. As soon as this... this all blew over. If only he could have gone with, to be with her, to let her know that he loved her.

Suddenly, he became fearful and protective Should he have sent Ella out into the fields like that? He would never forgive himself if anything happened to her. But he had to stay here - and get back on top as soon as he could and take command.

Hurrying back through the deserted cowsheds, Itzik felt his legs heavy and his head burning. No lowing. No scuffles. No clinking of chains and tags. He looked into the empty yards, instinctively searching for one cow humping another to see who was on heat. Nothing. Just silence.

Along the walkways, as his sandals squelched in the manure he thought of the herd, the millions of litres of milk they'd sent to *Tnuva*. Calves born and raised. His life's work – as though it had never been. Like those old movies of ghost towns when the gold ran out. Now, in one salvo of shells even this could just disappear.

Itzik slammed a gate shut and walked on. War. He knew war. War was for soldiers. With guns and tanks. But this? Women. Children. Animals. Houses. What kind of beasts waged war like this?

The black and white image of Guernica, Picasso's painting, suddenly flashed into his mind – like the colours of his Friesian cows.

Shosh had once tried to explain it, to make him appreciate modern art. He visualised the grotesque horse, the bull bellowing, the houses in flames. Yes. That was how it could all be – right here.

He glanced at his watch. It was half past two and he realised that hadn't stopped rushing around since late morning. And he must get back up top to take command. Make the decisions that others couldn't if . , .

Coming round the milking parlour, he was about to go up through the trees when a loud bellow split the silence. Kfir. The bull! What would happen to him? But there was no way he could let him loose out of the pen.

Kfir. He was almost like a son. Itzik's eyes grew moist, he felt he was about to cry. Three years of breeding from that long night they helped pull him out. What did those bastards want of them? What was the Egyptian army hoping to gain? God, how he hated them! The bull bellowed again. Itzik turned. He felt impelled to go down and see him.

For a moment, he stood, hesitating. He ought to get back up top. But he had to do something. Something. Running into the first cowshed, pulled the strings off a bale of hay and carried a huge armful down to the pen. As Kfir saw him coming, the bull pawed at the sand and snorted. Itzik opened his mouth to call, to reassure the beast. But no sound came.

A salvo of shells straddled the garages and the cowsheds. When the dust and smoke cleared, a bloodstained figure lay crumpled beside a huge crater. A short distance away, the stricken bull moaned dismally, its life-blood seeping into the sand through a dozen shrapnel wounds. It lay motionless, its head pointing towards Itzik's shattered body.

The sounds of the explosions echoed from the cowshed roofs and up over the hill. The dust settled. And the flies started to gather.

21

Another shell burst at the fringe of the wadi, showering earth and stones onto the heap of driftwood branches below. Ahmed woke, winced with pain and coughed as dust filled his nostrils, unable to believe that he was still alive.

Ever since he'd crawled under the tangle, he'd waited for the crunch of boots on the gravel, for the Israeli patrols to reach him – and for the final shots. Hardly daring to breathe, he'd waited. Then exhausted from the night's efforts and the wound he must have lost consciousness.

Slowly, he turned his head and looked through a gap in the branches at the far bank. Shadows had formed in the hollows and the near bank was completely in shade. He must have been there for over an hour. At first it seemed strangely peaceful but as his mind cleared, the sounds of gunfire reached him from beyond the bank and he heard the explosions in the distance. The soldiers must have taken shelter but they could still be near.

Ahmed raised his head a little higher to look down the river-bed towards the border, then tried to move. A sharp pain shot through his right shoulder. The arm was numb and he could no longer feel his fingers. He reached out with his good hand to pull himself forward. The sharp pain pierced his shoulder again, but he knew he had to move on whilst he still had the strength, take advantage of the fighting. It might not last much longer.

Carefully parting the tangle of twigs and dried grass, he squeezed out onto the stones. Keeping well into the shadows, he inched his way over the loose gravel and driftwood. If

Ismail's calculations were correct, he had about two hundred yards to the border. Poor Ismail, he had always been the lucky one. Perhaps now, he, Ahmed, would inherit his luck. *Insh'allah.*

As he pulled himself along towards the next bend, despite the agony, Ahmed felt a sense of elation, a conviction that he was destined to survive. Ahead, above the high bank, he could already see the border ridge. If only he could get close enough to leave just a short distance to cross after dark.

Soon, he had only fifty metres or so, but in pain and with having to lie absolutely flat without raising himself at all, each heave of his good arm and push with his legs seemed to take the effort of a hundred yards. But he would do it. For Ismail. And Fais. And Mahmud. For his father, somehow, he had to make it…

Half a mile to the rear of the front line, Major Salim's reports provoked frantic exchanges with headquarters. The fate of the Fedayeen no longer played any part as an artillery officer was despatched to the major's command post. In Gaza, the general staff had been summoned to an emergency meeting, High Command was on its way from Sinai by helicopter.

The generals studied maps and tried to analyse the reports. It was an entirely new situation. Their own forces had initiated the shooting, but events were now overtaking them. News of Israeli armour and troop concentrations was coming in, together with requests for heavy artillery support from at least two sectors. This would require approval from Cairo. Even from President Nasser himself.

The original spark to the confrontation also occupied little space in the minds of the Israeli General Staff, hurriedly convened in Beer Sheba. The security situation along this front had been quiet for some time and everyone was baffled by the sudden flare up. Meanwhile, the thinly scattered units along the border were being reinforced from Beer Sheba and Julis. Soon, all the roads running south-west were crammed with tank transporters and convoys of lorries, whilst Piper Cub spotter 'planes had taken to the air.

As reports came through of border kibbutzim under fire, the chief of staff left to telephone the Prime Minister. They might have to call in air strikes, but he would be reluctant, it always gave the world media a chance to blow up a purely local engagement into an international incident. Instead, orders were given for heavy artillery to silence the enemy gun emplacements.

Before long, Israeli shells were flying high over the orange groves where Harold and Ella were preparing to turn the herd away from the border.

The track through the groves was lined with tall cypress tree windbreaks and as the cattle jostled and heaved forward, a dense cloud of grey dust that shot up as from a wind tunnel, spreading high in the sky and almost blotting out the sun. As the shells fell on the cowsheds, Harold looked back. How lucky they were to have got them out in time. Itzik must be relieved too, he was thinking. But as the blast blew across the trees, the herd panicked even more, rushing towards the end of the track and the open fields.

At the junction with the new plantation, Harold bore off to the right, urging the colt through the young trees to get into the open before the cattle broke cover and came out into the beet field.

The huge green leaves glistened in the hazy sunlight as the horse picked his way between the rows of gold coloured beet each weighing more than fifty pounds apiece. Glancing at them,

Harold could help thinking of how the cows would reduce them to mere wet marks on the concrete troughs in a matter of minutes. Then he remembered the trailer still piled high by the barn and now drying out in the sun and cursed. What a waste.

By now, the colt's hide was chaffing his thighs. On top of it, castration on the beast's bony spine seemed even more likely. He should have persevered with the saddle like Ella said. But as he rode out onto the barley stubble, he was more concerned, wondering where she was? Spitting the dust from his mouth, Harold turned the horse to face the trees and waited.

Crouched in the lookout post, Major Salim pointed out the terrain to the newly arrived artillery officer. As a salvo of shells landed at the base of the small hill in front of them, the Major drew his attention to the village,

'Huh. That should shake them up,' he grunted. 'Now we'll see what they have hidden in there to throw back at us.' But, as the breeze began to blow away the dust of the last shells, a new, much denser plume of dust rose from amongst the dark green of the orange groves.

'Just look at that,' he snorted. Both men focussed on the column of dust that rose higher and higher into the sky. Slowly, it drifted across the fields, thicker and darker than anything they had yet seen.

'Well,' said the Major, 'What do you think?' The younger officer turned to look into his face. It was his first time under fire and he wanted to sound knowledgeable.

'Something large. On the move,' he replied. 'A column of trucks - or half-tracks. Even . . ' He paused. Major Salim slammed his fist into his palm.

'Even what?' he prodded.'

'Tanks, maybe?' said the officer.

'Exactly!' snapped the major, his eyes wide. 'Just like I was saying to lieutenant Faras, a short while ago. The cunning swine. Hiding armour in those villages all the time.' He smacked his fist against his palm again, 'I knew it. I knew it!'

As they watched, the cloud thickened and swelled, drifting downwind towards the east.

'We must catch them before they have time to fan out in the open,' snapped the Major, jabbing his finger in the direction of the fields. 'They think they are hidden. But we shall hammer them before they disperse.'

The artillery officer nodded. He wasn't absolutely convinced but a few rounds would soon reveal what was going on. He looked down and studied his map. Picking up the microphone, he barked the co-ordinates to the battery at the rear.

Reports of the huge dust cloud had also been received from two positions to the south and the officer's message provoked a scurry of activity. Israeli return fire had just put one battery out of action. As medical orderlies were carrying casualties to the dugouts, the commander made his decision. If it were tanks, there was no time to lose. The remaining battery of six inch mortars had been ranging on the village. Rapidly, it was given a new target, the centre of those dark green orange groves.

The dust cloud had now reached the fringe of the orchards. Up on the ridge Major Salim listened as the artillery officer continued to plot co-ordinates and radio them back to base. With silent satisfaction he noted the first flashes and smoke amongst the trees. This time, they had the upper hand. Now, they would see. This time, indeed it would be different.

In the armoury, Uri had finished handing out weapons and went outside where he was joined by Shlomo the electrician who doubled as the second armourer. As they saw the cattle stampeding out of the rear gate, Uri shielded his eyes.

'Where's Itzik?'

'There,' shouted Shlomo, 'going down to the bull pen.'

'Bloody cowmen,' said Uri, 'can't tear themselves away for a moment from their work.'

At that moment, they heard the whistle of shells and instinctively threw themselves on the ground, shuddering as the reverberations came through the ground again. When they stood up, smoke was billowing from below.

'The cowsheds!' they both shouted at once, 'right on the cowsheds, the bastards.' Then immediately looked at one another, 'Itzik!'

They started to run down the hill but suddenly Uri stopped.

'Wait. One of us. You go and fetch Reuven. And the stretcher. I'll carry on down.'

As Shlomo sprinted across to the first aid bunker, Uri started to run down again, then abruptly stopped dead, his head spinning. God forbid if anything had happened to Itzik, someone had to be in command up top. He desperately wanted to go down but Reuven and Shosh would be the ones to deal with it. And if they couldn't - he wouldn't be of any use either. Glancing down at the pall of dust over the cowsheds, slowly he turned and made his way up to the armoury again.

'Itzik,' he muttered, 'It'll be alright Itzik. I know it will be alright.'

Uri had been with Itzik through the last months of the '48 war. They'd had some pretty narrow escapes but always managed to come through. And when they'd left the army, Itzik had persuaded him to come and join the kibbutz. Looking back, he saw Shlomo and Reuven running down through the young pine trees with the stretcher. 'It'll be okay, Itzik,' he said to himself. But his stomach was turning. Between the cowsheds, nothing moved.

As he reached the armoury, three more shells landed, but this time amidst the orange groves. He shook his head, puzzled. Why there? Then he felt some relief as to the east, from the lines of trees by the main road came flashes of heavy artillery return fire, the army had woken up to the situation at last. To the west, the border ridge was enveloped in smoke and dust. It was the heaviest engagement in the six years he'd been here. And like everyone else, he was wondering: Why?

Uri went into the armoury and sat on a stool. Alone for the first time since he'd been rudely woken, Uri suddenly recalled the star-shell and the shots just before dawn. Was there a connection? Had it been brewing all night?

Bending forward, he held his head in his hands, his brain beginning to burn like a raging furnace. Yes. He should have woken Itzik. If he had woken him, Itzik could have phoned his old comrade at Magen to find out. They could have been prepared. And if they had, Itzik would not be down there now. He clenched his fists on his knees. It was his fault. And if anything had happened to Itzik, he would never forgive himself. Never.

At that moment, the angular figure of Stan blotted out the daylight. He had run down from the mortar pit.

'Bloody Mortar,' he cursed as he came through the door. 'Jammed. Just as we set it up on the sandbags. Gavriel asked me to get some spares.' Suddenly he saw Uri, doubled up. 'Here. What's up mate?' he said. Leaning down, he laid a hand on Uri's shoulder. 'You look real rough. What's up?'

Uri straightened back.

'No. Nothing. Just a bad headache,' he muttered. 'I'll get some pills from the shelters,' then stood up, his mind spinning. If anything serious had happened to Itzik, he had to snap out of it and take control until Meir got back from the fields.

'There's some spare parts in that cupboard, Stan,' he said.

'Take what you need.' Then wanting to do something practical he added, 'I'll go and make a round of the children's shelters. They must be worried about what's happening.'

On the steps of the babies' shelter, Uri almost collided with Rivka who was coming up. Her face was drawn and pale.

'What's going on,' she said, breathless. 'We felt the explosions. It's terrible being down there and not knowing. You know. . .' Then she stopped, he wouldn't understand. At times, in her nightmares she saw hordes of soldiers swarming up the hill, houses burning, shooting, children screaming. Now, down there in the semi-darkness, they'd surfaced again. Again and again she wished so much she were up in the dugout with Gavriel, however dangerous.

Uri tried scratched his head.

'Look. We don't know much ourselves, Rivka. There's a lot of firing. A few shells down by the orange groves and near the cowsheds. We managed to disperse the cows first though. Anyway,' he said, trying to smile, 'now the army is hitting back, they'll soon silence the bastards.' He didn't mention Itzik.

Rivka re-tied her headscarf, watching his face as he spoke. Was it only a few hours ago they had been drinking coffee in the babies' house in just another uneventful spell of night duty. Despite his lighthearted manner, Uri seemed to have suddenly aged.

'Anyway,' he asked. 'How are things down here?'

' Oh. Fine. Most of the babies are sleeping. But, like I said, we need to know what is happening, Uri.

'Sure,' Uri nodded. 'You're right. I'll make certain that someone pops in from time to time.' Then, as he turned to go, he called over his shoulder, 'Gavriel is up on the hill with the mortar squad. I'll give him your regards when I go round.'

'Thanks,' said Rivka, 'And don't worry. We'll take care of

things down here.'

Stan caught him as he returned to the armoury,

'I'm sure it's the firing pin spring. I'll take a spare up with me.' Lowering his voice, he added, 'heard something about Itzik?'

Uri shrugged.

'We'll know when Reuven and Shlomo get back up.' Bad news travelled fast. 'I'm going over to the first aid bunker to see Shosh.'

As Stan hurried away up the hill, Uri shouldered his Sten gun, locked the armoury and hurried across the lawn to the bunker, his head still burning with guilt. Why hadn't he woken Itzik that morning..?

At that moment, two further explosions came from the orange groves. He grew even more puzzled, the Egyptian gunners couldn't be that bad? Suddenly, he stopped and stared out towards the dark green trees. *Elohim!* Somewhere out there with the cows, were Ella and Harold.

22

Harold glanced back as he urged the colt out of the beet and across the parched stubble of the winter wheat. The huge plume of dust raised by the herd was moving towards the end of the track and the thunder of hooves grew louder. Ahead, the dusty green of the sorghum fields stretched away right up to the border.

The winter rains had come late that year but they were heavy. The sorghum was firm and green with swollen heads of small round seeds turning brown, ready for the harvest. He looked across the fields again, the first real crop after two years of drought was about to be trampled into the dust. Yoske and Uri would be devastated

Harold listened to the gunfire and explosions in the distance, wondering what it all meant. Living on the border, he'd become used to sporadic shooting and the odd detonation. Occasionally, a tractor left out in the fields at night was sabotaged, or aluminium pipes stolen. But continuous firing. Artillery? It was something completely new. And despite the heat he found he was shivering.

For a instant, the barrage reminded him of the Blitz on Manchester when he was a kid, the horrific noises at night and the ground shaking, then coming up from the shelters next morning to see gutted shells of houses and glass everywhere. Now, as he looked back towards the kibbutz, he tried to console himself that the explosions by the cowshed and in the orange groves were just stray rounds from the battle by the wadi to the north.

But as he looked, a cloud of smoke rose from behind the dining hall followed by the sound of two explosions. Perhaps Itzik was right and those gunners were trying to get the range of the kibbutz. His stomach turned. If they did, there would be nothing left of iit. He turned and glanced towards the border ridge and suddenly felt quite scared. In the heat of battle, a lone horseman or two would also be a target.

The next salvo of heavy mortar bombs landed right in the orange groves. Brilliant yellow flashes were followed by the noise and a blast of hot air and acrid fumes making the colt rear and buck. Harold fought to remain seated as his head burned. Those shells must have landed right amongst the herd. The carnage would be horrific but there was nothing he could do. Nothing. Except wait for Ella and be ready to head them away from the border when they came out into the open. But where <u>was</u> Ella? She should have ridden out by now?

A few seconds later, the cattle broke from the trees in a stampede and with them to one side, Ella, her red head-scarf tied across her face like some wild west outlaw. He shouted and waved. She saw and waved back, but a moment later was swallowed up by the dust. There was no point in trying to catch her, she was a much better rider than he.

As the animals poured out from the end of the track, Harold rode back and forth along the western edge, desperately trying to force them south and south-east, coughing and spluttering in the thick dust, hoping against hope that those shells were the last. Just then however, further explosions came from the trees, this time even closer – which convinced him that it was not by chance, the bombardment was moving their way.

His felt sick. First the cowsheds. Now the orange groves. Was this some new maniac master plan to destroy their livelihood? What kind of Ghengis Khan mentality wanted to return everything the arid desert it was before? And if the cows were the target, Ella and he were both in terrible danger. They had to get away but where was she?

Forgetting his sore thighs and painful crotch, Harold slapped the colt on the rump and galloped into the pall of dust in the direction he had last seen her. Cattle lay in pools of blood on the ground, panting their last breaths. Others hobbled along the rows of sorghum, lowing pitifully and dragging shattered limbs. The dust clogged his nostrils and stung his eyes. Harold couldn't think clearly. Barbarism. What kind of distorted minds could perpetrate such evil?

He had covered about fifty yards, when blinding orange flashes seared his eyeballs and the shock wave from three deafening explosions struck him like a giant hammer. The ground seemed to heave, the colt reared on its hind legs and Harold slid down the back, rubbing his thighs raw as he fell in a heap on the ground. When he managed to sit up, the horse had bolted, his right arm was numbed and everything around looked blurred.

Harold started to panic. His eyes. The blast had damaged his sight? He tried to stand up but lost his balance and fell down again. He was going blind. Blind!

Desperately trying tried to calm himself and raised one hand to his eye-brow anticipating open wounds and blood - and realised why everything was blurred, his glasses had gone. Kneeling, he searched on the powdered soil for a few minutes, then gave up. He was wasting time. Ella! Short sighted as he was, he could still manage to make his way about. He must find Ella.

Harold began to run along the rows of green plants. Soon they were green no longer but tattered and scorched brown. A carpet of tiny rust coloured seeds covered the ground as if blown from some huge threshing machine. He stumbled on, past torn scraps of black and white. And red. Past two enormous, black streaked craters, his lungs wheezing and burning and his legs pumping up and down, powered by some force way beyond him - and came upon the chestnut mare.

Ella's horse lay on her side, entrails spilling from a gaping hole, blood draining into the soil. Harold collapsed onto his knees, vomiting and retching until his stomach could convulse no more. Then, forcing himself to get up, he began to search in ever widening circles around the dead horse, his body trembling and his head burning, fearing to discover what might have happened.

Ella lay on her back, hair streaming out as if blown by a powerful fan. Her face was ashen, her legs bunched up and blood soaked. One arm lay across her stomach, the other covered in cuts and scratches was flung out pointing towards the west. And over every part of her lay a layer of fine, white dust.

Harold's knees buckled. He crouched down, gasping for breath and staring into her face, his brain in turmoil. She couldn't be dead, she wasn't gone... she mustn't...

The ground shook as more explosions came from the south where the herd was still running. But with the reverberations, Ella's hand twitched and Harold's heart began to thump and he leaned down and laid his head on her breast. It moved with shallow, irregular breathing. There was a heartbeat, faint but steady. He straightened up and unable to restrain himself, cried out aloud.

'She's alive. She's alive! Ella is alive!' He wanted to laugh. To shout it again and again, as tears ran down his face. But there was no one to hear. Then, just as suddenly, his elation turned to panic. Ella needed help. There was nothing he could do and without proper help she could die just as surely as if the shells had killed her outright.

Harold's throat tightened. He had to do something. Something. He reached out his hand and it hovered over her stomach, moving right, then left but he was scared touch her for fear of doing the wrong thing. He knew from the last manoeuvres that a wounded person shouldn't be moved, that he could disturb the very blood clots that might be saving her life. The hand dropped to his knee, helpless.

Warmth! He suddenly remembered, a casualty should be kept warm. It was still early afternoon, but the sun was pale through the dust haze and the sea breeze was quite fresh. Gently, he moved the outstretched arm to her side and taking off his shirt, laid it over her chest and shoulders.

He felt her hand. It was cold. The shirt wasn't enough, he must find something more. The horse! Ella usually slipped an old blanket under the saddle. Running back to the mare, Harold had to look away as he eased out the bloodstained threadbare cloth. Hurrying back, he spread it over the lower half then felt her forehead. It was feverish. Tearing a strip from the shirt, he moistened it with his mouth, held it in the breeze, then lay it across her brow.

Smoothing Ella's hair around her face, Harold then sat back on his heels. The dust settled over her face again like a death mask. He had to get help. He thought of running back to the kibbutz then realised that he could not leave her out here, alone. But he had to so something. Oh God! Something!

Sitting back on his heels he closed his eyes, desperately thinking what he could do and all the time murmuring to himself, 'Ella, it will be okay. Just hang on. It will be okay... Please.'

Suddenly everything seemed so quiet. No more shells fell nearby though machine gun fire still rattled in the distance as well as an occasional detonation, but that too seemed far away. He looked up towards the kibbutz. No more shells seemed to have landed there either, thank God. And surely someone would be looking out for them?

A scuffling sound made him look round. About five yards away, two calves wandered between the rows of sorghum. One, with long red streaks down its flank, stopped every few paces to reach round and lick its wounds. The other waited until it moved on, then followed, the two of them wandering like lost children across the scorched fields.

In the stillness, Harold wondered how long they had been out here. An hour? Two hours? Both their watches had been left hanging in the dairy from when they washed down. The sun had begun to dip. It must be around three o'clock.

He looked towards the orange groves. Cypress trees lay strewn on the ground as if felled by some giant lumberjack. Others stood stripped of foliage, like poplars in winter. And as the dust blew away with the sea breeze, all across the fields he could see black and white patches of cattle lying dead and dying, some trying to pull themselves along by their forelegs, wheezing and gasping.

He glanced up towards the ridge to the west. The nearby Egyptian positions were silent too. Nothing moved and columns of oily smoke rose into the haze. He looked down at Ella. They had come to bring life to this desert, now all he could see was devastation and death.

He looked up to the kibbutz again. Again, nothing stirred there but someone had to see them. They must. With what seemed to be a huge effort, he stood up and began to wave with both arms, screaming and shouting even though he knew that he was well out of earshot, perhaps some trick of the wind would carry his voice. But soon his head began to spin from the effort and he sank down again.

Just then, he heard a clinking sound to his right. It was the black colt, reins trailing in the dust and pulling at the chains of the bit. Harold's stomach turned as it limped towards him.

'Here boy. Come boy,' he called softly, *'Boh Hamud. Boh. Come sweetie. Come.'* Perhaps it was a sign, an omen. If that poor beast had survived all the carnage and destruction, he tried to convince himself, then Ella was destined to survive too.

The young horse came close and nuzzled its black head against his thigh. Harold patted the sweat-lathered neck as he looked down at Ella. Her breathing had grown more irregular. He put his ear to her breast again. The heartbeats were growing fainter but the blood on her trousers was still thick and sticky. If only the clots would hold. Tears welled into his eyes.

'Please, Ella,' he sobbed, 'Please don't die. Ella. Please. Someone will come soon. Someone will come, I know.' She probably couldn't hear, but he had to say it. For himself he had to say it...

Taking a deep breath, Harold forced himself to stand again. With the last reserves of strength left in him, he waved both arms in a crazy semaphore and, when his left arm became too painful, continuing with his right alone, back and forth, back and forth, until he could no longer. Then he sank down to his knees again, sweat soaked hair matted to his scalp, red-rimmed eyes peering through a mask of dust. There was nothing more he could do. Resting his forehead on his knees, Harold closed his eyes, exhausted.

After the two explosions in the courtyard, Gavriel had crouched with the other two in his emplacement and waited for more, his body trembling. The three-inch mortar bombs in his dugout were useless against long range shelling. But the next shell-bursts were further away. Surprised, he raised his head then saw the smoke and dust rising from the orange groves.

'Traversed the wrong way,' he muttered to Yoske, 'luckily for us.' But when the next salvo landed along the track through the groves, he realised that it must be deliberate. The orange flashes came from the midst of the dust raised by the herd and, a minute later, more from the end of the track.

'The bastards,' he snapped. 'Can't be! They're shelling the cattle!'

As the herd spread out into the fields, with the shelling following he felt sick and angry at his impotence. The prize herd was being cut down in front of his eyes, and there was nothing he could do about it. Their own mortar could barely reach the border and those six-inch mortars were well beyond range. And Ella and Harold were out there as well but he couldn't see them. Perhaps they were hidden by the dust haze?

'I hope they've taken shelter somewhere,' he murmured.

'Perhaps they're on their way back,' said Stan.

Gavriel was the eternal optimist but as the minutes passed and there was no sign of either of them, he became more and more concerned. Why hadn't they ridden to where they could at least signal back?

Some ten minutes later, there was a lull in the shelling.

'Probably realised their mistake, the Egyptians,' Stan grunted. 'Wait for it. They'll be back on us.' The words had hardly left his mouth when two shells landed between the main gate and the tractor shed. The three men huddled down in the bottom of the dugout again, bracing themselves. But those two shells were the last. Israeli return fire had silenced the heavy batteries in their sector.

After waiting another five minutes, Gavriel stood up on the sandbag parapet again and looked out over the plain. The dust had begun to disperse and for nearly half an hour, frantically he scanned plain, the shadows along the windbreaks and the gulleys in the nearby fields. Nothing, except patches of black and white amongst the sorghum.

Then, he saw it. A movement. About a mile away a lone horse was aimlessly moving across the sorghum fields, every few yards stopping for a few seconds before moving on.

'Look, Yoske,' Gavriel shouted. 'See that. There!' Yoske jumped up to join him.

'Walks lame. Must be wounded,' said Yoske and Gavriel grew even more worried. Whose horse? A moment later, he slapped Yoske's arm.

'There. Look there.' Where the horse had come to a halt, a figure had risen and was waving with both arms. Then with one arm.

'Harold,' Gavriel shouted, 'looks like Harold. But where's Ella?'

Both he and Yoske started to wave back, shouting and calling. Then stopped. At that distance, the wind would carry their voices to the east and with the trees in shade behind them, Harold would have a job seeing them. Leaping over the sandbags, Gavriel hurtled down the track past the dining hall and ran across the courtyard towards the armoury. No time to waste.

'Uri. Uri,' he puffed. 'Quick. It's Harold. And Ella. Out in the sorghum.'

Uri looked up from the deep slit trench. Thirty yards to his right, two small craters were still smoking, one on the remains of the laundry, the other by the shower block. All the glass had been blown out of the dining hall windows

'Get down. Get down Gabi. Headquarters haven't given the All Clear yet.'

Gavriel crouched by the lip of the trench, heaving and panting, his face flushed and agitated.

'To hell with headquarters,' he gasped. 'Damn the All Clear. It's Harold. Waving for help from the sorghum. I can't see Ella.' He stood up and lowered his voice, 'and there's only one horse.'

Uri had never seen Gavriel like this, almost threatening with the violence of his outburst. But he was right, Ella and Harold were more important.

'Okay. Come on,' he said climbing out of the trench. 'Luckily Meir has just come back with the jeep.'

A few minutes later, with Meir and Reuven, Gavriel sped out of the rear gate, negotiating the craters and fallen trees on the track through the orange groves and out to the fields, engine racing, wheels bumping over the rows of sorghum towards the motionless horse with the forlorn figure hunched beside it.

Harold heard the roar of the engine and looked up almost in disbelief. He saw Gavriel jump out, then Reuven and Meir with the stretcher. As he heard them call his name, he turned and pointed at Ella, then everything went black and he fell forward onto the scorched, parched earth.

23.

As suddenly as it had begun, so the fighting ended. The breeze dropped, the sun dipped beyond the ridge and set into the sea, silence returned to the plain. Darkness clothed the mountains of Hebron. The first stars appeared and the last grey light silvered a leaden sea, leaving the evening to anguish and to pain, to count its sorrows and salve the wounds.

Kibbutzim along the border tried to assess their losses, wondering what daylight would reveal. Out in the plain, jackals howled as they fought amongst the carcasses. Along the tree-lined boulevards of Tel Aviv, cafes were hushed as *Kol Yisrael* radio broadcast details of casualties and damage. The dairy herd merited one short phrase. Then the report ended. And the music resumed.

In the last hour of daylight, lieutenant Dani had resumed his search. The day's fierce engagement had not distracted him from his purpose. For Avi, for Orna and the baby, he would catch every one of those murderers, make sure they could never do it again.

Leaving the command car in the rear, he took his patrol slowly along the bed of the wadi. In the thicket, they found Fais, comatose but still with a faint pulse. Dani radioed back for a stretcher party. Thirty yards on, they found the body of Mahmud. Then that of Ismail.

Carefully, he searched further down. Nothing. They'd seen the fourth one fall, but he couldn't proceed further. Strict orders had been given not to approach the Egyptian positions. Picking up the two bodies and their weapons, the patrol made their way back. Tomorrow, he would continue the search.

Ahmed heard the distant footfalls on the gravel then muffled voices echoing from the high banks. It was almost dark and very quiet. The border must be less than fifty metres away and he prayed that they would not come this far.

All that afternoon, with the sounds of battle in his ears, he had slithered and crawled painfully over the stones and tangled roots, powered by a conviction that he would survive, to continue the struggle - and to spare his mother and father the grief that Abu Salah would now feel for Ismail.

He lay motionless behind a boulder, his teeth biting tightly together but gradually the voices grew softer and the footsteps vanished.

'*Ya Ismail*', he whispered, 'now indeed I must have your luck.'

Slowly, Ahmed edged forward, then stopped, his heart thumping. A huge, black and white shape loomed out of the semi-darkness. He waited, holding his breath but it didn't move. Cautiously, he crawled closer. It was a dead cow lying at the foot of an overhang, the kind the Israeli's kept. He guessed it had been killed in the exchange of fire but he wondered how it had got out there.

In the massive head, a bulging eye glinted in the last glimmer of light from the west, staring at him as he crawled past. The stench from blood and its burst stomach made him want to vomit. Somehow he managed to control himself, but the smell clung to him long after he'd left he caracass behind.

Where the wadi cleaved through the ridge, the river-bed was blocked with barbed wire entanglements. There could be mines there as well and Ahmed knew he would need the help of the Egyptian sentries to get him through. He waited until it was completely dark, then with his good arm he clapped a stone three times against the pebbles.

'*Min Hada*!' A voice called high from above as the sharp

clack split the silence. 'Who goes there?'

Ahmed raised himself on his elbow.

'*Fedai. Fedai*. Don't shoot,' he shouted, '*Fedai*.'

A narrow torch beam sliced the darkness. He heard voices. As they approached, he shouted the password that Ismail had gleaned from a sympathetic intelligence officer. More voices sounded above, this time closer. Boots scuffed down the slope and hands grasped him under the armpits. Ahmed gasped and fought not to scream as the pain knifed through his right shoulder. But he was safe. And knowing that made him bear it.

As they strapped him to a stretcher and pulled him through the wire, Ahmed felt a strange sensation of weightlessness, as though he was turning round like a leaf on deep still water. The stench from the dead cow seemed still to be with him but as he turned his head towards his shoulder, it grew stronger. It was the smell of gangrene - coming from his own wounds.

Exhaustion dulled his panic and his eyes began to close. The last thing he remembered was the half moon climbing in the sky. And the pale glow from the white sandstone beneath.

In the first-aid bunker, Harold had lost all sense of time when he woke and slowly sat up on the narrow bed. He stared at the whitewashed wall, dimly lit by two oil lamps, the power lines had been blown down. In one corner sat Reuven, head down and silent as he wound up some dressings. Beside him, Shosh was writing notes on a pad. She looked up and nodded..

'Ella is in hospital,' she said as she leaned across and handed him a cup of water. 'She'll be well looked after.' Harold glanced up. Her eyes were wet and red-rimmed and he surmised that it was because of Ella. Taking a few sips, he handed back the cup then lay down again and closed his eyes. It wasn't until later, when Reuven saw him back to his room, that he found out why...

Some thirty miles across the plain and cloaked in a white sheet, Itzik's body lay where he'd always wanted to be, close to Ella. Just a few feet and a thick wall separated him from the underground operating theatre of Beer Sheba hospital where a team of surgeons was fighting to save her life.

With the power lines down, the kibbutz was in darkness. Back in his room, as Harold blew out the candle and lay back in bed, the full horror of the day struck home, Itzik was no more, Ella was hovering between life and death and the dairy herd had been decimated.

Images from the day churned through his head, stirring up the morbid thoughts that returned to plague him often at night, was his struggle to continue was worth all the suffering, all the uncertainty? Soon however, despite his mind still in turmoil, exhausted by the day he fell into a deep sleep.

A tractor working in the courtyard woke him next morning. Harold threw open the shutters. Bright sunlight glared outside. He didn't know the time, his watch was still down in the dairy - if that was still standing.

The cold water at the veranda tap felt good and the long night's sleep had refreshed him. Shosh's pain-killer tablets must have knocked him out. But the bandage around his elbow and the general stiffness, reminded him of that fall from the colt and he walked awkwardly across the courtyard, his thighs still chafing.

Where the laundry had stood, a front-loader tractor was filling in a crater. Scorched clothing was strewn across the sand. Everywhere, cables hung from power and telephone poles. On the far side of the courtyard, a second crater gaped by the shattered front wall of the shower block. Five months to build, two seconds to destroy. Was it only the day before that Ella had had gone there to rest after breakfast? At the dining hall, a workman was removing what glass remained in the windows. Everywhere he looked, debris and destruction.

Harold hurried on, every movement and action from the moment he'd woken driven by a determination to get to the hospital in Beer Sheba. Shosh could have telephoned for him to find out, but he wanted to see Ella for himself, a desire to be with her and a compulsion he had never felt before, for anyone. A conviction that his being there would ensure her recovery.

In the dining hall, the clock showed seven fifteen. The cooks were preparing breakfast over paraffin stoves. Nodding 'good-morning', Harold put a few slices of bread, a hard boiled egg and two small cucumbers into his khaki haversack and hurried out.

In the porch, all the notices had been removed. Just one small, black-bordered page was pinned to the board. Itzik's funeral would be at three that afternoon, the heat of the Holy Land didn't allow for lying in state. Harold made a rapid calculation as he hurried down the track to the road. It would be tight, but he must try to be back in time.

By the eucalyptus trees, he glanced to his right. Jagged outlines and gaping holes showed in the cowshed roofs. Shouts of workers came up as they started on repairs. He wondered how many of the cows had managed to survive, but his mind couldn't take in any more. Quickening his pace, he strode out onto the road.

At the junction with the 'Hunger Road', built by the drought–stricken Bedouin for the British Army in the Thirties, Harold hitched a lorry from a neighbouring kibbutz. They travelled in silence broken only by the throb of the heavy diesel engine, neither wanting to talk about the previous day. Luckily, the truck was taking eggs to Beer Sheba and by mid morning, he was there.

Inside the new hospital, Harold felt awkward and out of place in the cool, pristinely white lobby - a real *'shlumper'* in his faded navy zip-up jacket and dusty sandals.

'Her situation is stable,' said the sister who came out to see him, 'but she can't receive visitors yet, I'm afraid.'

'I know,' Harold said softly, 'I know the rules.' He took off his glasses and wiped them, thankful that he'd had a spare set in his wardrobe. 'But I've come in specially,' adding without thinking, 'we were together, yesterday, you know. When the jeep picked her up.'

The sister sucked in her breath and clasped her hands, suddenly realising that this small, quiet man had been the one who had stayed by her. Probably saved her life. Suddenly, she felt quite humble - and embarrassed.

'Well. Er. One moment. I'll see if you can have just a few minutes.'

Alone again in the ante-room, Harold wondered whether he should have come. The hospital must have its hands full without having to deal with him. Perhaps it was better not to see her so soon. And for a moment, he became scared of what he might find. But as he shifted his weight from one leg to the other, the desire to be with her made him impatient, the seconds ticking away with the jerking red hand on the electric clock over the doorway.

The double doors opened, the sister's head poked through and he followed her to the far end of a small ward where a white screen was drawn around the bed. As they approached, a nurse came out carrying an empty plasma bottle. The sister put one finger to her lips.

'Just a few minutes, please,' and padded away down the ward.

Harold slipped through the curtains. Ella's small, round face was all he could see above the sheets, her lips and cheeks almost as pale as the pillow and her auburn hair matted against her forehead. Slips of white gauze were stuck to the side of her jaw and taped onto on her cheek. Alongside, drips hung on bright steel frames and a thin plastic tube disappeared into one nostril.

Harold eyes followed the contours of her small frame and her arms under the sheet down the bed, then stopped halfway. He clenched his fists, feeling he had been punched in the stomach and closed his eyes. Tears seeped through his eyelids as he remembered the blood-soaked trousers in the dust, desperately hoping that what he'd seen wasn't really there, that when he opened them again, it wouldn't be. But when he forced himself to open them, his worst fears were confirmed. Further down one side of the bed, the sheet lay flat on the mattress. Ella's life had been saved - at the cost of her leg.

His stomach heaved, but at the very moment he thought he would be sick, her eyelids flickered and as if she felt his presence there, her lips twitched in what could have been the trace of a smile – or was it just his imagination? Then, her eyes firmly closed she relaxed again, breathing silently.

A nurse came up and touched his shoulder. Without a word, Harold turned and walked down the ward, his eyes blurred, seeing nothing until he was outside in the hot, dusty street.

He stood for a moment, wiping his eyes on his shirt-sleeve before heading for the bus station through the broad gridwork of duty streets laid out for the Turks by German engineers at the turn of the century.

Cars, carts and people passed him but he saw nothing except the white sheet where it lay flat on the bed. He hadn't known what to expect, but he was still trembling. She was lucky to be alive, the sister said. But was she? With such deformity? And as the soul-searchings and doubts mingled with his own feelings, Harold became even more confused and disconsolate.

On the way home, Harold was hardly conscious of the crowded bus. Automatically he got down at the junction with the Hunger Road. Still in a daze, he waited for a lift. Luckily, there was much military traffic and soon he was speeding down the narrow road at the army driver's usual breakneck speed, the army suffered more road casualties than those killed in action.

Over the roar of the engine, came sharp reports of gunfire from the plain to his right. Puffs of smoke showed where Israeli self-propelled guns were in action. Harold wondered if fighting had broken out again.

At the turn off to the kibbutz, he jumped down and thanked the driver. As he did so, the soldier sitting alongside looked him straight in the face and their eyes met in instant recognition. It was the young Algerian immigrant with whom he'd argued only the other night.

'Hey. Kibbutznik,' the man half-smiled, 'treat them like human beings, eh? So much for your brotherly love for the Arab boy!'

Harold didn't bother to respond. What could he respond? That he hadn't changed his basic beliefs? That he wouldn't let his grief turn to hatred? He just shrugged and said nothing. As he turned to walk away, the young soldier opened his mouth to add something but the driver dug him in the ribs.

'Stuff it, you idiot!' he hissed. 'Didn't you hear what happened to that girl?' But as he engaged gear and drew away, the soldier shouted.

'Never mind. Hear those guns? We'll plaster them so hard, they'll never dare do it again!'

Harold walked slowly up the side road, hoping for another lift, his head swimming and his sore thighs prickling from all the walking. From all around came the booming of the heavy guns and distant thuds from the north-west where, beyond the ridge, smoke rose over Gaza.

'Revenge. Revenge,' boomed the guns. 'Revenge,' shrieked the shells as they flew over the Bedouin tents and fields and down into the centre of Gaza. It was market day. An eye for an eye, a tooth for a tooth.

'Blood into blood and under blood to lie . . ,' murmured Harold as he walked, the sun beating on his head. Would all the casualties over there prevent Itzik from being buried that afternoon? Would all the blood now being spilt bring back even one toe of Ella's leg. And would all the slaughtered goats and sheep over there restore the dairy herd to its former glory?

Harold thought again of the young soldier. Could they just sit on their hands and do nothing? His throat was dry and his head spun from the contradictions to which he had no simple answer.

A tractor turned out from the maize fields on its way back to the kibbutz, everyone was finishing work early. Harold climbed up and sat on the mudguard. He would just make it in time for the funeral.

24.

Ibrahim sat outside his hut looking through the vine-covered trellis to the sea. He saw neither the green leaves nor the deep blue of the water as he stared into space, waiting. Waiting for his wife to return.

Jamilla had gone to Gaza, to the market. Everyone would be there, she said. It was the best place to find out what had happened yesterday, to know if Ahmed or his friends had been involved. Ibrahim looked up at the sun. It was past noon, she should be back very soon. He wished she were here now.

Just two months ago, Abu Salah came to congratulate them. Ahmed had been chosen for an active unit of the Fedayeen at Beit Hanun. Ibrahim should be proud, he said, he and Jamilla. Their son was fighting for his people's honour. For their land, *Insh'Allah*.

Jamilla thanked them as she handed round small cups of Turkish coffee, accepting their good wishes. But why should their son be the one to put his life in danger, she asked when they'd gone. Ibrahim couldn't answer.

Last night, after the gunfire and the Egyptian army ambulances hurrying back and forth along the nearby roads, she'd grown anxious. Said she felt something, how Ahmed hardly talked on his last visit, had hugged them both for so long when he said goodbye - even kissed her hair.

After he had left, she and Ibrahim sat outside the hut in the darkness, around them the flickering oil lights from the nearby huts and the lamps of the fishermen bobbing out on the sea. She remembered that long goodbye, wondering at the time why

Ahmed was more tense than usual. She'd seen it in his eyes but tried to hide her own anxiety from him.

To her, Ahmed would always be the baby, the youngest of her children, his large brown eyes always wondering and questioning like he did as a child. She always felt the other two would manage, but Ahmed – for him she was always worried. And now all that fighting yesterday, it might just be a co-incidence, but...

Ibrahim told her not to worry, the Fedayeen didn't have cannons, only the Egyptian army had been involved. It didn't help to calm her. She knew that the Fedayeen never released names of casualties until long after. And as they went in to go to sleep, she told him she would go to town and find out for herself.

The breeze rustled the vine leaves. Ibrahim turned his head and looked along the rows of tin shacks and tents. Abu Salah used to boast back in the village how they would drive the *Yahud* into the sea. Now he, Abu Salah and all the rest of the village were only a few yards from being thrown into the sea themselves.

No. It was like he always said: War is War. And whoever wins, we the *felaheen*, the peasants, are always the losers. He tried to explain that to Ahmed, but the boy had his own ideas. *Ma'alesh*. So be it. He had hoped that Ahmed would come to visit them soon. Now he was just hoping that Jamilla would return quickly.

It was now midday, the sea breeze beginning to blow stronger and the refugee camp still and quiet with the men out working – or looking for it. Suddenly the ground trembled as huge explosions came from the direction of Gaza. Ibrahim jumped up and turned round. Two columns of smoke rose to the east.

Holding up his long cloak with one hand, he climbed the slope to the top of the dune, the wind blowing sand against his ankles. Flames and smoke mushroomed into a thick, crimson-bellied black cloud that spread high into the sky over the town. And from that moment, explosion followed explosion in a continuous roll of thunder.

Ibrahim stood and stared. The Israeli's were shelling Gaza yet not a single gun was firing in reply. So much for the Egyptian 'victory'. So much for the bragging from *'Saut Al Arab'* Cairo radio last night. After a while, his hand shaking, Ibrahim took out his old brass watch. It was gone one o'clock. The blood throbbed in his temples, his wife should have left the market over an hour ago. She must have. But if she didn't get back soon, he would go out and look for her himself.

Jamilla had set off early, wanting to be there and back before the midday heat. It was a good hour's walk into Gaza and she was not as strong as she used to be. Ibrahim didn't want her to go. The town would be crowded and dusty, he said, bad for her lungs, already weakened by the damp air through the thin walls of their hut. But she had to go, she said. Had to find out if Ahmed had been in the fighting yesterday.

Ibrahim had tried to make out that he wasn't worried. He never admitted he was worried, though he worried all the time about his children. Worried and sad. Saddened as his hopes of leading them all back to the village before he died faded with every day passing. He still talked as though they would return, but Jamilla sensed that deep within he had already despaired.

In the village, he'd been the *Mukhtar*, his word as good as law. Here, in the camp, who cared who was *mukhtar*, who was *mu'alam*, the wise one. Those growing up respected no one. Sought only to make a few piastres, to squeeze more rations from the UNWRRA stores. The boys hung around with nothing to do all day, the girls with faces uncovered and skirts up to their knees. Everything was falling apart.

Jamilla too was thinking about their children as she walked down the road to Gaza, her long black dress flapping about her ankles. Hussein was a teacher in Kuwait. He would stay there with his Jordanian wife. Grandchildren, she had never seen, only photographs. Mona, their daughter was married to a clerk at the UNWRRA offices in Jabaliyya, her husband a refugee from a village she'd never even heard of. And now Ahmed, the youngest – gone to be a fighter.

As she entered the town, Jamilla turned into the vegetable market. Barefooted urchins ran between the canvas-covered stalls trying to snatch fruit. Loaded donkeys and men bent double under huge sacks pushed between crowds haggling with the stallholders. Smells of cardamom and cumin. Just like any other market day - except for the knots of agitated young men on the street corners, arms waving, hands pointing towards the border.

Jamilla edged close to a small group sitting outside a bar.

'*Ya'allah*. Hundreds of *Yahud*, they killed yesterday,' one was saying.

'Ha! The *Jish* gave them a real pasting,' said another. 'Fifty tanks destroyed at least.'

She hurried away. It was the bragging of the ignorant, she could hear that any day. Real news would only come in hints and whispers.

Jamilla walked on through the alleyways, observing and listening. Outside a coffee house in the Goldsmiths Alley, two men in light grey suits played with amber worry beads as they talked. Jamilla set down her basket and fumbled inside, as though she was searching for something.

'Covering the retreat of a small group. Near Abassan,' one was saying.

'Mmm. A new policy, you think?' said the other.

'Who knows? About time the Egyptians took a real stand.'

Just then, an onion slipped from her hand and rolled between their legs.

'*Rukh. Rukh,*' they snorted. 'Off with you, stupid woman.'

Over the next two hours, Jamilla went purposefully back and forth through the narrow streets. Between buying four large radishes, some flour and a small bag of chickpeas, she gleaned scraps of information. The 'group', were Fedayeen. Some had been killed, others rescued. Israeli villages had been shelled. Many Egyptians killed and wounded. Everything was fitting into a picture that served only to increase her anxiety. Who had been saved? Who had died? She had to know.

Jamilla left the market and began to make her way back to the road to the sea-shore. It had taken longer than she'd intended and she knew Ibrahim would be anxious – but at least she'd found out something. That afternoon, she would make Ibrahim go to the camp at Beit Hanun. He was a father. Still a *mukhtar.* They would tell him if it was Ahmed. If he had been wounded. Or if... No. She didn't want to think any more. She would pray that he was safe. Her son. Her baby. Just a boy still.

The sun was high as it crept towards midday and the heat radiated from the stone and mud walls. In the shade of an overhanging bougainvillaea, Jamilla rested for a few minutes, chewing on one of the radishes. The purple flowers glowed in the sunlight, so lovely, so peaceful. Yes, her search took longer than she expected but she couldn't understand everyone's complacency. It wouldn't stay that way. The Israeli's were sure to retaliate, probably that same night, like at Khan Yunis. Yet no one seemed concerned or taking precautions.

Her eyes were heavy and for a while she dozed. People passed by as though she wasn't there, just another old refugee woman from the camps. A camel passing by snorted and woke her. She sipped water from a green plastic bottle in her basket, then rose and re-tied her white *keffieh*. It was past midday, Ibrahim would be waiting.

As she bent down to pick up her basket, two huge explosions came from the centre of the town, then two more at the end of the street. Panic-stricken stallholders and shoppers rushed past, knocking her to the ground while braying donkeys scattered their loads over the roadway.

Struggling to her feet, Jamilla joined the mad stampede to get out of the town. Just then, the road in front of her erupted as if it were a volcano. When the smoke cleared, she lay blood-stained and twisted, together with five others. A donkey dragged itself past, wheezing its last breaths as the shells fell everywhere filling the ancient town with fire and death and destruction.

The gunfire continued to echo over the sandhills and across the plain as Harold walked through the main gate and up the track to the dining hall. He couldn't bring himself to go down to look at the cowsheds, or to collect his watch even though miraculously the milking parlour had escaped with just the windows shattered.

While he'd been away, all that morning neighbouring settlements had joined with jeeps and horsemen to comb the fields and wadis, rounding up what remained of the prize herd. By lunchtime, the survivors had been corralled in the old cowshed. The other two sheds along with the calf pens had been too severely damaged.

Menasheh had called and was patching up whatever he could. Others had to be put out of their misery, ending up in the huge pit that bulldozers had dug in the sorghum fields.

Harold went straight to the dining hall. He hadn't eaten since early that morning. There were only leftovers and cold tea but he didn't notice, his taste buds were dead, Everything seemed surreal as if he was floating as in a dream. But the booming guns and the echoes from across the border told him otherwise.

He leaned forward and laid his head on the table, trying not to think of the pale face on the white pillow. Of Itzik being no more. Then, as feet began to tramp past outside the window, Harold rose and went out to join the cortege up the dusty track towards the graveyard.

From below, smoke and stench rose from the pyre of hundreds of chickens in a trench beyond the poultry houses. Death, thought Harold, death everywhere, as they wound past the water tower and the clinic, through a gap in the fence and on through the young cypress and casuarina trees around the tiny graveyard. Only two others lay there, Shlomo's mother who had reached a natural end, and one small stone for Aliza's baby, stillborn the year before.

Soon, the whole kibbutz, together with settlers from surrounding villages, people from Itzik's home town and army comrades, were gathered in a huge circle many deep around the pit in the sandy ground. It parted as an army command-car slowly drove in, four soldiers on either side of the plain deal coffin.

In the front seat, leaning against Shosh's shoulder, sat a small hunched figure, white stubble on his face, Itzik's father. The mother was too ill to come. Harold thought how strange that this tiny man had fathered the huge, blond hulk of his son. The son that was now being laid across the two timber beams over the grave.

As well as Dudik, the area commander, there were at least four top brass, which meant that it had to be also a religious funeral, the result of coalition blackmail by the right-wing religious parties. Mercifully, it was brief and as the army chaplain stood back, Gavriel stepped forward.

Gavriel hadn't prepared a speech. He just wanted to say what he felt, what they all felt. But for a full minute, he stood silent, trying to control the pent up feelings and not to burst into tears.

He stared at the boards of the coffin lid, talking softly and addressing Itzik in the second person as though was standing there, telling of the first days of the kibbutz, how they'd had built up the herd together, the plans they had for the future and the void there would be in everyone's lives now that he had gone. And all the while he spoke, through the hushed silence around the circle, the sea breeze bore the distant thunder of the bombardment on Gaza.

When he finished, Gavriel stepped back, his eyes wet and his throat dry. Only now did the full impact of Itzik's death seem to hit him. Only now, was it for real, that they would never again work together, argue over new ideas and methods, laugh at Menasheh's quirks, be careful not to mention whatever it was with Ella. And then, he thought of her too. What would become of Ella?

As the soldiers raised their guns for the salute, four men went forward to pick up the ropes. But as they took the strain, the hunched figure suddenly straightened and shot forward from the car, throwing himself on the coffin.

'Yitzchak. Yitzchak,' he cried, scraping his nails on the wooden planks, 'You're not going. You can't be. You mustn't leave me... Your mother... Yitzchak. Yitzchak!'

Shosh ran after him and took his shoulders. The old man turned and fell against her.

'Yitzchak. Yitzchak!' the father cried, then tore himself away and flung himself on the coffin lid again, 'for this I brought you into the world? For this we came to our own homeland? Why you? Why you? God in heaven, why? Why? Why?' while all around people were crying, even Dudik, the veteran military figure taking off his beret to wipe the tears that flowed unashamedly down his cheeks.

For a while, no one moved as the old man lay on the box, clutching at the lid and sobbing out his grief, ever and ever quieter, until he was still, crying softly. Dov and Uri came forward and together with Shosh helped the old man back to the command car. He sat without movement, chin on his chest, eyes closed, tears streaming down his stubbly cheeks.

The soldiers raised their rifles again and as the box disappeared into the grave, three volleys rang out over the young trees, over the shattered cowshed roofs and across the scorched sorghum fields, then echoed away into the parched plain beyond.

Gavriel, Uri, Stan and Yoske took up the shovels and began to fill the grave as the command car drove slowly away. Everyone followed. Except Shosh. And when they had finished and gone down, she sat by the heap of earth, her arms clasped tightly around her, weeping softly into the dry soil.

Down in the kibbutz, people sat in small groups on the verandas. Silent. It had all been said. From the west, came the continued muffled thuds of explosions from Gaza.

For two hours, shells rained down upon the town. Then, as suddenly as it had began, the bombardment ceased. Survivors crept out from cellars and from under ruined houses, dazed and covered in dust and dirt, trying to understand what had happened and why. And over the next few hours, carts and lorries carried the dead to the gardens around the hospital, where they were laid out, waiting for relatives to come and find them.

While women wailed and prepared for the funerals, the young men gathered in the Liberation square, shaking their fists towards the east, swearing revenge. Calling for blood. Blood and more blood. The sands of the desert cried out for water, instead they were slaked with blood.

Ibrahim had seen the fire and smoke, heard the detonations, saw the shocked and smoke-rimmed-eyed who had run all the way from Gaza. He asked if they had seen Jamilla, wanting to believe that she had already left the town, had taken shelter or stopped to rest on the way. A thousand explanations for why she might not have yet returned. And as soon as the shelling ceased, he decided to go and look for her.

Letting their neighbours know in case she returned, Ibrahim headed out across the dunes, to avoid the army roadblocks that were bound to be around the town by now. As he entered Gaza, he grew even more anxious. Whole buildings had been destroyed. Everywhere, roofs were shattered and glass was strewn on the roads. Worse than he'd ever imagined. And the nearer he came to the market, the more he grew fearful, each crater, each patch of blood on the road making him more and more frantic.

By the time he was directed to the hospital by a policeman, the shadows were long and dark. Head bent, Ibrahim crossed the stretch of waste ground towards the cypress trees. In the space of two sunsets, he had lost his wife and perhaps, his son. It was as he had always said: Whoever wins, it is we, the *felaheen* who lose.

25.

Major Salim stood back and saluted. Two soldiers closed up the tailboard and the lorry drew away to begin its long drive to Rafiah then across the Sinai desert to Egypt. Lieutenant Faras was taking his last journey home.

The narrow tarmac road ran between shallow ditches and prickly pear hedges, over which peeped corrugated iron roofs of the mud-huts beyond. Along the roadside, eucalyptus trees hung limp in the midday heat. From the north, came the thunder of the bombardment.

As he walked in through the gateway, the major saw the smoke billowing in the clear sky. He knew it was market day and Gaza town would be crowded. But there was nothing he could do. Nor anyone else. Any artillery that had not been put out of action was being held in reserve in anticipation of an Israeli reprisal raid.

During the battle yesterday, Lieutenant Faras had come along to see him and the artillery spotter. He'd wanted to know why the gunfire had switched away from the dust cloud. Unknown to either of them, the positions further south had seen that it was cattle breaking from the dust and radioed direct to the batteries. The major hurried away to the signals post to contact headquarters and ask why. Five seconds later, his observation post, with Faras still in it, had been destroyed by a direct hit.

The artilleryman had been buried at Khan Yunis that morning. The lieutenant's family had 'made arrangements' for Faras's body to be brought back to Alexandria.

Major Salim couldn't help seeing the irony. Both he and Faras had fought against the bribery and corruption in the army, but money and influence could still 'arrange' anything. Yet he was not sorry. Faras was a fine officer and a friend. He would deeply miss him. Returning salute to the sentry as he passed, the major left the small group of officers who had been with him and strode across the square to his office.

Throwing his cap onto the chair, the he sat at the desk and took out a large notebook. The facts were grim, without gaining any real advantage, the army had lost men and much equipment, he must put in his own report immediately.

There were many at headquarters who would lay the entire blame at his feet and lose no time to settle old scores. His efforts to extricate the Fedayeen would be ignored. It was some consolation that one had reached safety and was in hospital in Beit Hanun

As his pen scratched across the paper, the shelling continued. The major looked through the small window. Smoke was rising higher and higher over the town.

'Never mind,' he muttered to himself, 'go in peace Faras. We shall avenge you yet. One day, we shall show them.'

Major Salim felt weary. Sitting back, he closed his eyes for a moment. Yellow lights shot across the blackness and through them he saw a fleet of assault craft, Egyptian commandos leaping ashore to storm the trenches, the green, white and black flag over Israeli positions. Soldiers cheering. The major opened his eyes. 'Yes. One day, soon,' he murmured, 'we shall show them.' Taking up his pen again he continued writing his report. Through the window, the smoke thickened and shadows began to lengthen.

Gavriel and Harold changed into working clothes as soon as most of the guests had gone. As they made their way down the track, the sounds of gunfire suddenly ceased, leaving a strange silence.

They stopped by the eucalyptus trees and stared. Gaping holes showed in the roofs of the cowsheds and a tangle of steel rails and tubing was all that was left of the calf pens. Gavriel shivered. What a slaughter there would have been if Itzik hadn't had the foresight.

Itzik! He couldn't imagine the dairy herd without him. Slowly, despite his not wanting to accept it, the loss was sinking in.

A cowman from neighbouring Tel Kerem had come over to help and as the first cows plodded into the collecting yard, Gavriel nodded.

'We'll take it slowly. *Le'at. Le'at*,' he said. 'See how they shape up.'

Harold gently slapped one of the cows.

'They'll get over it sooner than us.'

At any other time, Gavriel would have accepted it as his sense of humour. Not today. He ducked under the rails and went in to switch on the compressors. The electric cables were down, but a kibbutz up north had loaned them a mobile generator. The rest of the kibbutz was still without power.

In the milking parlour, Harold watched the first cows enter, licking the rails, ears twitching, nervous and hesitant.

'Better take only two at a time each side,' shouted Gavriel as he came through, 'the generator may not take all the machines going at once.'

Harold waved acknowledgement and swung the lever to close them in. Two cows had deep scratches painted over with Gentian violet. Another was trying to lick the remains of Menasheh's dressing off its stomach. It seemed more like a casualty station than a dairy.

Carefully, they fitted the milking cups. One set was kicked off immediately, but the cow settled at the second attempt. Hardly daring to speak, the three men waited. The rubber hoses quivered and jerked. Milk began to froth into the glass containers, rising steadily higher and higher. And they relaxed.

Two from the next batch were more difficult, heavy milkers, their udders swollen and tender from not being milked for a whole day and now taking twice as long. But eventually they too went on their way and gradually the routine took over.

Gavriel lost count of the patches of gauze, the bandaged forelegs, the red weals on the black and white hides. And when the last cow swung out and down the ramp, there was no real joy. No sense of satisfaction, only a numbness, an emotional exhaustion. Out of the hundred and twenty, only about sixty cows had passed through. The rest were too badly wounded. Or were no more.

Harold leaned back against the concrete stall, watching the last container empty into the milking line. His stomach churned and his head was beginning to ache. He'd been pushing himself to the limit again. But this time he'd take notice of Ella.

'I'd like to go up top, Gabi,' he called across the parlour, 'if that's alright?'

'Sure.' Gavriel squirted the hose onto the ramp. 'Dudick and I can finish off. And Nahum will be down later.' As Harold climbed the steps, he added, 'I've put you down for late morning shift. Okay with you?' Harold waved.

'Fine. See you later.'

Candles lit the tables in the dining hall as Harold glanced through the doorway. At any other time it might have been romantic. Now, it only added to the sense of desolation. He didn't feel hungry and carried on across the courtyard.

The blast from the shell by the showers had reduced the reading room hut to a tangle of splintered timbers. Despite the weariness and pain, Harold almost smiled. In the end, Stan had beaten him to it, he would never finish that 'New Statesman' now.

Back in his room, Harold sat on the bed and kicked off his sandals. He switched on the radio and caught the announcer from 'Kol Yisrael' reporting the days events, his clipped staccato Hebrew like the chatter of a machine gun:

"... And whilst the settlements of the western Negev buried their dead and began to repair their shattered buildings, Israeli artillery has bombarded Egyptian forces in Gaza. The Prime Minister today stated that Israel would not stand idly by, whilst its citizens were murdered in cold blood..."

Only half listening, Harold wondered what they could make of it in Dizengoff Boulevard. Gaza was only forty miles to the south, yet light years away from the neon signs, the whipped cream and appfel-strudel, and the dark skinned Yemenite newsboys darting between the tables to shout the evening newspapers: *'Maariv! Yediot! Maariv!'* Making a living from headlines of blood, of fire. Of death.

Harold idly turned the tuning knob. An English voice came through. Glancing at the dial, he saw that it was the BBC overseas service, relayed from Cyprus, the cool, laid back, attempted objectivity: ".. Egypt has asked for an emergency meeting of the Security Council, condemning what it describes as an unprovoked attack on innocent civilians... BBC correspondent in Cairo reports over a hundred killed and many more injured in a day long bombardment of Gaza..."

Harold sat and listened. Would any of those out there in the wide world ever understand what this was all about? Would his Jewish friends in the British Communist Party be even more torn between their innermost feelings and the latest dictates of the Soviet Union? That Nasser's 'revolution' was the harbinger of peace and progress in the Middle East? Would it affect the intellectuals of the *Rive Gauche* in Paris as they ranted about Arab rights versus bourgeois Zionist nationalism? As though the Palestinian rights – just as they were - weren't just as nationalist?

Reaching out, he switched off the radio and sat hunched on the edge of the bed. Talk. Talk. Talk. Argument. Polemic. What has it all to do with Ella? With Itzik? With the new society they were striving to create in this desolate corner? Were all their achievements to be destroyed before anyone took notice? Did anyone care?

Like the winter floods rushing down the wadi, a torrent of thoughts crashed through his mind, carrying everything before it. Never to hear Ella's steps skipping along the path by his room. Never to see Itzik's plans realised. Gone. Everything gone. What hand had guided those shells to destroy two healthy people whilst he, Harold, with his affliction and his despair had been spared. Spared until the fits became more frequent, more serious, forcing him to work in the garden or a similar 'safe' job. For that he had come to the kibbutz? For that, he had been spared?

At that moment, he thought of his family. They must have heard the news. Knew where it was. Poor Mum. She would be worried sick. He hadn't ever given her much joy. Nor his father. As a teenager, bucking their religious beliefs, going his own agnostic way, giving up university to come out here.

When the first fits came, Mum dragged him from specialist to specialist, each time hoping to hear something encouraging. That it would pass, get better. Never able to come to terms with the awful truth. Yet unlike his father, not trying to stop him going to the training farm, especially when the doctor said it might help. But she too broke down when he announced his departure for Israel. Still wrote to him as though he was eighteen, wanting to know when he would go out and study, 'make something' of himself instead of working for others - which was how she saw the kibbutz.

Poor Mum. Now, in his own anguish Harold understood even more her suffering. Her sadness. When she met other Jewish mothers in Prestwich, Mrs.Epstein would boast of her son, the doctor, Mrs.Levy of her son, the solicitor and Mrs. Goldberg would prattle on about how much her son Hymie, earned as an accountant. And what could Mum say? That her son was milking cows. In the desert. For nothing...

One by one, Harold slowly opened the buttons on his shirt. Until that last relapse, he had believed in himself. Until yesterday, he'd had faith in the future. Now, he didn't know what he believed. Would they ever achieve what they had set out to do in the kibbutz? Would there ever be peace? And would he ever live a normal life?

His eyelids grew heavy. Undressing, Harold slipped under the sheet. Slowly, the dark ceiling faded into a mist. He was sinking down a deep, deep shaft of tepid water. And fell asleep.

It was dark when Gavriel came up with Nahum from the cowsheds and they went into eat together. Nahum was the most unlikely looking academic, short, with huge shoulders and a round face topped with a mass of bushy fair hair. 'Our genius,' Itzik would laugh. Gavriel realised that he must have missed his lessons at the Academy.

'How come you're back so early from town?' he asked. Nahum sliced a huge radish into his salad,

'I've decided to take a break, Gabi,' he grunted, 'for the time being,' his knife clicking sharply on the plate. Gavriel frowned.

'Won't that put you back?'

'Maybe. Oh. I don't know. To hell with it.' Nahum jerked his head in the direction of the graveyard, 'How can I concentrate on composition, on harmonics, when Itzik is lying up there.' He paused and looked into Gavriel's eyes, 'and poor Ella is fighting for her life in Beer Sheba?'

Gavriel looked at the flushed face. Just like the Sabras, deceptively hard and tough on the surface, but soft and caring inside.

'Anyway,' continued Nahum, 'I had a long chat with my tutor. He'll let me pick it up where I left off.'

'You should,' said Gavriel, adding as though it came by itself, 'I'm sure Itzik would have wanted you to.' Nahum winced. He idolised Itzik.

'You're right. But first I want to help sort out that mess down below. The academy won't run away.'

Rivka was asleep when Gavriel came in, light on, an open book face down under her hand. She woke as he tried to extract it and was wide awake when he came to bed. She lay with her head in the pit of his shoulder, comforted, but not at ease.

The trauma of the last two days had stirred up memories of Jassy, the sound of marching boots, shots in the street. Crumpled bodies. Gavriel longed to fall asleep, but felt the tenseness in her body. He stroked her hair, wondering how long it would take to erase the shock of these two days.

Suddenly she started to speak, her soft voice echoing in the silent room.

' Seems no point. None at all,' she said,

' No point in what?' he replied mechanically.

'In trying to sort out our lives,' she continued. 'Just as soon as there seems to be some purpose, some peace, it all gets blown apart again. We had no peace in the war. No peace in Rumania.

And now, no peace here.' She paused and turned her face towards him in the dark. 'Will it ever be any different Gabi. Will it?'

'Please,' he hugged her closer, 'please don't talk like that. It will be different. It is different. It has to be, Rivka. That's all I know.'

'Perhaps, Gabi. Perhaps,' she murmured, 'I wish I could be sure.'

'It will. It will be. For Udi. And this one,' he stroked her stomach, 'it has to be.' Despite his weariness, Gavriel fought to sound convincing. 'We just have to be, Rivka.'

They lay close. Silent. From the dunes came the wail of a jackal. Footsteps sounded along the path, then died away. Rivka sensed the bond between them. That, at least, she knew, would always be.

'Just, that I keep wondering,' she said softly, 'Wondering whether Udi will have to be a soldier when he grows up.'

Gavriel tried to phrase a response, but his mind was too fogged. Rivka raised herself on one elbow and brushed her hand across his forehead.

'I should let you sleep, my darling. You must be exhausted.' She leaned down and kissed his lips. 'I'll try to sleep too.'

Gavriel stroked the back of her neck and she put her head on his chest. He wanted so much to make love to her but just hadn't the energy. Instead, he wrapped his arms around her. And like that, fell fast asleep.

Rivka felt him relax and smiled to herself as she nestled against him. Although she could not sleep, the rhythmic rise and fall of his chest began to reassure her and she felt once more at peace.

Tomorrow, with Shosh and Miriam, she was going in the jeep to visit Ella in hospital. And as she started to make a mental list of what to take, worn out by the day, she too fell fast asleep.

26

Harold woke late but he didn't feel rested. He had the morning off but couldn't settle into anything, couldn't even bring himself to write to his parents even though he knew they would be worried. He tidied his room - just a little, collected up his dirty washing - but then there was no laundry to take it to .

All the time his mind churned with thoughts of Ella, of bending over her shattered body in the fields, seeing her tiny face with the plastic tube into her nose, the flat white sheet where he other leg should have been.

Aimlessly, he went out and wandered out across the lawn to the courtyard. A small bulldozer was clearing the rubble and filling in craters.

'Hey, cowman!' Baruch's gruff voice brought him up short. The plumber was cutting through a spaghetti of galvanised pipes, 'Don't just stand there,' he called in the inter-branch teasing that was part of their everyday humour, 'come and do some real work.' Glad of the distraction, Harold nodded and walked over to him.

'Okay, engineer. Just explain in words of one syllable!'

For an hour or so, he helped him free and cut the pipes so that they wouldn't foul the bulldozer's tracks.

'Right.' Harold dusted off his hands, 'want a new apprentice?' The plumber shook his head, grinning.

'I'll let the cows suffer,' then added, 'thanks for the help, Harold. Thanks.'

As he walked past the wreckage of the reading room, charred pages of 'Time' magazine, fluttered in the breeze. The world news condensed into the printed pages, now seemed so irrelevant to what was going on out here. Harold wondered who or what, determined which tragedies reached the pages. How many more went unrecorded. And if they were, did it help?

He glanced around the courtyard. Just two shells - half duds at that it appeared - had wrought all this havoc. He couldn't bear to think what might have happened if the barrage hadn't switched to the cows. It was as if like the scapegoat driven into the Judean desert in ancient times, the herd had been a sacrifice to save the kibbutz.

He stood and looked out to the south, from this distance the sorghum fields looked much the same. Beyond them, the grey, flat plain merged with the blurred horizon, much as it must have done for thousands of years and on out to the desert, the wilderness where father Abraham had sent Hagar and her infant son Ishmael to perish and chosen Isaac to succeed him.

Harold stared into the distance. Brothers. From Isaac had come the Jews, surviving thousands of years of persecution to return to this land, from Ishmael, the Arabs, enduring centuries of subjugation by conquerors and continuing to live here. A blood-brother feud, both laying claim to this tiny strip of earth between the desert and the sea. Surely there was enough land for them both?

Harold glanced at his watch. The morning had gone. Feud or not, the cows had to be milked. Jamming his hat on his head, he hurried down the track and through the eucalyptus trees.

Throughout the milking, Harold hardly spoke, not even one brief flash of humour. Gavriel was concerned.

'How about coming over for coffee afterwards?' he called across the milking pit, as the last group of cows came in, 'I'm taking a break before the evening shift.'

'Maybe,' said Harold, adjusting his glasses, 'but I'm a bit tired,' then wondered why he had refused.

'You can sleep later,' Gavriel smiled. 'Rivka says I'm working you too hard.'

'Okay,' said Harold, 'Hell hath no fury - and all that.'

That was more like Harold, Gavriel consoled himself.

As he used the showers in the dairy, Harold winced, Ella's wash bag still hung on the door. But as he climbed the track, the afternoon breeze seem to revive his spirits. Children ran past him to their parents' rooms. Shrill laughter and shouts, just like any other afternoon. But on the lawns, the adults talked in low tones, no jokes, no anecdotes, the shattered courtyard and Itzik's funeral still hung heavy in the air.

Gavriel was pulling weeds in his tiny flower patch. He straightened up as Harold came across the lawn.

'Glad you managed it.' He grinned, 'kettle's boiling'.

Harold followed him into the room, feeling slightly awkward. Like most of the bachelors, he rarely joined the families at tea-time. They were so pre-occupied with the kids and the children, sensing that these few hours were theirs alone, demanding undivided attention.

Rivka was on the floor with Udi, his blond curls contrasting with her black hair.

'Have a seat,' she nodded towards the bed, 'you must be tired from afternoon shift,' then stood up, 'English tea?' adding with her lovely smile,' I've brought some milk from the kindergarten.'

'Thanks. No. I'd prefer black coffee if that's alright with you?' Harold felt guilty as he declined. The milk would have been boiled to keep it from going sour, he couldn't stand boiled milk in tea. 'Need a stimulant,' he added, smiling.

Gavriel took her place on the floor, helping the boy fit wooden pieces into a puzzle. With no electricity, Rivka brewed the coffee on a paraffin stove and between playing with Udi, they carried on fragmented small talk.

'Hey,' said Gavriel grinning as Harold took his turn with the boy and seeming to enjoy it, 'we'll have to invite you in more often. Give me a break.'

The sun dipped towards the sand-hills and shadows lengthened across the lawn. Gavriel went into their small shower and changed into working clothes. He came out, crouched and took the boy in his lap.

'Daddy's going down to milking, Udi. *Beseder?*' The boy raised one hand up to his father's face and fingered the stubble.

'Kiss?' he whispered. Gavriel picked him up and, turning him around, hugged his son close and kissed him on the forehead. The boy broke away and fell against Rivka.

'See you later.' Gavriel waved and went to the door. Harold sprung up to follow him out. 'No. No. You stay,' he smiled, 'bad enough I have to go.'

Harold sat down again on the bed. He and Rivka talked a little - as far as Udi let them - discussing some of the books on her shelf. Harold felt he was intruding on the child's time and sensed Rivka's apprehension as the time to return him to the children's house approached. Like most of the mothers, Rivka was ambivalent about her young child sleeping in the children's house. It was part of kibbutz life and she too accepted it. But after the recent events, she was more than usually anxious.

At half past seven, she stood up.

'Come, Udi,' she held out her hand, 'Let's go.' Unlike the mother, the boy was only too ready to go back. He'd had his reassurance and enjoyed the attention and love. Now he wanted to go back and meet up with his friends, talk about what they had done in the rooms, how many biscuits they'd eaten. Rivka looked at Harold, 'Why don't you come too.'

Harold raised both hands.

'No. No. It's okay. I'm going up to the dining hall.'

Rivka wasn't put off. She ruffled the boy's hair.

'What do you say, Udi? Shall we show Harold your children's house?' The boy twisted on one foot and pressed his face into her thigh, then he spun round, reached out and grabbed Harold's hand.

'Bo. Nelekh,' - let's go, he said, tugging them both out through the doorway.

Along the pathway, they joined other parents taking the children back for supper. The boy swung between them, with boundless energy, right up to the doorway to the children's house, a single storey concrete building. A wide, cantilevered roof projected out like broad brimmed hat. In the surrounding lawn, stood a climbing frame, sandpit and swings.

It was nearly dark and a soft yellow light from paraffin lamps shone through the windows. Could have been a Christmas scene, thought Harold, as the light reflected from the children's pictures pinned to the walls inside. But the dim light now seemed only to add his sense of gloom.

Rivka was pleased to see that Offra, the regular *metapelet* was working that evening. Udi felt at home with someone he knew so well and sat down easily at the supper table. Whenever a temporary replacement was on duty, the parents were more anxious and the kids picked it up as well.

While the nurse tied a bib around his neck, Udi started to chatter to a girl across the table. Rivka spoke a few words to Offra, then leaned down and kissed him on both cheeks. The boy reached up his hands, stroked her face, then took them down again and carried on talking where he'd left off. This was his house, his friends with whom he'd lived since he was a toddler. Here, he felt completely at ease.

Not all the mothers were as reassured as Rivka. Two fussed

and hung around, saying goodbye, passing on their anxieties to their children. When they finally tried to go, the kids ran after them, demanding yet another kiss. And another. Eventually, Offra had to coax them back to the table.

'As if the situation isn't tense enough,' Rivka exploded as she came out, 'some idiot parents have to make it worse.'

The dining hall was beginning to fill, but the hubbub was subdued. People still talked softly, or not at all, as if all the trivia and gossip had become redundant in the wake of the tragedy. And about that, no one was as yet prepared to talk. Three others sat at their table, but they ate quickly and were soon gone, leaving the two of them silent around the glow of the candle. Harold ate a white cheese sandwich, all he had the energy to prepare. Rivka ate an omelette with some salad. Half-way through, she broke the silence.

'Takes a while for things to return to normal, Harold.' She half smiled. 'Have to give yourself time. Don't force it.'

For a moment, Harold said nothing. When he looked up, his eyes were damp. He knew that she could see that but didn't care any more.

'It's not the just physical effect, Rivka. The loss, the injuries, the damage. It's how I feel inside. Kind of hopeless.'

'I know. And I know what that feels like. . .'

Harold cut into her words.

'Yes. But you could see an end. A new beginning.' He paused and looked straight at her. 'I can't, Rivka. I just can't. Not for me, anyway.'

Rivka didn't respond immediately. This wasn't going to be an easy conversation nor a short one, she'd planned to go and see Udi before he fell asleep. But she had to stay - as though it were another child that needed reassuring – and wondering whether in this case, she could.

Gavriel told her about Harold's bouts of melancholy. His fears of what the man might do. True, she had overcome her own self-destructive moods, but she had Gavriel's love and support. Now she strove to find the right words, the right tone.

'Look, Harold. You have so much to contribute. To the kibbutz. To yourself. And you survived in one piece. Sometimes, you have to take that as a sign. Not God, or anything like that. Just a signal. A pointer. That you were meant to go on giving and creating. That is life.'

'Fated... In one piece. Yes,' he murmured, 'sure. But I feel that Fate would have been kinder to let that shell fall on me - not her.' Harold didn't wait for her reaction but carried on in a low monotone. 'Look Rivka, I don't know you that well, yet I feel I can say these things to you, things I would usually confide only to Ella.'

'Women can generally listen.' Rivka smiled. 'And we allow our feelings to show.'

'Yes. And I'm grateful to you. But now she has gone.'

'Look. Ella will come back. Shosh and I talked to the surgeon at Beer Sheba today. She will recover . . .'

'Recover?' Harold blurted out, 'which part of her will recover? To ride horses again. Marry a nice chap. Have a family? Do all the things she wanted to do?'

Rivka leaned across the table.

'Yes. Lots of things. Don't you remember your famous British fighter pilot. He lost both legs, yet look what he has done with his life. Ella too will do things. Use her brain and her talents to live as full a life as she can.' She reached out and touched his wrist. 'Listen Harold. This may seem unkind and harsh, but you can't transfer your own feelings to Ella's situation. Leave her to make her own decisions. Being so full of self-pity can only colour your thoughts - distorts perspectives, if you like. But it will pass. Believe me Harold. I know. It has to.'

Harold glanced around the dining hall. People were sitting in twos and threes at half-empty tables in the dim lighting, sipping tea, smoking, talking softly - some not at all. It was as if they were avoiding going back to the separateness of their rooms, wanting to restore the camaraderie of the dining hall, yet not quite able. He thought of Rivka. How painful it must be for her to listen to him with her own childhood. Yet she had. And he felt a sudden surge of warmth for her as he expressed his feelings and despair to her over the table.

Rivka stared at the candle. It was almost down to the saucer. She wondered how she'd been so positive, almost as if it were Gavriel speaking through her. Playing the part of healer, of life-saver even. Yes, she recognised the symptoms - and perhaps that was what had given her the strength.

'Look,' said Harold, 'sorry to have unloaded this onto you Rivka. 'And yes, perhaps you are right.' Harold pushed the glasses back onto the bridge of his nose. 'I just wish I could feel it.'

The server had come round and was waiting with his trolley, ready to clean off their table.

'Heck.' Harold glanced at his watch. 'I've kept you from going to say goodnight to your son!'

'*Ein davar*,' no matter, she said as they got up. 'The least we can do for one another in times of crisis, is talk things through, Harold.'

All the lamps were out in the children's house, except one by the sink where Offra was washing the dishes. The children had had their bedtime story and were tucked up in bed. If she went in now, it would only unsettle Udi for the night. Carefully, Rivka-tip toed to the shuttered window of his bedroom, which he shared with four classmates. She did this with Gavriel sometimes after supper, to listen to their burblings.

One of the girls was talking slowly, disjointedly as they did just before falling asleep.

'... And they are going to bring the biggest, biggest tractor to build up the laundry in one day... my daddy said.'

'Yes,' butted in a deeper voice, 'It will so big... so big, it will take only two hours even...'

'And there won't be any more bombs. Never..' she heard Udi say.

'No more shells either. No. Because we smashed all the Egyptian guns. All of them,' said another.

'And we'll have the biggest guns. Bigger than.. than...'

'As big as the tractor?' asked another voice, even sleepier.

'And we'll buy lots and lots of new cows,' said Udi.

'Huge. Bigger than the caterpillar tractor,' came a murmur.

'*Gadol. Gadol. Gadol.*,' said the deeper voice. Big. Big. Big. Then there was silence.

Rivka waited a while. Not a sound. Despite her doubts about collective education, she loved to listen to these last moment conversations, the children giving voice to their innermost thoughts and craziest fantasies to each other and themselves, across the darkened, silent room.

It was growing cooler. With a last glance at the shutters, Rivka stepped away from the window. As she turned to go to her room, the rising moon showed through the young pine trees. Suddenly, she thought again of Harold. Saw his pale, downcast face. Felt his despair. And, remembering her own desperation at the camp in Cyprus, she grew more fearful of what he might do.

27.

The weekend passed quietly, the border slept. On both sides the dead were mourned - and the living prepared to face the coming week.

Having sent his report through to headquarters, Major Salah Salim spent his time supervising reconstruction of the battered trenches and bunkers. The best way to restore morale was to keep busy – and to be ready for the next time. For surely, there would be a next time.

On the Monday, the Major allowed himself ample time to arrive at the inquiry. On his way into Gaza, things appeared to be back to normal. The diesel pumps in the well-houses chugged smoke rings into a cloudless sky, *felaheen* tended the orange groves and fields, and lorries passed to and fro laden with sacks and produce.

In the town, it was different. People were digging in heaps of rubble that lined the narrow streets near the market. Around the mosque, workmen pulled charred beams from shattered buildings, in a treeless land, every piece of timber was valuable.

As he drove through in his Soviet-built jeep the Major was met with sullen stares and grim faces. His army had provoked the Israelis and then had done nothing to halt the death and destruction that rained down upon the town. And what could he say? Tell them that the army was here to stop Israeli expansion, that it was preparing to recover their lost lands. Would that comfort the bereaved? Bring back their loved ones?

They ought to all be in this struggle together, brother Arabs. Instead, the Palestinians mistrusted the military, the officers in turn looked down on them as ignorant and ungrateful refugees, and the soldiers took advantage of the local women whenever they could get away with it.

Yes, without the Egyptian army, they would never be able to return to their towns and villages. But the army had to earn their respect by becoming strong and efficient and treating them as brothers, not as vassals. The Major glanced down at the leather briefcase resting on his knees. A copy of his report was inside - and it dealt with all this too.

As the jeep left the centre for the northern suburb of Jabaliya, a tall, white clad figure strode along the side of the road, head down, shoulders drooping. After a moment's hesitation, Major Salim motioned the driver to stop.

'*Ya sheikh*,' he called softly, using the respectful title for an old man, 'can we offer you a lift somewhere?' The driver sat bolt upright, staring straight ahead. Why bother for some old *felakh*? The Major studied the leathery, wrinkled face. It was full of character, noble even. And hadn't his father too been a peasant?

Ibrahim turned and looked at the smartly dressed officer. He was wary, the army sometimes made fun by stopping, then shooting off in a cloud of dust, laughing and catcalling.

'I am going to Shaati,' Ibrahim replied, still suspicious. But he had walked most of the way from the *Fedayeen* camp at Beit Hanun and his legs were very tired.

'Well. We can take you a mile or so,' said Major Salim, 'hop in the back.'

As they drove on, the streets grew broader. Large white villas and trees had replaced the narrow alleys and brown houses of the town centre.

'Been to market?' asked major Salim.

'Wish to Allah that I had,' muttered Ibrahim, adding, 'not

that much of it is left now anyway.'

'Well, we shall show them next time,' said the Major.

'Show them what?' Ibrahim leaned forward. 'I have nothing left to show. My wife was killed in the shelling. My son, Ahmed ...' He paused for a few seconds, wiping his eye. 'My son. He could still die. *Insh'allah,* he will live.' He reached into the folds of his cloak and pulled out a folded sheet of green paper. 'Now. I have nothing. This is all I have to show.'

Major Salim opened it out and read it carefully. On the top, was the crest of the Fedayeen. Beneath, a typed citation of honour: Wounds received in the glorious struggle for our land. Name. Date. Signature. He closed his eyes for a moment. This Ahmed must have been the one who had been saved from the wadi. He was about to tell the old man, then stopped himself. Instead, as he handed back the certificate, he touched his hand.

'*Ya sheikh*. Your son is a hero.'

Ibrahim took back the paper.

'Maybe. But he has lost his right arm. Will this piece of paper earn him a living? Keep me in my old age? Make him *mukhtar* in our village after I am gone?'

The major nodded.

'But at least, he fought for his people. For your land.'

Ibrahim didn't respond at once. Heroes? Land? He was thinking of that evening outside the hospital in Gaza. The rows of dead, amongst them Jamilla, torn and bloodstained. He leaned forward again, his face close to that of the Major.

'Honour. Hero's. Yes. For you military men, maybe. You say we shall fight again. More wars. Fight until we win back our land. Maybe. But when you have seen as much as I have, *ya* Major, you will know that war solves nothing. Had we chosen to talk to the Jews in '47, instead of running after that fanatic Haj Amin, we would not be rotting out here now. That's all I can say ...'

The driver gripped the steering wheel and stiffened. How dare that ignorant peasant talk to an Egyptian officer like that? But again he said nothing as he slowed down at the turn off to Jabaliya and stopped.

For a moment, there was only the sound of the engine ticking over. Then the Major turned in his seat.

'I understand what you say, ya sheikh. But one thing I do know. The Israelis will never give you back your village. Not unless we defeat them militarily and force them to. Of that I am certain.'

Ibrahim slid from the seat and stood on the sand by the road-side, holding the canvas top with one hand.

'Maybe. Maybe. But for you, the army, war brings glory. For us, it brings only ruin. Whoever wins, ya Major, it is the *felaheen* who loose.' He glanced at the driver, then back to the major. 'I thank you for taking me along my way. Would that there were more like you.' As he stood back, the major smiled.

'*Be'hatrik*. Blessed be your way.'

'*Ma Selameh*,' go in peace, said Ibrahim, and raising one hand, turned and walked away.

Major Salim sat quietly for a moment, listening to the engine purring as the tall white figure strode away across the dunes towards the sea. Then he nodded to the driver and they pulled away, heading for the large, three storied villa surrounded by tall cypress trees. To the inquiry.

Ahmed lay back staring up at the whitewashed ceiling. The saline drip bottle rocked as he moved his hand, the one he still had. All through his father's visit, he had tried to keep up appearances, re-assure him that the Fedayeen would look after him. Money had been coming in from Saudi Arabia. He would be provided for. Given a grant to study. Cairo. Or Damascus.

Assured a teacher's post in one of the schools if he wished.

He'd told him how he had survived - the only one. How everyone in the camp would be so proud of the family. But he knew that he hadn't been able to shake off his father's sadness, a deep, silent sadness from the death of his mother that seemed to have aged him in just a week. Poor father. He'd pinned so many hopes on him, his youngest son. But Ahmed also knew that they lived in different worlds and that perhaps Ibrahim would never understand.

Alone once more, Ahmed thought again of that night, the strange, evil smell, which he now knew was gangrene. He remembered the terrible pain as the soldiers lifted him up over the wire. Then the emptiness at his right side when he woke the next afternoon in hospital. His panic and his crying himself to sleep.

The relief nurse came down into the room and changed his drip. He was lucky, she said. So many casualties from the shelling and so many demands on medical supplies at the main hospital, but the Fedayeen had procured their own.

As she took his temperature and straightened the pillow, their eyes met.

Liela? It couldn't be? He remembered the tiny girl with short dark plaits playing in the dust by the well. Could this slim, dark eyed woman be her?

'You are Iqbal's daughter, maybe?'

The nurse started and blushed for a moment. Everyone in the small hospital knew his story and was so proud to have him there. A true hero. And he actually knew her?

'Yes,' she replied, embarrassed, 'and I know your father too.'

Now that reality was sinking in, so much he needed the gentle comfort of a woman.

'Perhaps,' he said softly, nodding at the bottle, 'perhaps, when this is all over, we shall meet. Somewhere more pleasant?' The nurse adjusted the drip and placed a hand on his forehead. A cool, soft hand.

'Yes,' she smiled, 'We might. But for now, you must rest. Get rid of the fever.' She turned and glided away down the ward, the long white coat dancing around her tiny ankles. Ahmed watched her go. Yes. They would meet again, once he was out of here. Of that he must make certain.

Ahmed felt sleepy. His eyes closed and once more, he saw the torch beam stabbing down through the darkness. Heard the Egyptian soldiers calling. As he began to lose consciousness, he wondered again which Egyptian commander had given the order to open fire, the man who had saved his life. He wanted so much to meet him.

As soon as the jeep turned into the gateway, Major Salim saw that this was no ordinary day. The compound was full of staff cars, most of them sporting insignias he didn't recognise. Top brass. From Cairo. Suddenly it hit him. This was going to be no ordinary enquiry. It was going to be like a court martial. And he would be the defendant!

It was hot and stuffy in the narrow corridor outside the inquiry room. Major Salim was wiping his neck with a handkerchief, when a door suddenly opened beside him and a young captain came out. He was clean shaven, hair brushed back giving his head a flattened appearance.

'Captain Shasli,' he said sharply, holding out his hand. 'Intelligence. Kantara.'

'Major Salah Salim,' replied the major took it, noting that the handshake was firm. The officer was obviously here to assess him. The major didn't mind. At least he was not from the local Intelligence mafia whose knowledge was confined to the Gaza drug rings and brothels.

The two men spoke about Kantara - which the major knew well, of President Nasser's plans to widen the Suez canal and then the border situation in Gaza. The Major felt the man was gauging his views and outlook and he remained cautious and circumspect. A sergeant came out to call in the captain. Ten minutes later, they called for him.

At the far end of the long, high ceilinged room, six staff officers sat behind a green baize covered table. Two were from local headquarters. Not much help from there. The others though might at least be neutral. At one end sat a clerk, ready to take notes, at the other were two men in civilian clothes, making the Major a little uneasy. The young captain sat over to the left, slightly behind him. In his entire career, the major had never felt so isolated.

A local colonel opened with an account of the two days' engagement. Major Salim knew him well and fought to remain calm as the puffy-faced man related in sarcastic tones, how a herd of cows had received the army's fire-power, allowing the enemy to regroup and return fire unopposed. He made much of the major's unauthorised decision to open fire, avoiding his repeated requests to H.Q., and mentioning the Fedayeen only in passing.

Throughout the major maintained his self control, tried not to react and made occasional notes on a small pad as the colonel read from his prepared text, stumbling more than once and taking over an hour. The major could see the impatience around the table. Then he was called upon to speak.

The Major spoke freely and to the point, glancing at his watch from time to time to keep to his planned thirty minutes. He gave his reasons, stressing the plight of the Fedayeen, the complete lack of response from H.Q. and finally, to his considered judgement, together with Lieutenant Faras, to open fire.

He admitted his mistake regarding the cattle then paused for a moment and looked up, adding softly.

'Lieutenant Faras was a dedicated and courageous officer, sirs. A great loss.'

He wished Faras could have been here with him, for he knew he had to attack now, or he would lose all. And with Lieutanant gone, instead he drew strength from that tall white figure striding off across the dunes and gave his opinions freely on the situation of the army in Gaza. He told of the lack of training, the alienation of the local populace and the corruption and smuggling. Carefully, he avoided naming anyone or pinpointing particular ranks but backed each observation with specific facts. Finally, in the last few minutes, he returned to the battle, mentioned that one of the Fedayeen had been saved, then sat down.

For the next two hours, questions and cross-questions flew across the table and around the room. The clerk scribbled furiously, the captain made notes. One of the top brass was making notes too. Someone was listening, thought the major as the local general mopped sweat from his forehead. He would have a lot to answer for.

The questioning ended. His part was over. The others would meet again that afternoon and he would be informed of their decision that evening. Despite his spirited defence, Major Salim knew that the wheels of the establishment ground in their own grooves. There was no knowing what the outcome might be. He stood up, saluted and went out.

When the captain followed a few seconds later, the major turned to face him.

'Every word was true, captain, I swear. But I realise that a general's word carries more weight than mine.'

The officer smiled.

'Well. I wouldn't count on that. Not this time.' He glanced

over his shoulder at the closed door then continued in a lower voice. 'Entrenched positions are always difficult to dislodge. But their time will come. So will yours Major Salim.'

'Thank you,' said the Major 'This will remain strictly between the two of us.'

The captain smiled again.

'I know it will.' He stepped closer. 'President Nasser has need of men like you, major.' He handed him a slip of paper. 'This is my direct line number. Obviously, I can't give you my unit.' They shook hands.

'I hope we shall meet again,' replied major Salim.

On his way out, the major thought it through. It could have been just an Intelligence ploy to test him out. But if it were genuine, then again it was a kind of conspiracy, even if in the right direction. Plots and subterfuges. Would it ever change? He put on his cap and walked across to the jeep.

At the road junction, the major pointed to the right.

'Sir. But that way is to the sea?'

'I know,' grunted the major. 'I'll tell you when to stop.' They drove for about two miles along the narrow, undulating strip of tarmac across the dunes. Beduin with their camels clustered around low, black tents and scraggy sheep nibbled at dry grass in the hollows.

The road ended in a rough gravel track just as the deep blue showed between the sand. To his right and left, rows of sun-bleached tents and corrugated iron huts stretched over the dunes.

Major Salim motioned to stop the car and swung out of his seat. Shielding his eyes from the glare of the white sand, he looked beyond the last row of huts, up to the crest of a high dune. An old man sat on his haunches, staring out over the sea, the stiff breeze pressing the white cloak against his lean body.

Ibrahim had been sitting there all afternoon. There was no reason to sit by the hut. Without Jamilla, it was so cold and empty. Neither could he bear to see Abu Salah now so crushed and broken with Ismail gone.

His old adversary had come to meet him as he walked into the camp. His son's body had been handed over by the Red Cross at the Erez checkpoint that morning.

'Ya Ibrahim,' he called out, tears in his eyes, 'Ismail is dead. Tomorrow, he will be buried.'

Ibrahim gripped his hands, trembling, tears coming to his own eyes.

'May your son sit at the right hand of Mohammed, Abu Salah.'

'Insh'allah,' said Abu Salah. Then he leaned forward. 'Our sons fought together, Ibrahim. Now, we shall live in peace together. The time has come to bury our differences.' Spontaneously, the two men embraced, heads on each other's shoulders and united in their tears.

Ibrahim's eyes were still moist as he stared out over the sea into space, seeing nothing. Down on the road, Major Salim stood for a full minute, looking up at the old man.

'No, *ya sheikh*,' he murmured, 'we haven't done much for you, have we?' Climbing back into the seat, he raised his hand and they drove away.

28.

Throughout the weekend and the days following, volunteers arrived from kibbutzim all over the country. Each day, new faces appeared in the dining hall, to be replaced by others as new arrivals gave up their Shabbat rest days to come and help clear up and begin the rebuilding. As if in the face of disaster, the old pioneering spirit had been reborn.

On the Sunday, Gavriel arranged for everyone to work extra shifts in the dairy. All that Shabbat, he'd been psychologically preparing himself for the day he'd been fearing ever since the bombardment, Judgement Day.

He'd almost put it off for another week but knew it had to be faced. Now, in the cool morning, Harold, Nahum and he made their way down through the dripping eucalyptus trees, each sunk deep in their own thoughts. Menasheh was coming to make a final cull of the injured cattle.

A loud hammering came from number one cowshed. Three men from their neighbouring kibbutz, with cutting and welding gear were sorting out the tangle of roof trusses and purlins.

'*Boker Tov*,' shouted Gavriel, 'Can't you lads sleep?'

'*Boker Tov*, to you,' one shouted back from his perch, his heavy French accent mixing the Hebrew 'R's and the 'Kh's. 'We knew you Kulaks wouldn't manage without us.' He nodded at the steel sections. 'We need to get as much done before the sun makes metal gets too hot to handle.'

'Thanks. Thanks for coming over. There's cold milk in the tank. Help yourselves,' the early morning banter providing light relief from what was going to be a heavy day.

As the man waved back, Gavriel recognised him. Eli, one of the ultra leftists whose cow naming had so incensed Menasheh that day. He wondered how the vet would react when he arrived later.

The milking started as usual, but this morning Gavriel was noting the scars, limpings and lacerated udders one by one as the cows came through, details which they noted on the record sheets and would decide their fate. They'd already lost more than a third of the herd, killed outright or put down the same day. How many more would have to go he wondered?

They went up for breakfast early, to be down again in time for the vet. The three neighbours came up with them, bringing their politics too. Gavriel knew that for the Tel Kerem boys, everything had to have a dialectical explanation. Their general meetings inevitably continued into the early hours, debating principles and ideology with intense heat.

This morning was no different and once at the breakfast table, the three were soon arguing over the previous week's events. Ehud, with his mass of curly brown hair and horn-rimmed glasses, was holding forth.

'Look. It's obvious that Ben Gurion deliberately engineers border incidents to gain military assistance from the Americans.'

'Hang on,' said Nahum, 'Look at Syria. They shelled our bull-dozers on the Jordan water project. We didn't start that.'

'Maybe,' said Ehud,' But the British and the Yanks would love to use Israel to topple Nasser.'

Gavriel winked across the table at Harold as he spread cream cheese on his bread. Harold decided to risk a soft boiled egg and cursed. It was runny. Gavriel played safe and took a hard one. Meanwhile the discussion grew more and more animated.

'Listen,' snapped Ehud, pointing his knife at Nahum, 'long

before Russian involvement in the area, Britain was pouring arms into the Arab states, financing the Jordanian Arab Legion. Soviet weapons are given only to those fighting Imperialism.'

Harold reached out and smiling, lowered the knife.

'No violence whilst we're eating, please.'

Gavriel smiled too. The other three didn't.

'If you ask me,' said Harold, deciding not to finish his egg, 'those Russian weapons will just as easily be turned against Egyptian trade unionists, as against Israel. Nasser is no socialist. Each side is merely furthering its own national interests.'

'Bullshit!' Ehud slapped his hand on the table. 'Nasser is heading the progressive, anti-Imperialist forces in the Middle East. Ben Gurion is just a lackey of American Imperialism!' he snorted. 'Soviet weapons will only be used to further the forces of progress and revolution!'

Harold's head began to burn. He put down his slice of bread and turned to him.

'Then tell me,' he said, the blood rising to his face, 'just you tell me. What blotted out Itzik's life? And crippled Ella? Eh? Your revolutionary Russian shells? Or Imperialist British ones?' Without noticing, his voice had risen to a shout as he repeated, 'just you tell me that, Ehud, will you?'

Abruptly, the dining hall fell silent. Everyone turned to look in his direction. It was the first time anyone had ever heard Harold raise his voice. Embarrassed, Harold jumped up from his seat, strode out and ran down the track to the cowsheds, his head burning - annoyed more at his loss of self control, than with Ehud. The man was an immature ideologue – what Lenin had called 'an infantile disorder'. Wasn't worth losing his temper over – but he had. Diving into the compressor room, Harold put his head under the cold tap and kept it there until he had cooled off.

Gavriel stayed with the others and finished eating. Ehud sat head down, chewing quietly. Nahum stood up, said he would see them below and went out and Gavriel turned the conversation to how much of the steelwork they could re-use and how long the reconstruction would take. By the time they all came down to the dairy, everyone was back to the thinking of the work at hand and Harold and Nahum had already brought along the next group of cows.

With the milking over, the smelly, dung-strewn stalls washed down and the parlour transformed into clinical white tiles and gleaming stainless steel, they three went through into the office.

'Right,' said Gavriel, 'now we're ready for Menasheh.' He glanced at the other two and smiled, 'you can see why he lost his temper with that lot.'

'Yes. Only too easy,' said Harold. 'Still, I don't suppose we were any less dogmatic a few years ago.'

At that moment, a tall girl, with bronzed face and long blond plait coiled high in her head walked in.

'Hi,' said Nahum. He turned to Gavriel and Harold. 'Meet Gila. A fellow student at the conservatoire.' He grinned. 'She's come to give a hand.'

Gavriel and Harold tried to suppress their smiles, the girl's neat sandals were already spattered with dung.

'Well then, ' said Gavriel, 'Shalom Gila! Get Nahum to find you a pair of boots. You can help feed the calves, eh Nahum?' Nahum nodded and the two went out.

'One way of learning harmonic scales,' murmured Harold.

Whilst Gavriel stacked the record cards required, Harold wandered into the machine room and took up a plastic mug. Lifting the lid of the stainless steel refrigerating tank, he carefully skimmed off the thick, creamy milk pushed to the corner by the huge revolving paddle. Closing the lid, he leaned back against the cool, tiled wall, the ice-cold liquid trickling down his throat. One of the few fringe benefits of working in the dairy, he would joke with Ella.

Ella! Through the open doorway, he saw Nahum and the girl walking across the yard. She was wearing Ella's blue boots. Harold closed his eyes to stop the tears. Ella would never need them again...

Brakes screeching outside cut off his brooding. Menasheh had arrived.

'*Nu, kinderlekh*,' the vet called, sliding from his seat, 'let's start. First things first though,' he muttered taking out his A.I. kit.

The vet and Gavriel worked together as they had always done. As Itzik had done. As if nothing had happened, each avoiding talking about what was to come. Above them, the three boys continued cutting out the tangled steels.

Menasheh glanced up at the men, then nodded to Gavriel.
'I was there on Friday. Think anything has changed?'
'I know,' sighed Gavriel, 'but their heart is in the right place.'
The vet shrugged.
'Maybe,' he said. 'After all, I suppose they could be living a soft life in Paris, instead of coming out to this desert.'

Harold joined them as they went across to the undamaged part of the second cowshed where the injured beasts were yoked in, quietly chewing on hay and oblivious that their fate was about to be decided.

Menasheh examined the record cards, then checked the wounds and the joints for stiffness, slowly moving his hands over the black and white hides and after each cow, muttering a few words for Gavriel to mark the card.

'Like playing God,' the vet muttered as he progressed down

the line. 'No man should have to do that.' He straightened up and glanced across the yard. 'Those Egyptian soldiers should only know. Great deeds for their country. For progress. For their Nasser. Another Hitler, *yikmakh shmo!*'

Harold took the cards from Gavriel and sorted them into two packs. By the time the vet finished, together with the original cull, the herd had been reduced to half what it had been.

'Nu. At least Itzik's new cow is amongst the reprieved,' Gavriel said to Harold as they crossed the yard.

'Maybe a good omen,' said Harold. But it did little to lift the gloom, as the three men reached the end of the cowshed and looked at each other, silent. The slightest thing could have plunged them all into tears.

Perhaps they would have, had they not seen Nahum and his fellow student, spreading straw in the deep litter. Whilst he carried on bull headed, pulling strings off the bales and breaking them apart, the girl was trying to step gingerly from one dry patch to the next while scattering handfuls of straw, hair falling down loose her back and golden skin streaked with manure,.

'With such young heifers,' muttered the vet as he caught them up, 'you should be okay.'

Gavriel laughed, breaking the tension.

'Just an exercise in composition that Nahum found amongst his studies. Still,' he smiled, 'she is trying.'

Harold couldn't even smile. He saw only the blue gumboots and couldn't stop himself thinking about Ella and what had happened. Wondering why it affected him so much more than Itzik's death. It was as though she were part of him and suddenly realising that he felt lost without her.

In the office, Menasheh wrote out his own notes, hurriedly looking again through the cards and confirming the final list of those to go.

'I have to be at the ministry offices in Beer Sheba by one o'clock,' he said almost apologetically to Gavriel, 'I think you can sort out the rest.' Gavriel meanwhile had noticed the way Harold had been gripping the record cards' box as they walked back to the office, his knuckles turning white.

'Harold,' he said softly, 'I think Nahum and me can manage now. Why not take off the rest of the shift?'

Harold looked up from kicking off his boots.

'You sure?' he said. 'I'm feeling fine.'

'Yes. Certain. Then you can start the evening shift and we'll be back to normal.' To Gavriel's surprise, Harold agreed without further persuasion. For as soon as the vet had mentioned his going, other plans for the day had formed in his head

'When are you leaving Menasheh?' he asked, as if by the way.

'Fifteen minutes. Why?'

'Could I cadge a lift perhaps? I'd like to visit Ella.'

With all his delicate equipment in the car and the passenger seat piled high with notebooks and files, the vet disliked giving lifts. For a split second Menasheh squinted through his spectacles, hesitating.

'Alright. If you can be ready in time.' He said, breathing out. 'Wait for me at the gate.'

Harold ran out and up the slope. When he had gone the vet looked at Gavriel.

'Not his usual self today, our friend.'

'No. Very cut up at what happened to Ella.'

'Hmm,' Menasheh murmured, 'you should keep a close eye on him. Shock, works in strange ways you know.'

Gavriel couldn't hide his surprise at the vet's concern. Menasheh noticed and smiled, showing a gold tooth.

'So. You think I have dealt only with cows all my life?' As Gavriel opened his mouth to protest, the vet placed a finger on his chest. 'In Leipzig, I was a doctor. When I came to Palestine, the country was full of refugee doctors. You know the old joke: When a woman fainted in a Tel Aviv cinema and they asked if there was a doctor in the house, half the audience stood up!'

Gavriel had heard the joke before, but coming from a supposedly humourless Yecker like Menasheh, it sounded special.

'Anyway,' continued the vet, 'we all had to find new professions. So I became a vet. Some couldn't take it. Went back to Germany.' He looked down. 'They never became anything - except ashes.'

The vet finished his notes, then talked a few minutes about which cows to send first. Throwing his boots in the rear of his car, he cleared the front seat and drove out onto the road.

Gavriel watched him go, then went over to tell Nahum to unyoke the cows. He ought to 'phone the abattoir today. He couldn't. Tomorrow, he would do it. Yes. Tomorrow.

29.

Harold waited by the main gate, dressed in the kibbutznik's standard khaki trousers and light blue shirt. It was a hot day but he'd also taken a casual jacket. He might not get back 'till evening. What a stroke of luck that Menasheh was going to Beer Sheba. It would have taken him 'till afternoon to get there otherwise.

Menasheh roared up from the cowsheds and twenty minutes later, they had left the Hunger Road were speeding along the ancient highway that once connected Gaza to Beer Sheba, Hebron and up to Jerusalem. Jerusalem. To make that journey now Harold mused, one would have to cross two borders and three countries.

Harold stared ahead at the winding strip of black tarmac. The old British Mandate road dipped and curved between the numerous small wadis and crevices and with every few miles east, the roadside trees grew thinner and more stunted, the plain more parched and grey.

For a while, neither felt inclined to talk. Menasheh was concentrating on the driving, slowing down as each heavy lorry thundered past until they had to stop for a moment at the junction with the Kastina road. The road along which Avi's truck had been ambushed.

'Was that only last week?' Menasheh said suddenly, pointing to his left. Harold nodded. 'Terrible that. Wife and young baby... And now Itzik. Such a disaster,' he continued, 'a catastrophe. A man like that. Gone. The finest dairyman I ever met..,' talking as if to himself, his voice barely audible above the engine noise. 'What a waste. What a terrible waste of life. And Ella,' he raised his voice, half glancing at Harold, 'she will be alright though, won't she?'

Harold started, surprised at the vet's direct question as much as by his sudden talkativeness.

'Well. Yes. She is off the danger list,' he paused and looked down. 'But she will be disabled for the rest of her life.'

'But she will live, no?'

'Why, yes,' answered Harold, thrown off balance by the question. Then, more sharply, added, 'but what kind of a life? To live like that? I'm not so sure.'

The older man didn't respond at once. He changed gear and accelerated to pass a truck loaded down with green striped watermelons, then eased back in his seat.

'Look, my friend. Life is hope. God has given us life. Only He can take it. Ella lives. That is His will and she will make as much of her life as she can.' He paused. 'We all have to. And believe me, Harold, sometimes it is very hard.'

Harold half turned towards him, his face muscles twitching.

'God's will Menasheh? Last week's destruction? Itzik? And Ella? Was that God's will too? How can you believe in some divine purpose after all this?' Suddenly, he stopped and blushed, then put out his hand. 'Look. Sorry. I didn't mean to offend you. Or your beliefs, Menasheh... I apologise.'

To his surprise, the vet just shrugged.

'Huh. Don't apologise. I've heard it too often to take offence. And as to your question? It has no answer. I too could ask: Why did six million Jews perish? My own family? No one can question God's will. But He is there. All creation is His, us included. Especially us.'

They travelled on in silence. An ancient acacia tree flashed by and to their right, the old Turkish railway embankment snaked across the desert. Harold suddenly broke it, speaking in a monotone.

'You are fortunate, Menasheh. I can't find any such comfort. And if what happened is the will of God, I just want no part in it.'

The vet nodded and pursed his lips.

'So. What do you believe in, then?'

'In Man,' said Harold sharply. 'In his innate goodness. His creativity.'

'So I will ask you the same question. Was last week a revelation of that goodness? Of his creativity?'

'Of course not.' Harold leaned towards him. 'Things like that happen because Man is corrupted and debased by an acquisitive society. A soulless capitalist world. When we have built a just and egalitarian society, wars and poverty will be a thing of the past. If we can do it in the kibbutz, one day, everyone will.'

The car slowed down to take a sharp curve in the road. Menasheh smiled again.

'Huh. The kibbutz? You are a small group of idealists. Think that ideologies will provide all the answers: Marx, Lenin, Herzl, Borochov. Great thinkers, maybe. But creation is much more than that, Harold. And without a purpose, without God, there is nothing.'

The tower of Beer Sheba police station stuck up in the distance. Harold stared through the windscreen.

'In a way, Menasheh, I suppose I envy you. To be able to feel that Itzik has gone to a better place. To me, he has just gone. Forever. And Ella has been crippled. For good. And,' he paused, sensing the vet half-looking at him, 'and I suppose I can't accept that finality, Menasheh. Not at all.'

A few minutes later, they were in Beer Sheba, turning the corner by the old Palestine Police fortress and down the broad, steep main road that led to the bridge over the river bed. On either side were one and two storied houses of brown stone pillaged by the Turks from the Roman ruins at Kurnub.

The car bumped against the kerb and stopped. Menasheh climbed out.

'*Rega!* Just a minute. I'll drop you off at the hospital.'

'No. Please. Don't worry,' Harold protested. 'You have to get to the ministry offices.'

'Ha. They won't run away.' He dived into a small shop, reappearing with a white paper package, then drove off again.

Dodging the donkey carts and lorries, they were soon outside the wire mesh fence of the hospitaL

'Thanks a lot for the lift, Menasheh. It was a great help.'

'*Lo davar,*' said the vet. 'It was good to talk. Made the journey shorter. Here.' He thrust the package into Harold's hands, 'give this to Ella. Wish her better from me. eh?' As he drew away, he called out, 'and look after yourself too, my friend. *Shalom.*'

Harold waved and stared after the car as it turned away. The Ministry offices were away on the far side of the main road, the man had deliberately gone out of his way. He looked down at the package. Just one week ago, whoever would have thought it?

Pushing open the door of the ward, Harold felt apprehensive and at the same time quite excited at seeing Ella again. And there she was, wide awake and propped up on two pillows. The drip had gone and so had most of the gauze, leaving pink patches on her face. But a steel frame held the blankets tented over the foot of her bed.

Hearing his footsteps, Ella turned and smiled and all the carefully prepared phrases flew out of Harold's head, leaving him strangely tongue tied, so that it was she who spoke first.

'Hi. Sorry I don't look my best.' She pointed to a stool by the bed. 'Take a seat. Thought you were coming tomorrow.' The face was still puffy but her hair was neatly brushed and her eyes, wide and bright. After a short pause, she added softly. 'Glad you came, Harold.'

And she was glad. Really happy to see him. After Rivka and Shosh had told her what happened, Ella knew that she owed her life to him. Now, lying here with so much time to think, she'd begun to realise that it was not just his quick mind, his humour, his repartee. Nor was it in any way some kind of pity for his affliction. It was him. Harold. The whole person that she respected. Liked. Even, if she were able to admit it, loved... God, what was in a word. Just that she felt so good when she was with him. Close to him. As though the space around them was warmer, brighter, less sterile.

'Well, yes. I did intend to come tomorrow,' said Harold, regaining the power of speech. But I cadged a lift with Menasheh.'

'How is the old Yecker?'

'Surprisingly human.' Harold winked, 'We had a deep discussion. On God. The meaning of life and all that. Yes. Very human in fact. Here!' He handed her the package, 'taken quite a shine to you.'

Ella opened the packet and took out a red and white box of 'Elite' chocolates.'

'Ah. He's a real sweetie.' Opening the box, she held them towards Harold, 'Go on. Have a few.'

'No. They're for you.'

'Nuts,' she said. 'Anyway, I've got to keep my figure.' Harold looked down at the silver paper, silent. My figure! The words reverberated inside his head.

It was Ella who began the conversation again.

'Nu?' she said softly, 'Any aches and pains still?'

'Me?' Harold thought fast, 'Me. Oh I'm fine. Slept it off over the weekend. Too busy otherwise to think about it,' he lied. 'And you?'

'How am I,' she said matter of factly. 'Well, the surgeon talks to me a lot. He was in the last war and in '48. Operated on quite a few like... like me.'

'And?'

'Well, he talks more about what I will feel, than what I will be like. My mental, rather than my physical state.'

Through the churning maelstrom of thoughts and feelings, Harold tried hard to listen to what she was saying, how they could perform such wonderful deeds with bodies but do so little for the mind, how each person was different, how important was the human will...

Suddenly, as though reading his mind, she stopped and looked straight into his face.

'You know, Harold. When I first woke and saw that,' she nodded towards the foot of the bed, 'I just wanted to go under and never wake up again.'

Harold nodded.

'I can understand that. I would probably feel the same.'

'I know you would,' Ella said, almost in a whisper, 'we've talked about it often enough, eh? But now the boot is on the other foot and...' She stopped abruptly and smiled, 'God. what a slip! Now I am the one who is...' She didn't finish the sentence Harold's eyes were drawn towards the raised blankets. How could she bear to joke about it. 'Anyway. How are things back there?'

He nibbled a chocolate then wiped his glasses. Replacing them on the bridge of his nose, he looked up at her.

'You've heard about Itzik, I suppose?' Ella nodded. Rivka had told her.

'Poor Shosh,' she said softly. 'And, stupid as it seems, I have my own guilt feelings, not resolving it sooner and all that.'

Much as he had sworn to be positive before he came, Harold's own preoccupations began to take over.

'Yes. He's gone. And nearly half the herd. And . .'

Ella laid a hand on his wrist.

'And poor Ella is lying here. Crippled. Is that what you wanted to say?' She half raised herself. 'Then for Pete's sake just say it Harold! We've always been honest with each other. Now isn't the time to hide feelings. Is it?'

Harold, didn't react. He looked away, his own self-pity raising its head again. Then he felt Ella's fingers curling around his wrist as if to reassure him. Strangely, at the same time Ella she felt comforted by it herself. Or was it so strange?

'Look, Harold,' she began, lying back again, 'I know the score. And I've decided to live with it. Dr.Yacobi is helping and we make plans for the future. It's the only way to get through, he says. And he's right.'

'Look. I know, Ella. I know he's right . . .'

'But you think I have yet to realise it,' Ella cut in, 'to suffer the full effects of the shock. That I will soon relapse into feeling hopeless. Suicidal even. Isn't that what you mean, Harold?' She was quietly angry with him. These bloody English, so uptight, never let themselves go.

Harold turned back.

'I don't... I didn't say. .' he stammered, 'I . . .'

'No. But that's what you feel.' She shook his hand. 'Don't you realise that I want to start afresh. Perhaps go on to finish my studies. Perhaps to pot, again.'

'To what?'

'Pot. Ceramics. I was quite good, but threw it up. Wanted to live the hard life. Hump bales of straw. Prove something or other.' Ella stopped and breathed, deeply. 'Now, I can't. So I can go back to it.'

'Well yes. That's great. I hope it all works out.'

'It won't just 'work out', Harold. Don't you see. I have to make it work out. Sure. There will be crises. And I'll have to face them when they come.' She paused and gripped his wrist again 'That's me. But what about you?'

Harold sat up, as though stung. Then hunched forward again.

'Me? Oh, me. Well. I'll carry on much the same. Until they put me in the flower gardens, or working something as safe, I suppose...' Abruptly he stopped, annoyed at himself for sounding negative when he'd promised himself to be positive and not load anything onto her. But being so close to Ella and the way she was taking it all, had disarmed him. No He couldn't play act. Not with Ella, whatever her condition.

Ella wasn't in a mood for playing either.

'You're being bloody flippant, Harold. For God's sake! The doctor told me they are discovering new drugs for epilepsy. You're not alone. There are millions like you. And facing up to it. Why not you?'

A woman in the bed opposite stared at them as they argued and muttered to the patient next to her. Ella noticed. She smiled at Harold.

'God. If we row like this, they'll think we're married!' Harold winced. That phrase had touched a raw nerve and they sat in silence for a while. Then as her shoulder began to ache, Ella slowly drew her hand back to rest on the mattress. Harold let his hand follow, to rest on hers and like that, hand in hand they sat, silent.

A nurse padded down the ward and came up to the bed. Harold glanced round.

'Throwing me out,' he said. 'Riotous behaviour again.' He rose and slid the stool against the locker.

'Shalom Ella.' He stroked her forehead. It was so cool. He had a terrible urge to lean down and kiss it. To kiss her. But it was enough for one afternoon. 'Look after yourself,' he said slowly. '*Lehitraot*'

'Glad you came,' she said. 'Shalom, Harold.' Then, as though slipping out by itself added with a smile, 'come again, Harold. And soon.'

Ella watched him go out through the veneered doors, then turned on her side as the nurse prepared a hypodermic. She needed it. The pains in her legs had increased - in both of them, the 'ghost limb' syndrome, the doctor had warned her of.

The nurse finished, re-arranged the pillows then went away. Ella closed her eyes. Harold's visit had left her feeling warm inside yet drained. How cheerful she must have seemed to him. How encouraging. She wanted to believe it herself. But now, with him gone, came the sadness. The doubts. She thought of Harold. He so needed her. And she needed him. And as she closed her eyes, they filled with tears

30.

Harold left the hospital and made his way along the dusty streets to the bus station. Left, right, left, right again, crisscrossing the regular grid of streets.

An area of rough tarmac in the middle of the old market square served as the bus station. Half an hour later, jammed into a crowded bus he was heading west along the old road to Gaza.

A large woman with a baby on her lap took up most of his seat, on the baby's round almond-coloured face were two large sores splashed with Gentian violet. The woman leaned across the aisle, speaking loudly in a hoarse, Arabic dialect. The boy opposite answered in Hebrew, but again, with that throaty intonation. Probably from Morocco, thought Harold.

The birth of Israel and the subsequent War of Independence had inflamed passions in the Moslem world. Jews fleeing riots had come in a mass migration to Israel. To avoid overcrowding the already well-populated central areas, they were being distributed throughout the country.

Destitute and often illiterate, many had been sent to new villages created over-night in this desolate, flat plain of the northern Negev. Harold clung to his bit of seat. Kibbutzniks like him had chosen to live a pioneering life, these people were out here whether they liked it or not, reluctant pioneers.

The old *Egged* bus hurtled around bends and up and down the dips of the wadis, its roof piled high with cases and bundles, the passengers suffering on the wooden seats. About an hour later, after stopping frequently at side tracks to the new villages, it eventually deposited him at the junction of the Hunger Road before turning north towards Ashkelon.

As it drew away, faces peered at him through the dusty windows with a mixture of curiosity and also admiration gleaned from radio about the battle. Harold walked across to the verge of the road avoiding their glances. No, he didn't feel at all like a hero at all.

The last bus along the border road had long gone. It had to get way down to Dangoor before dusk. Luckily, a small truck passed on its way to a neighbouring kibbutz. Harold managed to find a place amongst the sacks and tins, hanging on for dear life as it bumped and swerved over the potholed roadway

Having had to walk the last five miles, he arrived at the gates just as it was growing dark – and noticed that the fence lights were shining, the power was on again. Climbing the slope to the dining hall, Harold felt his stomach rumbling, he hadn't eaten since that hurried sandwich before leaving with Menasheh.

After the days of eating by candle-light, the electric light was dazzling, the faces paler. The bright lights also showed up the shattered windows, many still covered in hardboard. In a way, it had been more relaxed in the subdued atmosphere.

Harold was tired. With the journey to and from Beer Sheba, on top of working that morning, had been overdoing it. But more than anything, he was emotionally drained from the meeting with Ella and the mental turmoil left in its wake.

He hadn't stopped thinking about her all the way back and with every mile under the wheels of the bus, it became more and more clear that his feelings for her were much deeper than he had been prepared to admit. Much more than just liking her company, respecting her views and ideas, and her sense of humour, he knew now that she was someone very, very special to him, that he really did love her - whatever that word meant.

And from her hand on his wrist, the way she asked him to come again soon, was he someone very special to her too? Could he hope that perhaps she really felt the same for him.

Harold ate quickly then hurried straight down to the dairy and changed into his working clothes. With the smaller herd, the milking took less than two hours, working silently with Nahum while his girlfriend Gila helped bring the cows along and wash down. Gone was the joking, the bantering, just heads down and silence. And exhausted from the day's journey and feeling a headache coming on, Harold preferred it that way.

As he climbed the track to his hut, the headache grew worse. A faint humming started in his ears and his vision grew blurred. Harold recognised the signs and this time he began to run down the path to get to his room, fumbling with the handle as desperately he tried to get inside and lie on his bed. But he remembered only pushing open the door. Then everything went black.

He woke a short time later, a bump on his head where it had struck the edge of the chair and a sore shoulder. Thankfully, his glasses weren't broken. Without waiting, he undressed and slipped into bed, but he couldn't sleep and lay wide awake, brooding.

Would there ever be a miracle pill? Was Ella just trying to raise his spirits? Even with all her own troubles, she would still be like that. No. His reality was that at any time it could happen – even at work. He might fall off a tractor. Worse still, pass out and run someone over. No. His fate would be to end up working in the gardens, or at odd jobs helping out with someone nearby all day. Chaperoned like an invalid.

His melancholy deepened as he churned over again and again, why he with his affliction been spared, when two such healthy people had been destroyed? And with the despondency, came doubts about Ella. What a fool he was to delude himself. It was just pity. That was what she must feel for him. Pity - and the desire to save him from himself - from what he might do.

Harold stared at the dark ceiling. Voices echoed along the path, then died away. The longer he lay awake, the more he convinced himself that the whole carefully constructed fabric of their mutual affection was just a web of pity and compassion and that he was a idiot to even think of love. No. Tonight's fit had been sent to remind him of the reality of his situation. And there was no solution. Except one.

Suddenly he recalled that day, long, long ago. After a bad attack on the training farm, he'd stood at the roadside in Bedford, waiting for a heavy lorry. One step into the road and there would an end to it. Somehow, he had eventually turned away, gone back and said nothing to the others. Yes. But he'd been younger then, hoped that he would grow out of it. Now, he knew he never would. No. This time, he wouldn't step back...

The next morning Harold woke early. It was quiet outside. A bird chirped in the oleander bush. He thought again of his decision the evening before. Now, even after a good night's sleep, he still felt the same, a sign that he was doing the right thing.

Washing and dressing quickly, he made his way across the lawn to Itzik's room, hoping it wouldn't be locked up. But at the edge of the veranda, he stopped short. The door was open. Someone else was in there. Stepping back into the bushes, he watched and waited.

Two minutes later, Shoshanah came out, closing the door quietly behind her. Wiping her eyes, she glanced round but didn't see him. Then holding a few things in her hand, she hurried away. Waiting until she was out of sight, Harold went in. On the table in a small white vase, was a single red rose from the rambler by the clinic.

Shoshanah didn't look back. Head bent, she walked up the path and climbed the hill towards the small graveyard. There she sat down beside the grave her fingers playing with the freshly turned earth. She came every day and knew she would continue to come and be with him for the rest of this summer and right through the cold winter. When spring came and the tiny, blood red Adonis flowers quivered in the breeze she would stop, leaving the wild flowers to keep a vigil over the broken soil. In death, he would be hers, forever.

Making sure no one else was around. Harold crossed the small lawn and quietly closed the door behind him. He looked across to the far wall – and held his breath. The nails in the wall were still there but it had gone! Oh God. Had she taken it away? Kneeling down, he looked under the bed and breathing a sigh of relief pulled out the Sten gun. He opened the few drawers but couldn't see them. His head began to burn. Bullets. They must be here. He knew they were here somewhere. Frantically he searched the wardrobe and finally, under a neat pile of clothes, he found what he was looking for, the small cardboard box.

Hands trembling, carefully he took out the snub nosed bullets and pressed them into them into the magazine, five, six, seven. At ten, he paused. Wouldn't even need that many. Slipping the magazine into his trouser pocket and tucking the gun under his green working jacket, he went out, quietly closed the door and hurried across the courtyard.

By the avenue of eucalyptus trees, Harold turned left, putting the Dutch barn and the shattered calf pens between himself and the dairy. By the loading ramp, Gavriel and Nahum were coaxing the injured cows onto an open green lorry. The second consignment to the slaughter-house.

Gavriel urged the last beast up the slope and slammed the tailboard closed. He glanced at Nahum then quickly looked away so that he wouldn't see his eyes. Every cow he knew by name, had raised many of them from calves. Now, as each one of them limped and stumbled up the ramp, it was taking away a part of himself. A third load would go on Thursday. Thankfully, that would be the last. Only one thing had broken the gloom of that week, Daliah, the new cow that Itzik had bought was already fighting for her place amongst the leaders. At least something personal of his would remain.

Gavriel signed the docket and the driver climbed into his cab and drew away. Before going back into the dairy, as always, he glanced around the cowsheds and the yard. Suddenly a movement beyond the calf-sheds caught his eye. Someone was hurrying down beside the avenue of casuarinas towards the rear gate. Harold! It couldn't be? But it was. He recognised the walk.

Gavriel glanced at his watch. At this time of the morning? In a working jacket – and on his day off? As he went in to help wash down for the next batch, he tried to dismiss it as just one of Harold's quirks. But something nagged at the back of his mind. Something that Itzik had once said?

The damaged leaf still hung askew as Harold strode past the rear gate and out into the orange groves, stumbling over the roughly filled-in shell craters along the track. Ragged gaps showed in the cypress tree windbreaks, it would take a long time for the scars to heal.

Motti and Shlomo, their shirts soaked, were passing aluminium irrigation pipes between orange trees to reconnect in a new line. Shlomo waited for the first flow of water to flush out the sand, before plugging the end. Then, as the pressure rose and the sprinklers began turning, Motti ran between the trees, checking any that were stuck, cursing as sharp jets of cold water struck his sweaty body. He noticed Harold hurrying past out towards the fields but didn't give it a second thought. No knowing what those cowmen would be up to next.

Reaching the edge of the groves opposite the sorghum fields, Harold stopped and looked towards the scorched patch where he had knelt that day. Then turning left again, he made his way beside the tall cypress windbreaks, keeping close to the trees. About fifty yards along, he knelt down in the shade, took out the Sten and slipped in the magazine. He glanced around. Not a soul. He'd picked the time well. This time, he wouldn't step back. Not this time.

Harold fingered the shiny, black metal. Not a lot to do now. Barrel in the mouth. Squeeze the trigger. And it would be over. Tears welled into his eyes and ran down his cheeks, bringing the taste of salt to his mouth. He closed his eyes but through the blackness, all he could see was Ella, Ella in a wheel-chair, the blanket hanging flat against the front and her lovely face scarred. He brushed the tears with the sleeve of his jacket. No. This time he would do it.

With his eyes still closed, he felt down the cold steel, gripped the knob of the cocking handle and he drew it back. The bolt engaged with a sharp click. With his thumb, he pushed out the safety catch. Then turning the gun towards him, he closed his mouth around the cold steel barrel and felt for the trigger, his temples throbbing and his head like a furnace.

As his finger curled round the trigger, a sharp scraping sound came from the trees beside him. Opening his eyes, he looked down and saw a huge snake squeezing between the bole of a cypress tree and a fallen branch, a brown, zig-zag stripe running down the olive green back. It was a fully grown viper.

Sensing his movement, the reptile stopped and with a sudden jerk, coiled itself against the foot of the tree, its triangular head pointing towards him, fixing him with tiny, yellow eyes and its forked tongue flicking in and out.

As the head quivered as though to strike, instinctively, Harold swung the gun down and squeezed the trigger until his knuckles hurt. A sharp burst of gunfire shattered the morning stillness. Birds flew from the trees and two hooded crows rose and croaked their protest over the fields.

Gavriel had been fitting the condenser pail to the vacuum lines when he thought again of Harold hurrying down the track. So early? On his day off? And the bulky green working jacket? What was he hiding? Suddenly Itzik's chance remark sprang into his mind again: 'If I had something like that, I'd . . .'

Calling to Nahum to carry on, he hurtled out of the dairy and down through the rear gate, his heels chafing in the heavy rubber boots.

'Seen Harold?' he called to Motti as he ran past him up the track.

'Sure. Went to the end. Turned left, I think.' He held up a damaged sprinkler, 'Haven't got a wrench in the dairy, have you?' But at that moment, shots rang out.

'*Elohim!*' Gavriel yelled. 'Harold!' He hurtled up the track, Motti and Shlomo following closely behind.

Harold sat back on his heels, acrid smoke stinging his eyes. When it cleared, the snake writhed, coiling and uncoiling, blood oozing from its shattered body. He stared at it. One bite and he would have been as dead is if he had shot himself. Twice over he should have been killed. Instead, he had slain one agent of death with another. Why had he not ignored it, just bitten on the muzzle and pulled the trigger? Why? Why?

Once again, like all those years ago, he had stepped back from the roadside. Now, even if he renewed his resolve, it wouldn't have helped, in that short burst, all the bullets had gone. Resignedly, he clicked out the magazine and tried to see the logic in his actions, as if it were a dialectic negation of the negation.

With the adrenaline gone, Harold suddenly felt weary. He closed his eyes. Ella was smiling. She'd been right. Wasn't she always? He'd been judging her by his own despair. Using Itzik's death and her terrible injuries to justify his own feelings and actions. He was a cheat. A lousy cheat. To her. And to himself.

As the smoke cleared, the sun rose above the cypresses, warming the back of his neck. From the orange groves came the tck, tck, tck, of the sprinklers. Water, giving life to the parched soil, driving the snake to seek a drier spot and saving him from his own destruction. Was Menasheh right? Was there some hidden purpose? Were we meant to cling to life and to hope, whatever?

At that moment, shouts came from the end of the track. Harold opened his eyes and turned his head. Gavriel ran up, heaving and panting, quickly joined by the two others.

'My God,' said Motti, looking down at the snake, 'what a monster.' He broke off a branch and picked it up, 'That's the biggest Viper I've ever seen. One bite would kill an elephant.'

'Lucky he wasn't coiled round one of your pipes,' said Gavriel. 'Fine job you did there Harold.'

'Yes. S'pose so,' Harold smiled. 'Call me any time,' and they all laughed, breaking the tension.

Motti and Shlomo walked off holding the snake high in the air on the end of a branch. Gavriel waited until they turned into the orange grove.

'That was a pretty close thing,' he murmured, looking straight into Harold's eyes.

'Yes,' said Harold, 'it was. It was.' He looked down and they both stared at the blood spattered trunk. When he looked up again, he shrugged. 'I don't think it will happen again.'

Gavriel smiled and slapped him on the shoulder.

'See you on evening shift,' he said and they parted at the rear gate.

As he came back into the milking parlour, Gavriel took up a hose and started to wash down.

'Everything okay?' asked Nahum, who with the noise of the compressor had heard nothing. 'You shot out like a bullet from a gun.'

'Yes. Something like that,' Gavriel murmured as he squirted water on the white tiles, 'but it's all sorted now.'

31.

The sun glared from the sand dunes, blinding against the dark blue of the sea beyond. Ahmed pulled down the peak of his cap to shield his eyes. He'd made the taxi stop on the main road and was walking the last hundred yards to Shaati. He might have lost an arm, but he was not going to be delivered like some helpless invalid.

Children were the first to see him as he climbed the rough track, his left sleeve pinned to his khaki shirt. They burst out of the whitewashed huts and tents, clustering around and whooping, touching him and calling others, the noise deafening after the silence of the hospital.

He'd been given permission to make a short visit to his father. His wounds still needed care and his body was weak and Leila had made him promise to be back by noon.

It wasn't until Sunday that Ibrahim had broken the terrible news about his mother. He'd asked to see her every day but each time his father or the doctors, fearing a relapse, had made excuses.

When he heard, Ahmed had tried to get out of bed. He remembered shouting and swearing revenge, he would run to the camp at Beit Hanun, grab a case of grenades, kill all the Jews - every one of them. With his own life he would avenge her! As they had restrained him, he broke down crying, the helplessness of lying there and the sharp pain in his shoulder making it even worse. Eventually, after an injection, he remembered nothing else.

Now, as he walked through the gathering crowd, Ahmed winced. He didn't want a hero's welcome, he'd come only to see his father. Poor Ibrahim. Hadn't he suffered enough. And now

Jamilla dead and his youngest son, on whom he had pinned so many hopes, disabled.

The noise followed him up the slope, adults crowding to the doorways to shout greetings, children tugging at his clothes: 'How many did you kill?' 'Where did you get to?' 'How did you get back?' Question after question.

Ahmed suddenly stopped and raised his good arm. The tumult abruptly ceased.

'*Min fadal*. Please. In good time, I will tell you. But now I want only to see my father. Please.' A few of the older boys took over, shepherding the others away, everyone staring after him as he carried on. Ahmed. A fighter. Their hero.

Ahmed turned and thanked the boys. Yes. They were the future – and he'd had plenty of time to think of the future as he lay in bed.

His father's generation was of isolated villages, of enmity between the towns and the 'ignorant' peasants, of rich effendis exploiting the peasants, a third of all produce to the land owner, a third to the owner of the well and then, if he was lucky, the *felakh* kept a third to feed his family.

In the towns, it was no better. Poverty stricken, casual work undercut even further by cheap labour brought in from Egypt or the Hauran in Syria. No one felt part of anything. Now, after the '48 disaster, everyone was crowded together, *felakhin* from villages all across the land, merchants from Jaffa, textile workers from Majdal. All were refugees alike.

Ahmed looked east, towards the ridge of sandhills, beyond which lay his land. He glanced right and left at the tattered tents and miserable huts. Yes. From this misery would be born a new nation, a proud nation that would fight to return to their land. A nation that would learn to use technology, that would make up for the hundreds of lost years rotting under the

Turkish yoke. And they would do this all in one generation. Now. He would teach the youth. He and hundreds like him. That was his dream.

Ahmed carried on between the huts and up towards the crest of the dunes where Ibrahim was sitting on the sand with Abu Salah, his old adversary. The week before, Ismail had been buried with full military honours. But the shots over the grave had done little to comfort either of the old men.

The two men rose to greet him and stretching out his one arm, he went to hug his father, then Abu Salah.

'*Merkhaba*,' Welcome, said his father's old enemy. 'Come. You both will do me the honour of drinking coffee in my house.'

As they walked back down the slope to his hut, Ahmed smiled to himself. If these two old enemies had settled their differences and come together, anything could happen. It was a good omen for the future.

The sun climbed towards noon. The breeze from the sea strengthened and began to blow across the dunes and through the narrow streets of Gaza, up over the sandhill ridge and across the plain, sifting fine dust over the freshly filled graves of the dead and bringing relief to the living.

It blew against the shutters of the darkened room where Itzik's Sten gun lay once more silent at the bottom of the wardrobe. It blew through the fly netting of the small room where Harold had spent most of what was left of the morning composing a letter to Ella. He wanted to catch the post-van before lunch.

It was a difficult letter and three screwed-up sheets lay on the floor. For the first time in his life, he was trying to bare his innermost thoughts to another, to express his deepest emotions. – in writing It wasn't easy. He wasn't a hundred percent sure what she really felt for him. But the shock of his attempted suicide, the relief and Gavriel's friendship and understanding had been the catharsis, enabling him to take the risk. Now, he could tell Ella how he really felt - to tell her of his love for her.

With it finished and sealed, Harold hurried across the courtyard, letter in hand. A carpenter was fixing new glass in the shattered windows of the dining hall and a gang of builders from town was patching up the shower block.

'Hey, *kibbutznik*,' one of them flashed a gold toothed smile, 'You'll have no excuse to be dirty after tomorrow.' Harold smiled back and waved, then carried on towards the porch.

To his right, the sand hills shone in the morning sun. White and silent. Was it only last week they were shrouded in smoke, spitting death everywhere in a sudden burst of insanity, a battle which nobody had won. And as he walked onto the tiled porch, he wondered how many had been killed over there? If only those hills would stay quiet. *Hallevai*.

At that moment, the mobile post van pulled up at the back of the kitchen. Harold dashed round and thrust his letter into Khaim's hand as he passed the kibbutz post to the driver.

'The stamps are in the office,' said Khaim.

'I'll run and bring one,' gasped Harold. 'It must catch the post. It must!'

'Must be a love letter,' said the driver. Harold wondered whether he'd blushed. 'Never mind,' the man grinned, 'I'll stick one on. Khaim you can sort it out next time.'

Harold stammered his thanks and hurried away.

Khaim took the incoming post and as was his habit, started to sort it as he walked back to the office.

'Here!' he called, 'there's one for you, Harold. From Beer Sheba.' Harold ran back, his heart thumping. And in the shade of the porch, he tore open the blue envelope.

'My Dearest Harold,' the letter began. Harold closed his eyes, trying to stem the tears then, wiping his face, hurried down the path to read it in the quiet of his room.

In the cool of the dairy office, Gavriel sat down to write up the record cards. On the second one, Itzik's writing seemed still so fresh - as though he would soon be down for the next shift. As he filled in the details in his large scrawling hand, he knew there was no way he could match Itzik's native neatness. But at least, he could continue his work. In three or four, certainly in five years they could once more challenge for leadership of the league tables.

Having completed the records for the day, Gavriel kicked off his boots and climbed slowly up the track to the hilltop. By the dining hall, he turned and looked out over the shimmering, grey plain. To the east, shrouded in a dust haze, it rose towards the foothills of the Judean Mountains. To the south, extending for as far as he could see, was the endless expanse of the Negev desert.

He turned around and looked at the houses and trees of his kibbutz. He had survived the war and the purges in Europe. Managed to bring himself and Rivka out here to rebuild their lives together. This was his home, his homeland. He had no other. From here his forefathers came. Here, whatever, his children would grow up to be free and proud Jews.

Over to the west, the sand hills gleamed along the border. Those refugees, over in Gaza, it was their homeland also. They too had no other and they would not suffer endlessly without reasserting their claim. They too must have a future – with their own independent state.

Gavriel looked beyond the rooftops, towards the deep gash of the great wadi. Every winter, in just a few days, millions of cubic metres of water thundered their way down to the sea in flash floods, whilst all around, the land lay parched and deserted, crying out to be settled. Yet here was this borderline of senseless enmity and hatred. Surely there was enough land for them both, without precious life-blood being wasted in the barren sands?

A cow lowed from the dairy below. From the rear gate came the clang of hammers as Meir welded the hinges back in place. No. There had to be another way. A way in which they could live and work the land together. Use their energies to make the desert bloom, create a society which, as the great book said, would be a guiding light to the peoples of the world. Was that too much to ask?

Gavriel looked up the track that led past the water tower and beyond, to the graveyard. How many more would join Itzik up there before their time, how many more families be bereaved in Gaza until sanity prevailed? For there was no alternative. Either they would learn to live together. Or they would all perish in some new holocaust of weapons of mass destruction.

A tractor changed gear at the foot of the hill and began to grind its way up to the dining hall. He looked once more out to the south, to the great desert where the ancient prophets once went to recover their spirits and visions of hope. It was his vision too. That peace and friendship would win in the end. For Itzik. And for Ella. For all of them. It had to.

Turning towards the porch of the dining hall, Gavriel took off his old cloth hat and stuffed it into his pocket. It would be a hurried lunch, still so much to do.